BOT WARS

BOT WARS

J.V. KADE

DIAL BOOKS
an imprint of Penguin Group (USA) Inc.

DIAL BOOKS FOR YOUNG READERS
A division of Penguin Young Readers Group
Published by the Penguin Group
Penguin Group (USA) Inc., 375 Hudson Street, New York, New York 10014, USA

USA/Canada/UK/Ireland/Australia/New Zealand/India/South Africa/China
Penguin Books Ltd, Registered Offices: 80 Strand, London WC2R 0RL, England

For more information about the Penguin Group visit penguin.com

Library of Congress Cataloging-in-Publication Data
Kade, J. V.
Bot Wars / J. V. Kade.   p. cm.
Summary: In a futuristic world where humans and robots are at war,
a boy goes on a search to find his missing military father.
ISBN 978-0-8037-3860-7 (hardcover)
[1. Robots—Fiction. 2. War—Fiction. 3. Fathers—Fiction. 4. Missing persons—Fiction.
5. Science fiction.] I. Title.
PZ7.K116462Bo 2013   [Fic]—dc23   2012017682

Printed in the United States of America

1 3 5 7 9 10 8 6 4 2

Designed by Mina Chung

Text set in Perrywood MT Std

The publisher does not have any control over and does not assume
any responsibility for author or third-party websites or their content.

To Gavin and Bella

UNITED DISTRICTS OF AMERICA

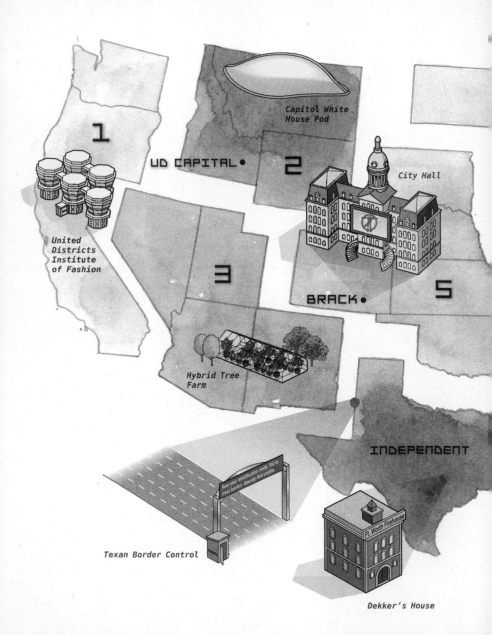

Capitol White House Pod

UD CAPITAL •

1

2

City Hall

United Districts Institute of Fashion

3

BRACK •

5

Hybrid Tree Farm

INDEPENDENT

Have your Identification ready. Toll to cross border. Seventy-five credits

Ft. Worth Firehouse

Texan Border Control

Dekker's House

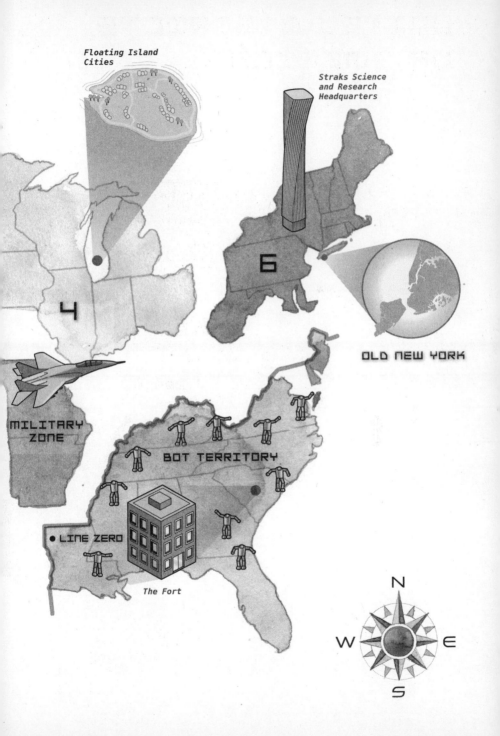

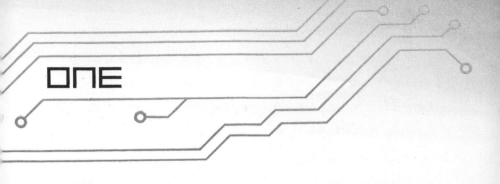

MY BROTHER LOST his leg because of the Deeta disease, but he tells everyone it happened during the Robot Wars even though his service only ran two months and he never even left the Military Zone. I call him Po now (short for Pogo, as in the old-fashioned jumping stick), because he used to hop around on one foot till he got his prosthetic leg. Which I sometimes accidentally-on-purpose misplace. Or steal.

"Trout!" he shouts as the sound of his one foot thumps across the floor. "Where's my leg?"

I can't stop the snicker from rasping up my throat and Po stops thumping around long enough to find me on the other side of the kitchen island. I laugh as he lunges for me and misses. His fake leg is heavy in my arms, and I hug it close to my side like a football as I duck left and run for the living room.

Po grunts. Thumps. Grunts again. "Stop being a bolt-head or I'll take your Net-tag away."

Whenever Po wants to threaten me with something serious, he goes to the Net-tag—the key card that gives me access to the Network and video games and, most importantly, my credits. A boy can't survive without money. Or vid games. Or the Net. Okay, so I can't survive without the Net-tag *at all*.

I stop running and toss the leg on the couch. "Dude, you're no fun."

Po frowns as he hops around the couch and collapses into it. He lets out a harrumph as he tugs the leg of his shorts up to expose the metal bracket his fake leg fits into. With a twist and click, the leg is back in place and he rises to his feet easily.

"No fun, huh?" he says right before he grabs me, looping his arm around my neck. He takes me down. My knees slam against the floor and a sharp pain shoots to my toes.

"Come on!" I shout.

"Lookit the little trout squirming!" Po sings as he scrapes his knuckles across my head. It's called a bolt burn and it hurts like crazy. I try to shake him off, but it's no use. Po is not only seven point five years older than me, he's also a foot taller and sixty pounds heavier.

"All right. I give up!"

He pulls back, fixes his hair with a quick flick of his

hand. It's still wet from his shower and it sticks up like porcupine quills. "Next time you screw with my leg, it's the Net-tag and a groundation."

"If you have my Net-tag, what else are you going to ground me from?" I challenge.

"From socks. And bread. And underwear. How about that?"

I snort. "That's stupid." I sit up and straighten my own crappy brown hair. "So what are we doing today anyway?"

"If you stop screwing around long enough to come back to the land of maturity, we'll go downtown to the Heart Office and see if Dad's thread has come online."

My stomach instantly goes squirrelly. Dad's been gone for over two years now and there's been no log of his thread in almost eight months. Not everyone has a chip in their heart (which gives off a frequency called a thread, which can be traced by the Heart Office), but Dad insisted we all get one right when the Robot Wars started. At the time I thought it was dumb because I didn't want Dad or anyone else being able to track me all the time like some lame-o dog that might get lost, but now I'm glad he made us. It gives us something to look for instead of just sitting round the house like a couple lumps of space junk.

The only crappy part? During the war, the bots used

scramblers to make it harder to track the chips, but the war has been over for six months now and the scramblers have been turned off. Dad's thread should have come on and stayed on, whether he was alive or not. I hate even thinking like that. I *don't* think like that. Dad is out there somewhere, waiting for us.

I push myself up to my feet and level my shoulders like Dad taught me.

Stand tall, like a man, he'd say. So I do.

"I'm ready," I tell Po. "I've arrived at the land of maturity. But I don't think they'll let you in."

Po laughs. "You're a trip, you know that?" He ruffles my hair one more time and we head out the door.

Downtown Brack is bustling with people even though the sky is the color of moldy doughnuts and threatens to spit rain any second. Above us, billboard screens flash ads from the tops of buildings as we head down the sidewalk. *Long trip?* one ad says. *Reserve your seat on the Tamer Rail and cut your travel time in half. Get to Denver in under twenty minutes!*

The Tamer Rail is supposed to be like the jet version of a train. Po keeps promising to buy us tickets, but he's always too busy working.

The billboard changes to an anti-bot ad. There's a menacing-looking bot in one corner, his eyes blazing red. *Robots are responsible for the deaths of thousands of United District citizens,* the screen says. *If you see a robot, call the emergency hotline.*

I don't remember much about when the war first started, since I was only like seven, but I do remember the news feed playing vid from Chicago, District 4, where the violence first started. Robots were fighting soldiers with laser guns, and people were running away screaming.

I shiver at the bot glaring down at me from the billboard. I don't like those ads. They gear me out. Thankfully, the screen changes again and pop singer Tanner Waylon comes on flashing his pouty face. A couple of girls across the street point at him and screech. I roll my eyes. That dude is a total drain clogger if you ask me.

Up ahead, the traffic light switches to green and hoverboards zoom past, the riders' eyes hidden behind slick goggles. Po and I don't have a hoverboard, but even if we did, I don't think he'd let me ride it. *Too dangerous,* he'd say. *You might lose a leg.* And then he'd snicker to himself like making fun of missing legs was the funniest thing he'd ever come up with.

I kick aside a bot gear (there are old pieces everywhere,

if you take a second to look) and it skips into the street. It hits the glowing blue hover rail that lines the curb, and the metal clangs like a bell in a boxing ring.

"Hey, come on," Po says, giving me a shove.

I look at him like, *What*? But he's totally forgotten about me already. He's locked his eyes on Marsi Olsen, who's standing at the next corner with a hoverboard tucked under one arm.

Po has the fiery hots for her and as she laughs, her dark red ponytail swinging behind her, Po turns into a drooling clanker.

Marsi's goggles hang around her neck. Her brown pants disappear inside tall brown boots, the buckles of which look super-complicated, like a puzzle I'd probably fail. A shiny white top is tucked into her pants, but the big sleeves flutter around her like wisps of smoke.

I think she's pretty, but not *that* pretty. I look at Po out of the corner of my eye. He's just standing there, hands shoved in his pockets, this blank look on his face. Like all the important stuff just zipped out of his head.

"What would you do if I yelled her name?" I say.

Po doesn't look at me as he answers, "Clock you one."

I breathe in deep and then say, "Ma—"

A sweaty hand clamps down over my mouth, cutting me off. Which is fine. Because I wasn't planning on say-

ing Marsi's name anyway. I just wanted to see Po gear out. Which he did.

"Come on, you little squirt," he says, tugging me in the opposite direction.

I laugh around his hand as we turn onto the next street. Finally he lets me go and hangs his head like he's all embarrassed. The sun breaks through the clouds for a millisecond and I squint as I glance over at him.

"I don't know why you don't talk to her."

"You're only twelve—"

"I'll be thirteen in ninety-seven days."

"So? When you're older, you'll understand it a little better."

I frown, because I don't think there's anything to understand except that Po is a big clucking chicken.

We walk another three blocks before we reach City Hall, where the Heart Office is located. It's this big building in the center of Brack, with curving stone steps that lead up to the front entrance. A gigantic screen on the front of the building flashes a pic of President Callo addressing some people in District 2, where the capitol is. His graying hair is swooped to the side and gelled straight out so that it hovers over his forehead like a diving board.

Callo announces budget cuts, the headline says below

him. Then, *Districts still feeling the pinch after Bot Wars.*

When the conflict started, and bots either fled or were dismantled, the United States fell apart like dry biscuits. Stores and factories and stuff had to shut down because they had no bot workers. That's when the states turned into the bigger Districts.

Sometimes I hear my friend Lox's parents grumbling about the "financial collapse" and how we became too dependent on robots. Once, when his mom caught us watching *Man vs. Bot,* she threatened to move Lox to Iceland, where the closest you come to a bot is a can opener.

Since we parked our ancient X55 outside the city limits to avoid a downtown parking tax, my legs are tired from all that walking and I trudge up the steps to City Hall, lagging behind Po. I don't know how he can walk all that way with a bum leg and not complain.

At the entrance, Po slides his Net-tag in the reader installed in the wall just to the left of the door. The machine beeps and whirs and the lock clicks once Po's been approved access.

The door rushes open and Po heads in, saying something about how hot it is in there. His voice bounces around the big space. It's like a cave, but a shiny, expensive cave that smells like lemons and old leather shoes. The floor is a black-and-white checkered pattern, and if

I stopped long enough to look straight down, I'd probably see my reflection in the polished marble. A big old staircase rises in front of us, branching off at a landing. We cut left, passing the stairs and the two security guards stationed there. All the important officials work on the higher levels, and they take security seriously. People like Po and me aren't allowed up there. I bet it's just a bunch of boring offices and stuff anyway.

I avoid looking at the guards because their metallic eye bands gear me out. They're special glasses that display information through the lenses, so a guard can look up anyone's information without going to a computer. Lox thinks they help with shooting and fighting too, but I don't know if that's true.

As we head for the Heart Office, I tap the stone statue of President Callo that stands just inside the hallway. Dirt and fingerprints cover his shoulders on both sides. People believe touching Callo is good luck because he got struck by lightning—*twice*—and lived. That sounds like bad luck if you ask me, but Dad said there's a belief that lightning doesn't strike the same spot twice, so that makes Callo about as lucky as a lottery winner. And I figure I've got nothing to lose.

Directly behind Callo is a picture of Sandra Hopper, the Head of Congress and governor of 5th District. Everyone calls her Beard though, because of her whiskers. Apparently she's never heard of a laser razor.

Po is the first one to reach the Heart Office, but he lets me go in ahead. Tanith, the clerk, smiles when she sees me.

"Good afternoon, Mr. St. Kroix. How are you?"

I smile big to match hers. I like that she calls me Mr. instead of Trout.

"Fine. How are you?"

"I'm well." She pushes a hunk of her wavy black hair off her shoulder and leans over the counter. "And how about big brother?" She winks at Po and Po blushes.

"I'm good. Thanks, Tanith."

She nods. "So, should I check the log for you?"

Po and I nod. Tanith taps in a few things on her computer. She waits, watches the screen, taps in a few more things. Suddenly my heart feels like it's going to burst outta my chest.

I swallow. Lick my lips. Every time we come here, and every time Tanith types in Dad's ID thread, there is this moment where anything can happen and it makes every nerve in my body hum. I want this time to be different from the hundred other times we've come here. I want Tanith to smile and give us the word that Dad's thread finally came back online.

I feel like I'm leaning in more and more, like I'm afraid if I don't get in close enough I might not hear her answer. But really I haven't moved at all. It's just the world that seems to have gotten smaller.

The frown on Tanith's face tells me what I need to know.

Nothing's changed.

"I'm sorry," she says, like she does every other time we're here.

"It's all right," Po says behind me. "Thanks for checking. We'll be back next week."

Tanith nods and her hair falls back over her shoulder like a curtain. "I'll be here."

I turn, and hurry into the hallway. I think about kicking old President Callo on the way out. Stupid statue and its stupid promise of good luck. It never works anyway. Like touching a hunk of stone will somehow change anything.

"Hey." Po catches up to me and sets his arm on my shoulders. "He'll come back online. I just know it."

I don't say anything, but I don't push him away either.

"Why don't we go across the street to the diner? Get some ice cream. How about that?"

I shrug, like I don't care, but deep down in the trench of my gut, I do. Po is usually so busy we don't hang out much except for on his days off. And usually we can't afford ice cream. Even though I know it'll take Po a good two hours to work off the price, my mouth waters thinking about it. If anything had the power to freeze this crappy feeling in my chest and turn it cold and dead, it's ice cream. Maybe.

"Can I get Bot-N-Bolts?" I ask. Bot-N-Bolts is this cool silver ice cream with little blue flecks of candy inside. If the Great Wall of China was made of Bot-N-Bolts, I'd eat my way through it.

Po pushes open the door and says, "You got it, little bro. Bot-N-Bolts it is."

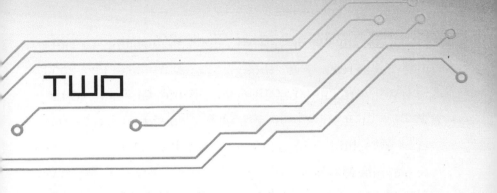

TWO

THE ICE CREAM sits like a hunk of space junk in my stomach as we head back for the car. Po walks slower than he did on the way to City Hall and I wonder if he's thinking about Dad too. Fact is, Dad isn't the only soldier still missing after the wars, but he's the only one with an ID chip who is.

It sucks not knowing what happened.

By the time we reach the car, Po has only enough time to drive me home before he has to head off to Chinley's, the restaurant on the west side of town where he works. It takes a good fifteen minutes just to get there.

We pull up in front of the house and Po starts in on his rules. "As soon as you get inside, lock the house down. Don't answer the door. No cooking—"

"On the stove. I know. I know."

"Hey. Big bro"—he points at himself, then at me—"little bro. Big bro gets to pester little bro about the rules whenever he wants and little bro will not whine."

I screw up my mouth as I look over at him, which makes him laugh real hard.

Once he's gotten control of himself he says, "I'll be home a little after midnight. Don't wait up."

"Like I would."

He ruffles my hair as I climb out of the car. I swing at him but he dodges the hit and laughs. "Hurry up! Before I'm late," he says, and I hop over the hover rail onto our brown lawn. The car door automatically slides shut once I'm clear of it and Po steps on the accelerator, zooming out of sight. Our street grows quiet as I stand there watching the spot where Po disappeared. I try to act like it doesn't bother me, being home alone, but sometimes I wish Po would call in sick so we could hang out. But Po never calls in sick. He doesn't have the time to cover it and we always need the money.

I head inside, shut the door, and pop open the security panel with the tap of a finger. The panel slides out of a niche in the wall and the screen lights up neon blue like the rails. I punch in my code and the pad beeps once the house is locked up tight.

With nothing better to do, I plop down on the couch, nab the remote now that it's mine and only mine, and flip through the channels. History show about the ancient

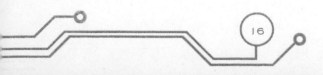

times. Lame. Home improvement show. Lame. Cartoons. Already saw 'em.

I land on the news feed. A reporter is standing outside a mansion in 1st District, over on the West Coast. Behind her, several UD officials file out of the house dragging a man, then a woman, and lastly a robot, onto the front lawn.

The bot is a small model, not much bigger than the woman. It has white silicone skin and big black eyes. I've never seen one like that, but then, I haven't seen a bot up close in a long time.

The woman starts screaming something at the officials, but they ignore her as the bot is zapped with a shock gun. The bot seizes and its fingers curl as it collapses to its knees.

The reporter raises her voice to be heard over the commotion behind her. "We're here in West Los Angeles outside the home of Mr. and Mrs. Miller. They're accused of harboring a robot. Though Mrs. Miller argues the robot is a nanny and is no threat to humans, sources close to the Robot Control Agency say there is suspicion surrounding the origins of the bot. Its design is unlike anything the UD has ever produced and some wonder if perhaps the bot came from Old New York, where it has

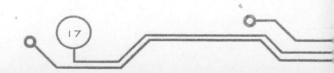

long been suspected bots have created their own factory.

"If you, or anyone you know, has seen a robot within the UD, please call the hotline . . ."

I flip the channel. I feel all funny inside, like I just watched a friend get yelled at by his mom. Most of the time bots freak me out, but I had a robot nanny before the war, and seeing that report makes me think of Cleo.

Dad saved up for a year to buy her after my mom died in a car accident. I was only two when it happened, so I don't remember her much. My nanny took the place of my mom. She had a funny voice, like the sound of a hundred toothpicks hitting the floor.

She came uploaded with over six thousand stories, and she read me something every night. My favorite was *Brent Billy Saves the Universe*. She'd project the book's vid on my bedroom wall. Her big owl eyes always got bigger when she read the part where Brent's spaceship crashed on Titan.

I was never afraid of Cleo. Even after the revolt started, when the UD said bots were dangerous.

I miss her.

After I've flipped through another dozen channels, I give up on finding anything that isn't about bots. I pull my Net-tag out for a round of vid games. I'm about to

connect it to the Net receiver when a familiar face comes on the vid panel.

"Welcome to another edition of *Getting to Know Brack*. I'm your host, Candu Rix. And tonight we're heading north of town . . ."

I sit forward. Candu Rix is the mom of one of the girls I go to school with. Tellie Rix. Tellie and I don't get along real well. She's kind of snotty and bolt-headed. And her parents are super-rich. Her dad is a congressman for 5th District and is second in command after Beard.

I knew Mrs. Rix had a show, but I thought it sounded lame, so I've never watched. On the TV, she leads the cameraman into a tiny apartment in Geissa, a poor neighborhood on the south side. She introduces the viewers to a woman whose son lost both arms to the Deeta disease during the war.

Somehow, I get dragged into watching and by the end of the show, Candu Rix has promised the woman and her son all the medical treatments they need for free along with a year's supply of groceries and a new apartment.

Talk about hitting the jackpot.

And it's not like the Deeta disease is rare or anything. Po had the same thing. People got it from the leftover blast haze from X-bombs. Something in the energy used in the bombs damaged the nerves and tissue in soldiers' limbs if they were exposed to it too long. The ones on the front lines suffered from it the most.

At the end of the show, Candu Rix comes on and says, "If you know of anyone in need of help, contact us at candu@gettingtoknowbrack.5dtr."

My hands start to sweat when I hear that. The credits zoom across the screen and a commercial comes on, but I'm already running for the computer.

It might be stupid. It might be a long shot. But I have to try. Because I need the biggest help of all. I need to find my dad. For me. For Po. But mostly, for Dad. Because if he's out there somewhere, maybe he's having a hard time getting to a Link. Maybe he doesn't have any money. Maybe he's hurt.

I log into the Net, open a new e-mail and start typing.

TO: Candu Rix
[candu@gettingtoknowbrack.5dtr]

FROM: Trout
[smarterkroix@zipspeed.5dtr]

June 11th 3:34 p.m.

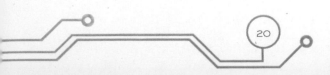

Dear Mrs. Rix,

I just watched your show for the first time. It was the episode about that guy with the Deeta disease, which my brother had too! He lost his leg.

You don't know me, but I go to school with your daughter, Tellie (if you ask her about me, she might not know me, because we're not friends or anything. Not that I don't like her!).

I need your help. My dad served in the Robot Wars, but he never came home and his thread hasn't come back online and it's just my brother and me now (our mom died a long time ago). And while my brother takes care of me and the house, he doesn't make pancakes like Dad and he doesn't even know the first thing about hy-breeds. Sometimes, my dad and I would stay up late studying new breeds and making up pretend ones.

We need our dad. So if you could help me find

him, or at least get the word out about him, that'd be really great.

Thank you for your time. I hope you pick me to be on your show. It'd mean a lot to us.

Sincerely,

Trout St. Kroix

THREE

I DON'T TELL PO about the letter I sent to Mrs. Rix because he'd think it was stupid. But it only takes him a day to notice my obsession with the computer.

"Hey, gearhead," he says, "you think I can get the computer for five minutes? You've been hogging that thing all day."

I click on my e-mail box one more time, even though I have the auto-ding set up so the computer will chime when a new e-mail arrives. I only got one message since last night and it wasn't even from Mrs. Rix. It was from Lox.

> Yo! The ocean is so wrenched! You're missing out! I BET YOU WISH YOU WERE HERE! Cuz I would.
>
> Have fun living the lame life, bolt sniffer!
>
> —Lox

"I'm done," I say to Po and log off. The desk chair spins a circle when I clamber out of it and Po stops it with a hand.

"What's up with you?" He narrows his eyes. "You're acting weird."

"Nothing." I head into the kitchen. "I was looking to see if Lox e-mailed me and he didn't." The lie slithers over my lips like a snake. I used to hate lying to Dad—the guilt would sit in my chest like a bolt—but lying to Po is easy. It's like a game to see what I can get away with.

I hear Po's fingers tap against the keyboard as I inspect the food in the back of the fridge. Old breadsticks from Chinley's. A dried lump of spaghetti. A cup of yogurt. I check a block of cheddar cheese but spy a bit of mold and toss it back in.

"Hey," Po calls from the living room, "I don't have to work tonight. You want to hang at the park for a while?"

I pull an apple from the crisper drawer and give it a squeeze to see if it's mushy. Seems all right. "Yeah. I guess. Nothing to do around here." Besides, I can check my e-mail through my Link. And it might help if I'm doing something besides checking it. Before I drive myself nuclear.

Po and I spend the rest of the afternoon melting into matching puddles of TV goo. We watch several hours of

Man vs. Bot, and, after a nap, we finally peel ourselves off the living room furniture to head out.

I follow Po down the front walk to the driveway and climb in the passenger side of our car. The engine click-whirs to life when Po presses the ON button and The Rezzies blast through the speakers. Po taps on the steering wheel in time with the music and I can't help but bob my knee.

We make our way toward Ryder Park, but take a detour when the car's navigation system warns us of a traffic jam on the freeway. Po cuts through a neighborhood he calls The Glitz. The houses there are constructed of recycled material and, on sunny days, the glass shards in the buildings' exteriors flare up like glitter. If you don't have sunglasses, you're practically blind when you drive through.

When we reach the park, the lot is packed with cars and it takes Po twice as long to find an empty space. Finally, we climb out and Po grimaces as he stretches. His bum leg gets stiff and sore when he's been sitting for a long time, and considering we wasted the day on the couch, I'd say his leg is probably feeling like an old prune by now.

We cross the parking lot, stopping once for a crew of kids on hoverboards. I watch them zoom past, jealous that they have boards, and jealous that they're hanging out. I don't have a lot of friends, at least not ones that I hang out with outside of school. Lox is my closest friend and he's been gone on a family vacation for a good week already with another week to go.

We enter the park beneath the metal archway. The pavement stops and grass takes over. It's thick and green and I can tell it's been cut with a laser-mower because each blade looks exactly the same height as the one next to it. We still have an old electric mower that takes out random chunks of grass. Po kicks it every chance he gets.

The sun shines over the treetops and I slide on my sunglasses. The lenses adjust to the perfect shade of dark and I feel instant relief. As we head farther in, I scan the people hanging round, trying to see if I know anyone.

There's a group of guys Po's age playing hover-bee off to my left. A mom and dad sit beneath the big oak tree straight ahead, their kids running circles around them chasing a flutter-fly, its shiny mechanical wings glinting in the light. It's always busy on the weekends. It's one of the reasons I like coming here. I'm alone too much as it is, and I hate silence.

Po hurries his steps and I have to jog to catch up to him. "What's the rush?" I say.

"You're just slow."

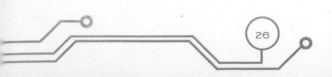

I snort and that's when I see her. Marsi Olsen. Of course! I bet Po checked her Luna page this afternoon and I bet she posted something about going to the park. Which is why Po asked if I wanted to go so he could pretend he wasn't stalking her like a bot-zoid.

"Oooh. Po's girlfriend!" I sing, and he punches me in the arm. "Ouch." I rub the spot where it aches. "Dude! That hurt."

When we make our way down the other side of the hill, the Maroz Fountain comes into view. It's constructed of the old bodies of robots left over from the war. Back before the fights broke out, everyone had a robot. Robots rang you up at the grocery store. They delivered packages. They walked dogs down any old street. Some were even teachers. That's why everything shut down after the bots were gone. People couldn't remember how to do that stuff for themselves anymore. Dad said it'd been a long time since a human ran the checkout scanner at a grocery store.

That's when the states collapsed.

The fountain is the closest I've come to a robot in five years.

As we near it, the piles of gutted torsos flash like the old warning lights used during the war. Not that there was ever any real threat in our territory. The battles were fought in Bot Territory southeast of here. The only part of the war I saw was on TV.

Po veers left, toward Marsi, and for a second I think we're headed for her, like he's gotten brave enough to talk to her instead of standing there staring at her while drool drips from his chin.

But then he slows and I see his group of friends lounging around a holo-fire, the computerized flames flickering even though the day is as still as butter. By the way everyone is grouped close around it, I'm guessing the heat feature is turned off.

Po's best friend Johz calls out to us. When Po joins him, they slap the backs of their hands together and hook thumbs at the last second in a gear-lock. Po tries to pretend like Marsi isn't twenty feet away. But I can see him looking at her out of the corner of his eye.

"Yo!" Johz says. "What's chopping?"

Po shrugs. "Nothing. You know. Just had to get out of the house."

"Here," one of the girls says to me, gesturing to her chair, "you can have my spot."

"No, that's okay," I start, but she cuts me off.

"I insist! I've been sitting around all day. Take a break, kid." She grabs me by the shoulders and directs me to

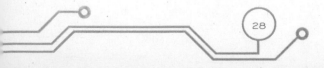

the chair like I'm blind as a banana. I plop down and the chair's auto feature molds to my body, holding my butt like a cloud. Lox calls these chairs butt-kissers. Most of the time Lox is crazy and obnoxious, but it's when he's gone for a while that I realize I miss having him around.

The girl who gave me her chair—Bims—offers Po a drink and he takes it with a smile. Po used to have a crush on her before Marsi (seriously, my brother's love life could be a Net-opera). But now I think Bims has a crush on Po. She leaves me behind in her chair and slides in next to Po all snuggly-like.

At a party Po took me to once, I heard Bims tell one of her friends she thought Po had "kiss-me lips" and Bims's friend agreed. I skeeze out just remembering it. I never want to hear my brother's name uttered in the same sentence as *kiss-me lips* ever again.

Po turns away from me to tell his friends some lame story about work, so I drag out my Link and log into the Net. It takes all of two seconds to check my e-mail, and a big fat zero stares back at me.

I sit in the butt-kisser chair for another hour, checking my e-mail, surfing the Net, and watching vids. Bims gives me a soda, which I down in 7.5 gulps. I catch Po checking out Marsi again, and then suddenly he's pointing at me and all his friends look over.

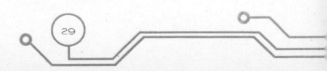

"What?" I say.

Po has a can of soda in one hand and his Link in the other. "Show everyone how you can climb like a monkey."

Back before Dad left for the war, he would take us to the virtual mountain at Kippy Creek Center and we'd climb till we couldn't feel our fingers. I was the best at it even if Po never wanted to admit it. Dad said it was because I was small and had hands like an octopus.

"You grab hold of something and you don't let go," he used to say.

That was true for other things too, like credits and food and vid games.

But we haven't been climbing since Po lost his leg, since Dad left. And I'm not sure I can hack it now.

"What do you want me to climb?" I say with a snort. "A tree?"

Johz pushes the hair out of his face with the flick of his hand. "How about the fountain?"

Everyone glances toward the middle of the park, to the Maroz Fountain. The bot shells are gray in the dusk. And look slippery. Po says it's supposed to be a reminder of the UD government's power and their zero-tolerance policy against bots.

Even though I'm not a bot supporter, I still think it'd

probably be wrong to climb it. I scrunch up my nose. "You're kidding, right?"

Po looks at Marsi before he says, "Come on, little bro. You can make that pile of bot shells look like space junk beneath you."

I purse my lips and squint over at the fountain like I'm trying to calculate how hard it'll really be. Hearing Po talk about my climbing skills like that, like I *am* the best, makes me really want to do it bad.

Plus, I think he wants to get Marsi's attention, and maybe helping him will earn me some brother points. Besides, there aren't any patrolmen out here, far as I can see. And even if there were, the worst they would do is fine me a few creds, maybe.

"All right," I say, and push out of the butt-kisser chair.

Po and his friends trail behind, cheering me on. Everyone within a hundred feet looks my way. I reach the base of the fountain and climb over the low concrete edge, splashing into the water. My feet squish in my shoes. I want to shuck them off, but wet bare feet on metal might not be a good idea. I can use the rubber soles of my shoes to grip.

Making my way from the base's edge to the bottom of the bot wreckage takes me a long time. People are definitely staring now, but the attention fuels my courage.

A crowd forms in a loose circle. I look over a shoulder. Marsi and her friends are watching me.

I avoid the side of the fountain where the water sprays out and head around to the back. This side is as dry as a rotted-out engine. *Here goes nothing,* I think as I climb onto the first bot shell. It's just a torso, with holes where the arms should have gone and one for the neck too. I put my foot on its chest and push up, grabbing the next shell at the armhole.

I clear two more shells and a leg. People cheer from the ground.

"Trout! Trout!" Johz and Po chant. Other voices join in.

My heart thumps a steady beat in my chest. I forgot how much fun climbing is and I want to keep going, right up to the top.

I make quick work of an arm and another shell. The voices from the ground sound farther away and I can see the tops of the trees through the spaces between the robot parts. I look up. Almost to the top.

I reach for a hollowed leg and catch my left hand on a sharp edge. It slices through my palm. Blood fills the cut. It stings instantly and I have to grit my teeth against a yelp.

"What's wrong?" Po shouts.

"Nothing!" I call back and keep going.

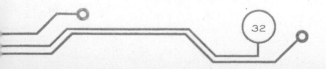

I scramble over another torso. Then another. Just one more to go. I dig my feet into a nook between two bots and push with a grunt. I nearly clear the top when I notice something in the rubble.

A robot head. Two giant owl-like eyes stare back at me. The mouth is contorted like it was trying to screech when someone smashed its body to pieces. It reminds me instantly of Cleo.

I shrink away, and my bloody hand slips. I lose my footing and suddenly I'm dangling from the mound of bot junk by one hand.

The crowd gasps. Po yells, "Trout!"

My fingers ache. I can't hold on anymore. I let go and slide down the side of the fountain. Water mists my face. I clunk against an arm, bang my elbow on a foot and thunk over a shell before I find something to grab hold of.

"Trout!" Po calls again.

I hang for a second before I find a spot for my feet and grab on to a neck hole with my other hand. I take a deep breath as the water trickles down my face. "I'm okay," I say, but I'm feeling the sting of the cut and the bruise of the hits.

At least I didn't crash to my death.

"Can you make it?" Po asks.

"Yeah."

My way down is slower than my way up. When I finally reach the ground, Po crushes me against him in a hug. "You okay?"

"I'm fine. But you're squeezing the air outta me."

People behind us are cheering. Johz whoops. Marsi and her friends clap. For a split second, I forget about the war and about Dad being gone, and scan the crowd looking for him. To see if he's proud of me too.

But he isn't there. Obviously. It's just Po and me now.

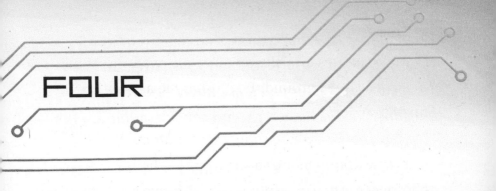

FOUR

JOHZ DUBS THE butt-kisser chair my throne. "Because the gnarly lad is King of Bot Mountain!" Any other time, I'd soak up the special treatment, but I'm feeling empty inside. What if Dad is never around to see the cool things I do? Like when I get my driver's license. Or when I graduate from high school. I never thought about all the things he'll miss if he never comes back.

As Johz and Po reenact a *Man vs. Bot* scene, I pull out my Link, careful of the cut on my hand, and check my e-mail. I refresh my in-box and one new message pops up. The subject reads: *Getting to Know Brack Submission.*

My heart war-drums in my chest. I click on the message, holding my breath as it loads. The world goes silent so all I can hear is the beating of my heart. This is it.

Dear Mr. St. Kroix,
We have reviewed your submission to the *Get-*

ting to Know Brack show, and must regretfully decline to feature you and your father on the show at this time. Please know that your submission was given careful consideration . . .

I stop reading. My legs go numb. I can't feel my toes. I can't feel my fingers. This was my last chance to get help looking for Dad.

Now my chance is gone.

How could they turn me down? The disappointment turns into a black hole in my chest, threatening to swallow me from the inside out. Tears sting my eyes. I have to get out of here. NOW.

I leap out of the butt-kisser throne. "Po!" I shout. "I'm going to the bathroom."

I don't wait for him to answer. I follow the winding paved path around the fountain and to the convenience center. I have to pass the concession stand in order to get to the bathrooms, and my stomach growls at the smell of French fries and cotton candy.

I skirt around an old lady as she tries to quiet her kid. He's wailing about getting a red snow cone when he wanted a blue one. I'm so focused on the kid that I'm not watching where I'm going and before I know it, I smack right into someone.

"Jeez, clanker!" a raspy, girly voice says. "Watch where you're going!"

I don't have to see the face to know who it is.

Tellie Rix.

I bounce back a foot and look up at her. Big blond curls hang around her face like a tangle of old computer wires. Her mouth is screwed up in a scowl, and the purple lipstick she wears only makes the expression scarier. She looks like an ocean monster drudged up from the trenches of the Pacific.

She holds her Link in one hand, while she fingers a cluster of charms hanging around her neck with the other hand. She pops a hip out, like, *Whatchya gonna do now, drain clogger?* But I've got nothing to come back with since she's pretty much the last person I want to see right now.

"Sorry," I mutter.

"Sorry?" is all she says, still playing with her necklace. "Gosh, St. Kroix, get your eyes checked before you find yourself stumbling into Bot Territory or something."

Hearing mention of the bots makes me want to cry harder and I don't want Tellie, or her friends behind her, to see me cry like that snow-cone kid. I rush past her, arm my way through a group of old people, and slam my way into the bathroom. I hide out in one of the stalls, locking the door behind me with the press of my thumb.

The toilet lid slams in place when I knock it down, and I plop onto it, holding my head in my hands, ignoring the stinging in my palm as the tears finally come pouring out.

I miss my dad more than anything in the world. And no one cares except for Po. People like Tellie Rix have their mom and dad and a big stupid house and they have no idea who Robert St. Kroix even is.

Two years ago, the night before Dad left, I cried really hard and Dad sat down with me on the stinky old apricot couch and said, "I'll be back before you know it. It'll be like I was never gone."

I had swiped the tears outta my eyes. "Promise?"

He grinned big, hooked me around the neck, and gave me a weak bolt burn across the top of the head. "How could I not come back when I have you and Po to pick on?"

I laughed and wrestled out of his grip.

I'd believed him when he said he'd come home.

But the longer he's gone, the more I think maybe he's gone for good.

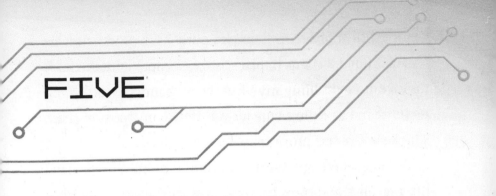

FIVE

IT SEEMS LIKE forever before I'm able to sniff back the tears and snot and show my face outside of the bathroom. Only three people stand in line at the concession center now. The smell of food turns my stomach into a snarling beast and I don't want to go back to Po just yet anyway. At least not until my eyes stop looking like juiced strawberries.

I get in line behind a burly man who smells like pizza and engine grease. As I wait, I check my cred balance, punching in the pin on my Link to log into my account. I have ten creds. I look at the menu board above the ordering window. The digital sign glows neon green like a radioactive dump.

I have enough creds for a bottle of water and a small bag of chips. I order, tap my Net-tag on the pay pad, and watch my creds count down to zero on my Link.

Outside, the sun is gone and the sky has melted to a

shade of dull blue. I follow the path back to Po and his friends, but I take my time getting there. I don't think they've noticed how long I've been gone. No one even looks at me as I plop back down in the butt-kisser chair. The holo-fire has grown since I left.

As Po relays his latest Chinley's prank (he stuffed his fake leg in a box of wrapped chicken so the other cook found it, which made her scream her choppin' head off), I finish my chips. All around me, voices rise and fall. Laughter and shouting and dogs barking and kids screaming. I usually like being in the park when it's like this, but all I can think about is Dad in Bot Territory and how geared out he must have been when he fought in the war. I can almost hear the sound of the laser guns in my head. *Thwip. Thwip. Thhhhhwip.*

Thinking about the war while sitting in the middle of a park is weird. It's like the war is a movie I watched on vid—a story someone made up. Because here everything is fine. Just fine. Even when the war first started, and bots were dragged out of houses and stores, not a lot of them fought back. At least not here.

All I want to do is go home and crawl into bed. Could I sleep the next gazillion years away? Maybe when I wake up, this stupid world won't be as nuke and doom as it is now.

"Po!" I shout, and he glances over a shoulder.

"Yeah?"

"Can we leave?"

His eyes dart to Marsi and her group. They're sitting around a holo-fire too, but their group is a lot quieter than Po's group. Dad would have said "civilized." Unlike Po's group, who's as loud as a pack of hyenas.

"It's still early," Po says.

"I'm tired."

"Aren't any of your friends here?" he tries. "Take a walk or something. How about that?"

"I don't want to."

He looks at Marsi one more time and then says, "Please?"

Like he's suddenly going to get brave enough to troop his way over there and talk to her. Like tonight is his last chance and if he goes home, he'll lose it. Like he even *has* a chance.

Every part of me goes wiry with anger. Ogling Marsi is more important than me, his own brother? I'd never choose a girl over him. Like girls are that important.

I get up and stomp right over to Marsi and her friends and announce in my loudest voice: "My brother has the fiery hots for you. He's just too much of a chicken to do anything about it."

Marsi and all her friends stop talking and stare at me like I'm a total space case.

And that's when Po yanks me back by the shirt and drags me out of the park.

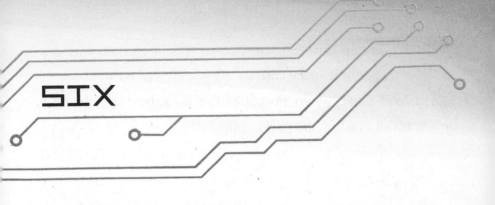

SIX

"**W**HAT WERE YOU thinking?" Po shouts.

The front door slams shut when he gives it a kick. I plop down on the couch and cross my arms over myself. This is stupid. This whole day is stupid. Sending the letter to Mrs. Rix was stupid. Why did I think my story was special enough to get on the show? If I had a vid account on the Net, I'd post my *own* vid and I'd get my dad home. I know I would.

I look at the arm of the couch, at the burn mark in the apricot-colored material from the time Dad accidentally set the iron down. He used to sleep on the couch so Po and I could have our own bedrooms. He used it for everything. Sleeping. Eating. Ironing.

Suddenly, I don't want to be here sitting on the same couch Dad sat on right before he left for the war.

I leap up.

"You made me look like an idiot!" Po says, and I realize

he's been talking this whole time and I haven't heard a word he's said.

"I'm sorry," I mutter. "I didn't mean to." Really all I wanted was to get his attention.

Well, congratulations, bolt sniffer, a tiny voice in my head says, *you got his attention.* And I kinda feel bad now that it's all over with. The look on Po's face is part angry beast, part sad puppy, and I wish I could take it all back.

Po stops pacing the living room and sets his hands on his hips. "What's gotten into you lately?"

My confession zooms through my head. I think about telling Po about the letter, about how badly I want to do *something* to get Dad home, about how I can't stop thinking about Dad at all.

But I'm scared he'll tell me it's pointless. Instead, I shrug and say, "I had a headache and didn't want to be there anymore, and you wouldn't leave."

He runs his hand through his hair. "How about next time you just say, 'Hey, let's get out of here before I gear out and ruin your life'?"

I fidget with a string hanging from my shirt, avoiding looking my brother in the eyes.

"I'm going to bed," he says, even though it's a good two hours before his usual bedtime. His footsteps thump down the hallway and into his bedroom. His bed squeaks

as he drops down on it. There's a click a second later as he undoes his fake leg, taking it out of the bracket.

I stand there listening to the emptiness of the house and the hollowness of my chest, like my heart ran off in the middle of the day because it was sick of hurting.

Not that I would blame it.

I wake the next morning feeling like a pancake, and it takes everything I have to crawl out of bed. It's a good thing it's summertime, because I would have missed the bus to school if it weren't. And then Po would probably ground me.

I trudge down the hallway and find Po in the kitchen making eggs. I stall a second to see if he's still mad.

"Yo," he says. "You want any?"

My stomach grumbles and Po cracks open two more eggs without me saying anything. So I guess we're all right. I do my part in our morning routine. I put the bread in the toaster and set the table. If you can even call it a table. It's just this tiny round piece of wood big enough for Po and me. I think it was supposed to be for a front porch and probably had some fancy-schmancy name like The Lily Garden Café Set. We bought it last year after our last set, the one with *three* chairs, finally bit the space dust.

When the toaster dings, I scoop up the bread and plop it onto two plates. Po slides the eggs out of the pan next to the toast. We sit and dig in like a couple of starving dogs. We don't talk. Just eat. And while I eat, I scheme ways to get Dad home.

I still think getting his name on the Net is the best way. Sometimes people make vids that spread through the Net like crazy, and pretty soon everyone is talking about them. And if everyone is talking about Dad, then everyone will be looking for him.

There's just one problem. Or two. Okay . . . a lot of problems.

I don't have a vidcam. I don't have a vid account. And it takes the United Districts Net Control, or UDNC as everyone calls it, weeks to approve new accounts. Half the time they deny the requests anyway. Plus the application fee is probably way more than my allowance.

I bet Tellie Rix has a vid account.

"Earth to Trout?"

I look up. Po is staring at me with his eyebrows scrunched together. "What?" I say.

"I've been talking to you for like five minutes and you haven't said a word."

I gobble up the last chunk of egg and shrug.

"You're still acting weird," he says. "I was hoping a

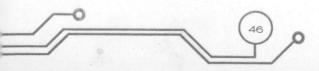

good night's sleep would bring you back to the land of normal."

All I say is, "You're weird all the time." Po wrinkles his nose at me.

When breakfast is done, I'm the one who cleans up and Po mutters something about needing a shower. When I hear the water running through the pipes, I hurry onto the Net and look up Tellie Rix on Luna. There's a vid on her front page of her and some of her lame friends shopping.

I knew she'd have a vid account. And I'm not surprised she uses it to post stupid vids of her and her friends picking out dresses.

Tellie Rix has everything. And all I've got is this old stinkin' house and a brother with one leg who tries to be my dad but can't.

I log off the Net, beat on the bathroom door, and yell to Po, "I'm going for a walk!" and hurry out before he can tell me no.

SEVEN

TELLIE RIX LIVES in the Outer Banks and it takes me a half hour to walk there. As I turn down her street, I'm surprised at how thin the hover rails are here. They must be the newer models I heard about. The upgrade is supposed to be more powerful (gives the cars and hoverboards a quicker boost, so you can get where you're going in less time). They break down less. Which is cool. Because the rails in our neighborhood break down all the time and then you coast along the road at the pace of a snail, running on nothing but leftover boost.

Even though I've never been in this neighborhood, I know exactly where Tellie lives. Lox had a crush on her last year, so I got to learn all sorts of random facts about her life. Her house is on the corner of Fifth and Ocean and it's easily three times the size of mine. The outside is the color of pineapples, and the trim is white and fancy.

A brand-new XR33 sits in the driveway. You don't

even need hover rails with that thing. They call it an off-roader. You can take it wherever you want without needing a boost, because it creates its own. It probably drives itself too. Lox's mom has an auto-drive car. Sometimes she lets us take it to the movies or the mall, but if they had an XR33, Lox and I could go anywhere we wanted. We could go to 4th District and see the floating island cities in the middle of Lake Michigan.

I hesitate as I stare at the house, feeling like a slug in a box of jelly doughnuts. I don't belong here.

Just go, gearbox.

I cross the street, but as I head up the front walk, an underground sprinkler system kicks on and cold water blasts me in the face. I screech like a little girl and run the rest of the way to the front door. But it's too late. I'm already soaked. My white T-shirt is plastered to my body and shows off my non-existent muscles. My brown hair is plastered to my forehead.

Maybe you should go home, that annoying voice in my head says. But I can't. I made it here and I need a vid and Tellie is the only one I know who has an account.

So shut up, I tell the voice.

I fix my hair and ring some of the water out of my shirt. As I stand there, the front door pulls open and an older woman (who isn't Mrs. Rix) looks down at me.

"Can I help you?" she says as she wipes her hands on a towel.

"Is Tellie home?"

"Are you a friend of hers?"

"Um . . ." I stall for a millisecond as I try to decide which is better—a lie or the truth? "Sorta," I say. "We go to the same school."

The woman opens the door wider and says, "Well, come in, and wait right here."

I step inside. The house is cold because of the air-conditioning, and gooseflesh pops on my arms. I try to make myself warmer by hugging myself and bouncing around on the balls of my feet.

"Here, dry off," the woman says, handing me her towel.

"Thanks."

As I scrub the water out of my hair, she goes to a monitor on the wall and presses a button. "Tellie," she says, "you've got a visitor."

"Who is it?" Tellie's raspy voice answers back.

The woman looks at me. I lick my lips. "Tell her it's Trout," I say.

A smile pulls at the corner of her mouth. "Like the fish?"

"Yeah. Unfortunately."

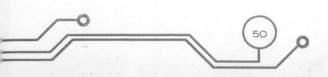

"Interesting." Through the monitor she says, "Says he's a fish."

"I didn't say that!"

Tellie sighs. "I'll be down in a sec."

"Where did you get a name like that?" the woman asks as she steps away from the monitor.

I just shrug. Po was the one who started calling me Trout when I was like one minute old, and everyone has called me Trout since then, even my dad. Unless I'm in trouble. Then he uses my full name.

"Well, I best get back to work, Trout like the fish," she says with a smirk. She disappears through a doorway on the left.

While I wait, I check out the house. To the right of the front door is the living room. A big couch curves around the room in a U shape. A massive vid panel hangs on the wall, surrounded by shelves that are mostly empty except for two family photos and a stack of books.

Directly in front of me are the stairs and farther back is a door that leads out to a patio and a pool. The closest Po and I have come to a pool is a puddle in the backyard.

Tellie stomps down the stairs a few minutes later and says, "What do you want?"

Up until this point, I was fine coming here. Tellie and

I aren't best friends or anything, so her opinion of me doesn't matter. Or at least it didn't. But now that she's staring at me, my heart acts like it wants to tuck its tail between its legs and take off running. My dad used to say that not one person was better than the next, that all human beings were created equal. But as I look up at Tellie standing there in expensive clothes in her expensive house, I can't help but feel like that same slug I felt like out on the sidewalk.

"Um . . ."

Tellie leans into the railing and cocks her hip out as she waits for my brain to start working. "Yeah?"

"Well . . ."

Silence. Tellie swings her weight to the other foot. Water drips from my nose.

"I need help making a vid and getting it on the Net." The words tumble out of my mouth like marbles on a Net game.

Tellie straightens and pushes her braided hair off her shoulder. "What kind of vid?"

So I tell her. In one long string of words. And she listens without saying anything. When I stop to take a breath, she comes down the rest of the stairs and looks me right in the face.

"You miss your dad?" she says.

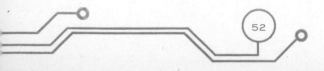

No one has ever asked me that. Po knows I miss Dad. And I'm sure Tanith at the Heart Office knows I miss Dad. But no one ever bothered to *ask* me how I felt. And I'm shocked right down to my toes that it's Tellie Rix who is the first person to say the words.

"Yeah," I answer as a leftover drop of water rolls down my neck. "More than anything."

"Well, come on then. My vid cam is upstairs."

If Lox knew I was in Tellie Rix's bedroom, he'd go nuclear. Her room looks the way I thought it would look—big and pink and fluffy—but there are things in here I didn't expect to see.

A hoverboard is propped up against the wall across from the closet, along with a helmet and goggles. I've never seen Tellie on a hoverboard before. There's a Rezzies poster hanging above her bed and a Junction Box poster right next to that. Both groups play reg-ray rock. I had no idea Tellie liked that kind of music. I figured she'd be in love with Tanner Waylon, that kid who sings dumb love songs about broken hearts and other lame stuff.

Tellie sits at her desk and pulls a vid cam from its charge plate. "Have you thought about what you want to say?"

I walk farther into the room feeling weird. Fact is, I never thought I'd get this far. "No. Not really."

She pulls out a SimPad and hands it to me. "Let's make a script. If you're going to do this, you should do it right."

I take it carefully ('cuz they're expensive, and all I need is to accidentally drop it) and then stare at it like it's an X-bomb. I've never even breathed the same air as a SimPad, let alone used one. Not that a SimPad needs to breathe.

Tellie looks at me like I just grew a set of horns and then sighs again before prompting the pad with the touch of her finger. The screen brightens as it comes to life. "Compose," Tellie says. A window opens and the pad projects a holo image of the document in midair. "Just press your finger to the orange light at the bottom when you want to speak. Press it again to stop recording."

I press my finger to the square of light and a cursor flashes on the screen.

I freeze like a Popsicle.

Tellie waves her hand, coaxing me to say something.

"Hello." The cursor writes out the word and the holo image shows a 3-D version of the text in thick white letters between us. "My name is Trout St. Kroix and I need help finding my dad."

EIGHT

IT TAKES US almost an hour to get the script right, and another to shoot the vid. In that time, Tellie rolls her eyes at least sixteen gajillion times and sighs at the end of every sentence. But when we replay the vid, I realize it was all worth it.

Now my face is on the vid panel, big as Mars. "Hello, my name is Trout . . ." vid-me says.

"I don't sound like that. Do I?"

Tellie looks at me, eyebrows scrunched together. "Yes. You're practically a chipmunk."

"Whatever," I say, and we turn back to the vid as the rest plays out.

"I haven't spoken to my dad since right before Thanksgiving. He said he was doing one more mission before going on leave. He was stationed in Bot Territory near the Mississippi River. He has an ID chip, but his thread hasn't come back online. The commander of his troop said Dad disappeared during the mission. I think he's still alive somewhere out there. I can feel it. So if you have any information, please contact me: smarterkroix@zipspeed.5dtr."

My face disappears and a picture of Dad flashes on the screen just above my e-mail address. The picture is from the summer right before Po left for the war, before he lost his leg, before Dad volunteered and changed everything. That was our last vacation together. We went to Lake Tahoe for a week, and I caught a total of seventeen fish. Po only caught three. It was the best week of my life.

In the pic, Dad's smiling, his arms around Po and me. Dad's hair is messy, like always, because he said brushing it was a waste of time.

A man has better things to do than preen.

When the vid ends, my eyes sting and I sniff back what I know are tears. I can't start crying in the middle of Tellie Rix's bedroom.

"So what do you think?" she says.

"I like it. It's totally wrenched." I duck my head, pretend I got something in my eye, and rub them both with the heels of my hands. When I think I'm good, I sit up straight, and meet Tellie's gaze.

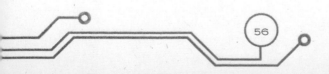

The look on her face says she knows I'm a big baby. She turns back to the computer. "You think it's ready?"

I nod, even though her back is to me. "Yeah, I think so."

She clicks a few things on her computer. "I'm uploading it to my Luna page. And I'll e-mail a friend of mine about it too. He runs a site and if he links up, maybe the vid will get some extra views."

I go to the desk and watch her work over her shoulder. For a girl, she's really good with computers. Her fingers glide over the keys, then she hits ENTER and a snapshot of the vid is up on her Luna page.

"Done." She smiles, beaming with pride, and I have to say, I'm really impressed.

"Thanks, Tellie."

She shrugs. "It's no big deal."

I fidget and then say, "I should probably go. I kinda bolted from the house before telling my brother where I was going. He's probably pretty mad."

At the front door, Tellie leans against the frame, arms crossed in front of her. The house is quiet behind us. I guess her parents aren't home yet.

"So, I'll see you later," I say, and step down onto the walkway.

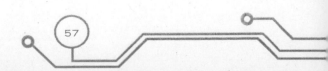

"Hey, Trout?"

I turn around. "Yeah?"

"I hope it works. The vid. I hope you find your dad."

"Thanks," I say. "Me too."

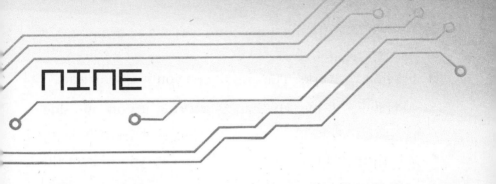

NINE

THE FIRST FEW days the vid is up, it doesn't get that many hits. Still, I stalk my e-mail like a bird stalking a worm. On the third night, I get so tired of watching my in-box that I go to bed early and read until I can't keep my eyes open.

The next morning, I wake to a dinging noise. At first I think it's my alarm clock, but then I remember it's summer break, so why would I set my alarm?

I sit up and blink back the sleep crusting in my eyes as I try to figure out where the noise is coming from. And then I realize it's the chime I set up on the computer to alert me to a new e-mail.

Ding. Ding-ding.

I throw back the blankets, rush down the hallway, hoping to reach the computer before Po does. I must have forgotten to log off last night! I'm such a bolt-head!

I tear into the living room. Po is already there frowning at the computer. I come up alongside him and freeze.

The little e-mail icon at the bottom of the screen says *373 Unread E-mails.*

Holy space junk.

Po turns to me. His hair is sticking up on one side, mashed to his head on the other. His eyes are still heavy with sleep. "Dude, what the chop? Did you kidnap the Pope or something?"

My fingers itch to click through the icon and read the e-mails. Any one of them could lead to Dad! But I don't. Because if Po finds out, there's no telling what he'll do. I log off with a tap of my finger.

"It's probably spam or something," I say.

Po snorts. "Yeah, sure."

Thankfully he lets it go and heads into the kitchen, banging pots and pans around. "You want some French toast?"

I'm still staring at the computer screen when I answer. "Two pieces."

"You got any plans today?"

"No. Do you have to work?"

"Yeah. Late shift again. I'll probably take a nap this afternoon. You got anything you need me to do before then?"

I check the clock in the corner of the computer. It's just

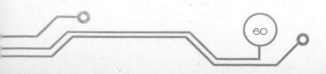

after ten. The late shift usually starts at five, so Po will probably take a nap from two to four.

"No," I say.

Why are so many e-mails pouring in? Tellie might be popular, but she's not *that* popular. I set the table like usual, but have a hard time focusing. I accidentally give Po two spoons and grab the salad dressing instead of syrup.

If Po thought I was acting weird before, he probably thinks I've completely geared out today. Somehow I make it through breakfast and clean the table as Po does laundry. And then I sit on the couch, my knee bobbing up and down.

I watch the clock like it's the last day of school.

Finally, after I straighten up my bedroom, vacuum, and put away the dishes, Po shuffles into the living room and says, "I'm gonna lie down. If I'm not up by four, will you get me up?"

"Yeah! Sure!"

He narrows his eyes.

"What?" I say.

"What are you up to?"

I let out a nervous laugh. "What do you mean?"

He sighs. "Never mind. Just, make sure I'm up."

"I will."

His bedroom door shuts. I wait all of a second to leap over the back of the couch.

When I log into my e-mail, it says I have 402 unread messages.

People are responding to my vid! Maybe Dad is out there somewhere. I read through every message carefully.

I don't know where your dad is, one lady wrote, but I just wanted to tell you, you and your family are in my prayers.

Yo, I hope you find your pops! a guy named T-Zone wrote.

Dude, your face is funny-looking. And your nose is shaped like a tuna fish.

I go cross-eyed trying to look at my nose. A tuna fish? Delete.

An hour later, I've read and responded to and deleted over a hundred e-mails and I'm no closer to information on Dad's location. No one seems to know Dad, or anything about Bot Territory. They only e-mail about the vid, or me, or to wish me luck.

There are at least a dozen messages about my face. That it's shaped funny. It's too pale. Too small. Too wide. One lady offered to bake me a casserole because she thought I was too skinny.

By message two hundred, I'm so tired of reading e-mails I start deleting them without responding. I can only write *thank you* so many times. And when I clear out the in-box, I check the vid one more time for messages left in the comment section.

I'm reading another one about my voice when I hear a gasp behind me. I whirl around in the chair. Po is standing in the middle of the living room, his gaze fixed on the vid, *on my vid face*.

Jam.

"What is that?" he says, pointing a finger at the screen.

"Nothing!" I start tapping at the board in a panic.

"How did you get a vid on the Net? What's it . . ." He reads the title of the page. "'Help me find my dad'? Are you kidding me? Trout! This is the last thing we need right now. Drawing attention to ourselves!"

I manage to close out the Net page. Po and I stare at the desktop picture of Lake Tahoe, the water glittering in the sunlight.

"Take that vid down," Po snaps.

"No way!" I stand up. "It might help us find him. If someone has seen him . . ."

Po lumbers toward me and gets right in my face. He clenches his teeth. "Take it down."

"Why?"

"Because . . ."

"Because why?"

His eyes are big now, fully alert. "Because we're not going to find him! Not like this."

I put my hands on my hips. "Do you think he's alive?"

Po pushes away from me toward the hallway.

"Do you think he's out there somewhere? Po? Tell me!"

In the doorway to the bathroom, he stops and takes a deep breath. His expression softens as the anger runs out of him. "Of course I do." He sighs. "We'll find him. Just . . . not like that. People on the Net are cruel, ya know? They'll make a joke out of it."

I already know that's true, because half of the e-mails and comments I've gotten are people making fun of me.

"Take it down," he says, and then adds, "Please."

This was supposed to be my big chance. I wanted to show Po that I could find Dad on my own, but maybe it *was* a dumb idea. And anyway, now I guess I have Po on my side. And a promise from him that he'll help me look. However he plans to do that.

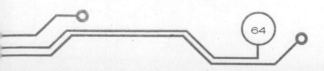

"Yeah, all right." I hang my head. "I just have to go to Tellie's to do it. She's the one who posted it."

"Sure. Just be home before dark."

Po shuts the door to the bathroom, and the shower turns on a second later. I grab my raincoat, remembering my Link warned of a storm later today, and start walking toward Tellie's.

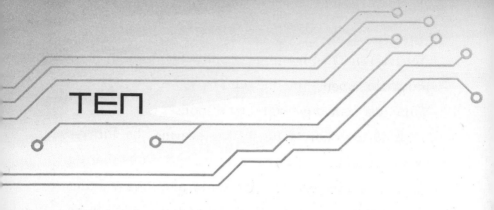

TEN

RAIN POUNDS AGAINST the window above the sink in Tellie's kitchen. Thankfully, I made it over here just before it started pouring. Tellie peels open an instant pizza and slides it into the infrared oven. I climb onto one of the stools as music plays from the Net station embedded in the counter. It's a new Junction Box song with bongos and quick, snappy guitar riffs. It's my favorite song, and judging by the way Tellie shakes her shoulders to the beat, it's a song she likes too.

"I guess I get why Po wants me to delete the vid," I say. "But I kinda want to keep it up just in case."

Tellie sits across from me. "Maybe he hates being in the spotlight. Like, having people pay attention to him."

I shrug as I wipe the sweat from my glass of water. "Maybe." But Po's not afraid of attention. The only time I ever see him acting like a silent weirdo is when Marsi is around. "Anyway, I guess we have to delete it."

"If you say so." Tellie comes around the counter to my

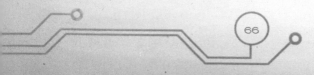

side and taps in a command on the Net station. A browser window pops open.

"How did the vid get so many responses today?" I ask.

"I don't know. This is the first I'm hearing about it, but maybe it's . . . oh."

I scoot in closer. "What?" My vid is up on the browser and I look at the number of hits on the lower right-hand corner. "Holy jet smoke," I breathe. There are 543,773 views!

"How did—I don't get—how—"

Tellie types in a Net address and pulls up the Dekker Site and there I am. My vid. The headline says: *FishKid Looks for Dad in Enemy Waters.*

"Aaron Dekker?" I say. "How did you get Aaron Dekker to link to my vid?"

The oven dings. Tellie goes around to pull out the pizza. "Well, when I first asked him to link to it, he said no. I didn't know he changed his mind."

I remember her telling me she'd ask a friend to link up when we first posted the vid. "Are you friends with him?"

Aaron Dekker is a Net star who lives in Texas, the only remaining state that's separate from the Districts. My history teacher said that Texas was full of a bunch of "no-good bot supporters" and that they thought "they were better than the UD." Texas is super-rich, and was during the financial collapse, so it didn't need to join with other states or the new Congress. Its government didn't one hundred percent agree with banning robots either.

Aaron doesn't have to follow the UNDC's restrictions, since he isn't part of the UD. He posts whatever he wants on the Net. That doesn't mean the UD doesn't try to stop him. His site is shut down like every day, but it usually only takes him three seconds to find a way around the block.

"My mom interviewed him forever ago," Tellie explains, "and I was traveling with her that day. We've kept in touch."

I lick my lips. "So he linked up to my vid?"

"I guess so, but I wonder what changed his mind." Tellie pulls the rubber band from her hair and the blond ringlets fall across her shoulders. I can't stop a stray thought from running through my head. *Wow, she's pretty,* the thought says. And then I squash it like a meaty bug.

"Before we delete it, want to do a search and see if people are talking about it anywhere else?"

"Sure."

After Tellie divides the pizza between us, we go to the living room. She brings up the Net interface on the vid panel and types in "Robert St. Kroix." A bunch of

results appear. Tellie picks the first link and it takes us to a site where people are placing bets on Dad's location. There's even an interactive world map where you can pin a virtual tack to any location and write in your name.

At another site, a girl named Heller tore apart the family photo from the vid and animated the three of us, putting us in some ridiculous Wild West action comic. Dad's name is Sharp-Shooter St. Kroix and Po is Po the Piper and I'm Wily Fish.

At first I think it's funny, because Po looks ridiculous in a cowboy hat and leather chaps, but the longer I stare at it, the angrier I get. Because my dad is missing and there he is dancing around, looking like a joke.

I grit my teeth, take in a gulp of air.

Tellie glances at me. "It's just a bunch of drain cloggers. What do they know?"

I can't stand to look at the screen for one more second. "My brother was right. We should take it down."

She types in two quick commands and when the screen reloads, it says: *Your media has been deleted.* The speakers belch out a crunching sound, like the vid was a piece of trash crumpled up and tossed into a Dumpster.

"There. Done."

"Thanks." But even though the vid is gone from Tellie's

Luna page, we both know the vid isn't gone for *good*. I wanted it to spread through the Net and I got my wish. It's all *over* the Net.

At least I did what Po asked.

"It was worth a shot," Tellie says quietly. "If your dad is out there somewhere, he knows you're looking for him. He knows you love him."

"Yeah."

We're both quiet for a long time. The air-conditioning turns on with a click, and whirs through the vents. "I wish I had a family like yours," Tellie says.

I frown. "What do you mean? I have no parents."

Tellie snorts. "Neither do I. I mean, yeah, they're here, but they're not *really* here. Which is almost worse."

"That's stupid." And unfair, I think, but I don't say that, because of the way her eyes get all watery-looking. Now Tellie is the one who's crying? "I mean . . . I'm sorry."

"No, you're right. That was wrong of me to say." She leaps off the couch and grabs both our plates. I follow her to the kitchen.

"Your mom and dad are never home?" I try. She's been a big help to me, and she's listened to me whine about my own family. I should have been more of a friend when she wanted to talk about hers. But are we friends? I still don't know.

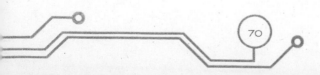

She slides the plates into the dishwasher. "I see the housekeeper more than I see my mom."

"That's notched."

"Yeah." She turns on the dishwasher and the light glows red. "And my dad . . . sometimes it's like he doesn't even know I exist."

I shove my hands in the pockets of my shorts. I don't know what to say. I guess it's better not to say anything. Tellie seems okay with that anyway. She quickly changes the subject and shows me her stash of chocolate. It's more candy than I've ever seen outside of a store.

We spend the rest of the afternoon stuffing our faces. And by the time I go home, I think maybe Tellie and I really are friends.

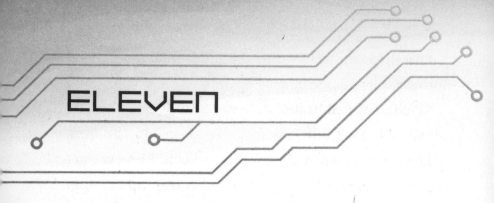

ELEVEN

OX CALLS THE next day. I grin big when I see it's him, and I can't wait to tell him everything that's happened. But when I pick up and his big face comes on the screen, he doesn't waste a second before opening his mouth.

"Thousands of girls all across the world are writing your name in hearts right now," he says. Then he raises his voice real high. "I heart Trout. XOXO. Forever."

I move outside of the phone's camera range. "Come on! Or I'll make you talk to the toilet."

"Trout is so cute!" he goes on. "Marry me, Trout!"

I go into the bathroom and point the phone at the toilet.

"Dude," he says, his voice echoing in the bowl, "you need to scrub that thing."

At least he isn't making fun of me anymore. I pull the phone back so that the camera points at me. "Can we have a normal conversation now?"

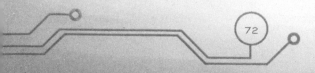

Lox scratches his scraggly blond hair and says, "Define normal."

"Well, if you shut up long enough to let me talk, I'll tell you all about Tellie's bedroom."

Lox's expression inflates like a balloon. His eyes get bigger, his nostrils flare, his eyebrows creep up his forehead. "YOU WERE IN TELLIE RIX'S BEDROOM?"

I laugh, because that's exactly what I wanted him to say. "You should have seen your face just now."

"You're changing the subject!"

"All right. All right!"

"Details, my friend."

I start by telling him about the hoverboard I found in her room the first time I was there, and then about the Junction Box poster. But somehow I veer off in a totally different direction about how funny she is, and how she started calling me Goldfish because she thought I looked more like one than a trout.

And before I know it, Lox is pointing *his* phone at the toilet.

"Hey!" I shout.

"You need to bring it back and take it down a notch."

"What's that supposed to mean?"

"You sound like a fangirl at a Tanner Waylon concert. You got the fiery hots for Tellie now?"

I snort and pretend like I'm turning off the Link.

"Wait!" Lox says.

I pause.

"All right, I'm done." Lox puts on his most serious face, which looks like a horse eating a sour gummy worm. "Any word on your dad?"

All the laughter dies in my throat. "No. Not yet."

"I bet news is just around the corner. Your vid is spreading through the Net like the screaming memes."

I wrinkle my nose. *Screaming memes* is Lox's term for the flu. And not the kind that comes out your mouth.

"That's gross." The doorbell rings from the front of the house. "Someone's here. Hold on."

I make my way down the hallway and to the front door. I check the tiny screen in the security pad to the right of the door. It's an old system. The screen is the size of a peanut and it's really fuzzy.

There's a woman standing on the stoop holding something in her hand.

"I think it's just a delivery person," I tell Lox as I open the door, but once I get a good look outside, I see that it's not a delivery person at all. And it's not just *one* person.

News vans hover along the curb. More people stand on the brown lawn. Cameramen zoom in on reporters. The woman in front of me leans in with her sleek micro-

phone. "Mr. St. Kroix, can you comment on the latest development on your father?"

"What's she saying?" Lox says. "Point me at the action!"

"What development?" I blurt.

A cameraman turns and the light on his camera blinds me. People rush toward the house once they realize I've opened the door.

The reporter looks pleased to spill the bolts. "Your father's ID thread came back online this morning." She jams the microphone in my face.

I stammer out several syllables, but none of them actually make words.

"Dude!" Lox shouts.

"Mr. St. Kroix!" someone else yells.

"Trout! Where did you get your nickname? What does it mean?"

The crowd is suddenly crushing. There are so many people crammed on the stoop and gathered around the three steps that I can barely see past them to the street. Their voices mix together in an ear-scraping sound. My heart hammers against the hill of my tongue.

I back into the house and slam the door shut. Lox yells through the Link to get my attention. I bring the phone back up so we can see each other.

"What was all that noise?" he asks.

I get far away from the door, taking off like I'm on a hoverboard, and hurry into my bedroom. I slam the door shut and drop down on the bed.

"That was crazy," I say. The reporter's words bounce around in my head like stray laser beams. Dad. Thread. Online. ZING. ZING. How? When? ZING. Does Po know?

"I gotta go," I say.

"What? Now?" Lox shouts. "You didn't tell me what was going on!"

"I'll call you later."

I hit the END button and the screen goes back to my default picture—a scientific diagram of a wolf monkey. Dad loved wolf monkeys.

My stomach twists up in knots thinking about him. Did his ID thread *really* come back online?

Is he alive out there somewhere waiting to be saved?

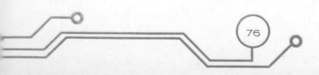

TWELVE

IT TAKES PO twice as long to get inside after work because of all the reporters and cameramen. And when he finally does burst in the door, his face is all screwed up and he's breathing like a racehorse.

"Mother son of a—" he shouts once he's safely inside, cutting himself off when he sees me. "You," he says, pointing. "This is your fault!"

I set down the box of crackers I'm feeding off of and jump to my feet. "I've been trying to call you. Where have you been? Did you hear about Dad?"

Po ignores me and disappears into the kitchen. I follow him and find him rooting around in the freezer.

"Dad's ID thread came back online," I say.

Po chips away at a mound of frost. I think there's a box of frozen macaroni and cheese under it, but I can't be sure.

"Are you listening to me?"

The freezer kicks on and cold white air pumps out.

Po makes quick work of the frost, tears out the box of macaroni, and rips open the top. He digs inside and pulls out a tiny black stick attached to a ball chain.

He presses his index finger to one end of the stick and his thumb to the other. When it beeps, a blue light . . . blinks on.

"What is that?" I ask.

"It's a scrambler. For your ID chip."

"You hid a scrambler in a box of macaroni?"

"It's pretty old," he says, totally ignoring me, "but it'll do the job." He slips the ball chain over my head. "Tuck it in your shirt. Keep it close to your heart."

I do as he asks. "Why am I wearing a scrambler?"

"Shh," he says, and points at the ceiling.

"I—"

He cuts me off with the shake of his head. He whirls around and taps the faucet. Water comes gushing out. Next, he pulls out his Link, punches in a few commands, and plays a French lesson. Marsi Olsen knows French, and Po bought an app a while back thinking he'd learn French too.

Lot of good it did him. How do you say "drain clogger" in French? Because that's something I'd like to know.

With the water running, and a dude rattling off French words, Po gets in real close to me and whispers in my

ear. "Just a precaution. You can never be too careful. Dad taught me that."

"Dad? When? I don't get—"

He points to his ear and I grumble before leaning in. He smells like fried food and cornbread. The smell of Chinley's always sticks to him after he gets out of work. I used to hate the stench, but now I think of it as the smell of my brother being home.

"You've notched this whole thing, you realize that?" he says.

I pull back and roll my eyes before saying, "Tell me what's going on then!"

"I can't!" Po whisper-shouts.

"Try!"

"Trout." He makes my name sound like a growl.

"Did Dad's thread come back online or not?"

The French lesson switches to popular phrases. "*Avec plaisir.* It was my pleasure. *Pas de quoi.* It was nothing."

Po stares at me for a long time and the longer he stares, the harder my heart beats. I can't tell if it's because of the anticipation of his answer or the chip in my heart reacting to the scrambler.

"Yes," he finally says, and all the air rushes out of my lungs.

"When?" I lean in closer. "Where is he?"

"It's probably a decoy, the thread. To move the attention away from where Dad's really at. Or maybe it's to lure us in . . ."

My eyebrows sink into a frown. "Where is he really at?"

"I've already told you too much. The less you know, the better. Trust me."

"Is Dad alive?" I blurt.

Po makes a face like he's afraid to tell me the truth. Finally, he nods his head.

I feel like my insides have turned to stone. I grit my teeth. "How long have you—"

He holds up a finger again, reminding me I have to watch what I say and how loudly I say it, even though I have no idea who would be listening.

All those months I'd been waiting around to hear the news that Dad was okay. And Po knew the whole time. The anger is like a cannon-laser bursting out of me. I shove him. He stumbles back, slamming into the counter. I throw a punch, but my aim is bad and it lands on his biceps. He grips my arms and pushes me into a chair.

"Calm down!" His face goes red.

"You knew! This whole time you were lying to me." I flail, kick, hit. Not that it does any good.

"STOP!" Po yells.

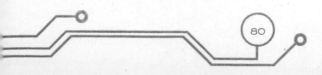

I slump against the chair and swallow a growl. I try to hold in all the things I want to scream. I'm so mad, I feel like an X-bomb about to go off.

"You won't tell me any of the important things!" I shout. "I'm not a little kid anymore!"

"I never said you were."

"Then tell me what you know."

Po shakes his head. "I can't, little bro. Not yet."

"Fine." I get up and shove the chair away. "Let me know when you *can* tell me."

"Trout," he calls as I stomp down the hallway.

I slam the bedroom door behind me and sink against it as I try to make sense of all the crud filling my head. All those visits to the Heart Office were pointless. I feel stupid now realizing I went in there all full of hope, wishing with everything I had for a different answer than *sorry*.

And Po knew all along.

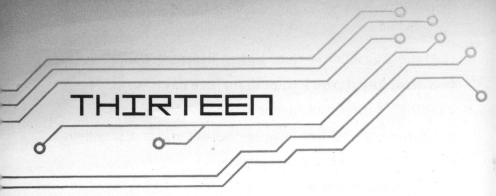

THIRTEEN

AROUND TEN O'CLOCK the next morning, my ex-brother comes out of his room. "I got some errands to run."

Errands is probably code for "I'm going to the Smoothie Shack to ogle Marsi while she works."

"Sure," I say, not even looking at him. If Po kept it a secret that Dad was alive, what else is he keeping from me? And why did he keep it a secret to begin with? I sit parked on the couch staring out the front window, my head buzzing like a broken hover rail.

Po stalls near the front door. "I'm sorry about yesterday."

I keep my face blank.

"I didn't mean to yell at you," he adds.

"Sure."

"Will you at least look at me?"

Sighing, I turn his way, arms crossed over my chest. "What?"

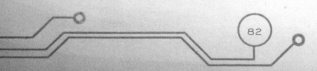

"I wish I could tell you. I do. It's just . . . it's better if you don't know. You'll understand one day."

"Fine." I turn back to the window. Part of me hates being mean to Po, but the other part of me is still ticked off, and that part is definitely winning.

"You want to come with me?"

"Nah."

He lets out a breath. "All right. Don't leave the house. I'll be back in a few hours."

I grunt as he leaves.

Reporters start showing up an hour later. Some of them ring the doorbell. I ignore it, wishing I had an underground sprinkler system like Tellie so I could turn it on. That'd send them running.

Two hours later, the doorbell has rung so many times, I start plotting ways to break it. But Lox is the one who's good with tools and electrical things. I'd probably burn the house down.

After three hours of cartoons, I realize it's closing in on dinnertime and Po still isn't home. I check the driveway and find it empty. There are still reporters hanging around, but they're thinning out. Probably because we haven't talked to them, and also because we're pretty boring.

When I've had enough TV, I search for my Link, thinking I'll call Lox or Tellie, but before I can find the stupid thing, it starts ringing. I dig it out from beneath my bed and see it's Po calling. I don't know if I feel like talking to him, so I let it ring a few seconds as I decide.

We're out of milk, so maybe I should tell him to pick some up. Course, it's not like I drink *that* much milk. But if I want a bowl of cereal later or something . . .

"Fine," I mutter, and pick up the call.

Po's face comes on the screen. He's at an odd angle, like he's holding the phone in his lap.

"What do you want?" I say.

"RUN!" he says, not looking at me.

"What?"

"Get out of the house!" he screams, shoving something away from him.

"Po? What the—"

There's a crunching sound somewhere out of range of the camera. A table topples over. Po throws a punch.

"Po!"

I clutch the phone harder, pull the screen closer to my face as if it'll help me see the whole picture, see who's attacking my brother.

An arm comes into view of the camera. A watch glints in the light. My brother ducks away, swings upward with

a fist. He's slammed back against a wall and the phone clatters to the floor.

The picture cuts out.

My Link goes blank.

Run, Po said.

So I run.

FOURTEEN

I SNEAK OUT THE back door and poke my head around the corner, surveying the street. Reporters run to the curb, their cameramen their shadows. A sleek black car with no official markings hovers in the middle of the street.

Patrolmen, maybe?

Fear does a nosedive down my spine. I press against the house, and the siding digs into my shoulders. Now what? Are they looking for me? Or are they here to shoo away the reporters?

I dare another look. Uniformed men make a path through the remaining crowd and hurry to the front door. I don't have time to think about why this is happening, or if Po is okay.

I break away from the house and run to the shed. Inside, I dig through some boxes as fast as I can. I find one of Po's old hats, a ratty fedora that molds to my head the second I put it on. I slide into a smelly jacket that's

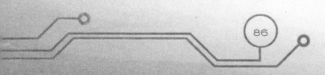

too big for me, but it hides how skinny I am, so I figure that's good.

If the police are looking for me, they're looking for a short, scrawny kid with short brown hair.

With my disguise on, I scramble out the tiny window in the back of the shed and leap over the fence into the neighbor's backyard, hitting the ground with an *umph*. Pain weasels into my knees.

I stumble to my feet and dodge a picnic table, then a kid's sandbox. I run along the side of the house and a dog leaps at a window, barking and scratching at the glass. My guts nearly jump outta my throat, and I slam into the fence behind me.

I get myself together and keep going. Staying on the street is dangerous, I think. Even though I have no idea what I'm running from or running to, I have a feeling I need to stay hidden, so I cut through yards and alleys. When I hit The Glitz, the clouds part and the sun blazes down on a two-story house to my right, hitting the shards of recycled glass. I tug on the brim of my fedora, using it to shield my eyes from the blinding light. I look for a yard to slink through, but the fences here are tall privacy fences, and I feel weird using someone's gate.

As I reach the end of the street, I hear the familiar

sound of a car on the rails, a soft whirring noise behind me.

I move faster.

A little kid rounds the corner up ahead on a hover-board.

The car closes in. Static fills the space around me like inflata foam, and it takes me too many seconds to realize it's the sound of a loudspeaker crackling as it's put to use.

"Identify yourself," a voice says through the speaker.

The little kid hops off his board. "Is he talking to you?"

My heart is beating so loud, I can barely hear the kid. I squeeze my eyes shut as a drop of sweat rolls down my face. I'm caught. And I don't even know why I'm being chased in the first place.

"Turn around slowly," the patrolman says. "Identify yourself."

My fingers shake. The big jacket feels like a wet towel weighing me down.

I start to turn when I hear Po's warning in my head again. *Run. Run!*

I push off the sidewalk like a sprint runner, my shoes digging into the pavement. The kid goes wide-eyed as he sees me barreling toward him. I snatch the hoverboard from his grasp and throw it down in the street so that it hovers on the rails.

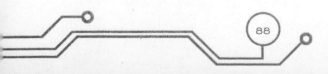

The loudspeaker crackles again. "Young man! Identify yourself!"

I hop on the board and it sinks before it adjusts to my weight. I've only been on a board once. It belonged to Nade Rybber and I nearly wrecked it when I crashed into a vending food truck. He wouldn't let me near it after that.

But I know enough about the boards to know how to use one.

I shuffle my feet into position and shift my weight forward, which commands the board to move. The board lifts in the back and shoots straight ahead. The kid yells behind me. The patrol car hums to life. I lean to the right to cruise around the corner, but I lean too far and the board wobbles like a plate of gelatin, like it wants to throw me off.

When it evens out, I lean forward more. Faster. Faster! I shoot through the streets like a laser beam. The wind rips the fedora from my head. I chance a glance over my shoulder in time to see the hat hit the ground and tumble over itself. But I also see the patrol car blasting around the corner.

I don't know how far you can lean forward before the board loses connection with the rails, but I push it farther, then veer to the left down a side street. My toes curl in

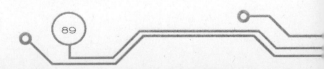

my shoes, my knees lock in place. I like the feel of soaring through the air like a hawk.

The patrolman's voice crackles behind me. "Pull over immediately!"

It's only a matter of time before they catch me or cut the power to the rails. I'm so deep in trouble. Po's threat of groundation seems like a party compared to this.

What was I thinking, running away? I could turn myself in, say I was scared or something and that's why I ran. I mean, how bad can this be? We're not in trouble. Po and I haven't done anything wrong.

But Po wouldn't have told me to run unless it was for a good reason. And I think maybe there's more going on here than I know about. Maybe it's all somehow connected. Dad's thread mysteriously coming back online and the police showing up a day later.

You have to keep going.

I double back to The Glitz, an idea striking like divine inspiration. That's what Dad used to say. I turn onto the street with the biggest houses and look up at the sky. Clouds cover the sun, and the houses barely shine.

The patrol car catches up to me. "You leave us no choice, young man," the voice says through the speaker.

I look up at the clouds and will them to part. Please.

Please. Please! If the sun falls just right on the houses, reflecting off the shards of glass, it might be enough to blind everyone on the street and give me a chance to escape.

I'm nearly to the end of the block when a second patrol car wheels around the corner, trapping me. My heart beats so hard, it feels like it'll hammer right outta my chest.

Just when I think I'm done for, the clouds finally thin and the sun hits the houses, turning thousands of shards of glass into mirrors, reflecting the light back. I throw my arm up, squinting against the glare.

The patrol car slows behind me. I tip back on the board just enough to slow it down and hop off. I snatch the board up, tuck it beneath my arm, and run, pushing through a gate, through a second one. Dodge left. Another gate. My lungs burn. My breath comes out fast and wheezy. I disappear inside another backyard and swing left once I've cleared the house.

Up ahead, I see an old church made of red brick with a big bell tower in the front. If I can just make it there . . .

Sirens wail from the next street over. Patrolmen call out orders. I blaze down the sidewalk and reach the church in a blink. I toss the hoverboard in the Dumpster and slam into the tower wall. The brick is old and pitted and I think I can make quick work of it if I can find a few good handholds.

There's a crumbling brick just above my head, and I stick my left hand there. The old cut from my climb up the fountain opens. It burns all the way down my arm. I clench my teeth and find another hole to my right. It's a stretch, and I feel like a bug splattered against the wall as I push up. The rubber soles of my shoes are good for gripping, and finding holes for my feet isn't as important as it is for my hands.

Sweat rolls down my forehead and into my eye, burning like pepper juice. I ignore it, and focus, zeroing in on the few crumbling brick holes left above me. The sirens get closer. I only have another two or three feet before the top.

"Over here," someone yells—a patrolman, I think—and I quicken my pace. The top is turreted and I scramble through one of the open notches, collapsing on the roof in a heap. I roll over onto my back and stare up at the blue sky, breathing in deep.

I made it. At least I think I made it.

Voices carry on from the ground. I lie there for what feels like forever, hoping and praying that the police don't find me. I pat my shirt, feeling the hard outline of the scrambler at my chest. I say a silent thank you to Po for

it, and then feel a familiar twist in my gut when I think about my brother, about him being trapped and beat up and . . .

I squeeze my eyes shut. If anyone can get away from the police, it's Po, right? Po is smart and strong. Except, he isn't fast, not with his prosthetic leg, so if it came down to a footrace, he'd definitely lose.

The day fades to night. I want to leave the roof when the street goes quiet, because my body is sore and my stomach is empty, but as I plot my escape, a sickening realization takes over me: I have nowhere to go and no one to go to.

I don't have any family besides Po. At least not anyone close enough. And Lox is still on vacation.

Tellie.

I used to think she was a bolt-head, but now, well, now she's my friend.

But would she help me? I picture my face plastered all over the Net and the evening news.

What have I gotten myself into?

My stomach growls again and every tiny movement makes my bladder shriek like a baby.

I have to get down and I need somewhere to go.

Tellie is my only option.

FIFTEEN

I STICK CLOSE to the bushes that line the sidewalk when I reach Tellie's street. I didn't see a single patrol car on the way over here, but I don't want to risk being seen out in the open.

When Tellie's house comes into view, I have to wrestle with the urge to run straight there and bang on the bell. There are no cars in sight, so I hurry across the street stealth-style, crouched low to the ground.

Tellie's house is lit up like a birthday cake. There's a light on in almost every window. The porch light blasts across the front lawn. Neon blue solar lights dot the yard like stars. At the front door, I press the bell and the house's security system announces my arrival.

"House guest has arrived. Goldfish," the voice says.

I cringe. Tellie must have programmed me into the house's system. At least she didn't use my real name, or Trout, which I'm sure is blasted all over the news feed right now.

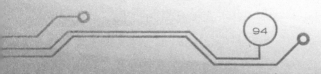

It says a lot about how much things have changed between us. If I'm programmed in, then that must mean she expects me to come over more often than never. But what does *that* mean? That she likes hanging out with me?

"Who's Goldfish?" a man says from inside.

"I got it!" Tellie yells, and whips the door open. When she sees me standing there on the front porch, she goes still.

"Hey," I mumble.

Tellie grabs my arm and wrenches me across the threshold. "It's just my friend!" She drags me toward the stairs.

Just then, a man comes around the corner wearing one of those slick black suits you only see movie stars and businessmen wearing. The kind that costs more than Po makes in a month. There's a short glass in his left hand with swirly designs etched into the base, and it's filled with brown liquid. He eyes me as I hit the stairs right behind Tellie.

"Nice to meet you . . . Goldfish," he says as we run past in a blur.

"Goldfish?" Mrs. Rix says as she clicks into the room on her high heels, her Link held in front of her. Her blond hair is twisted back in a fancy hairdo, and yellow lipstick makes her lips look radioactive. Someone is rattling off a to-do list on the other end of her Link, but pauses to say, "Candu! Are you listening to me?"

"We'll be in my room!" Tellie says.

So that's Mr. and Mrs. Rix. I've never met Mr. Rix, and he's rarely on TV like some of the other congressmen. Mrs. Rix looks scarier in person.

In Tellie's bedroom, she shuts the door behind us and whirls around. "What are you doing here?"

"I'm sorry. I didn't want to get you in trouble, but I didn't know where else to go!"

"The whole United Districts is looking for you! What did you do?"

"Nothing!"

"Well, you can't stay here." She huffs and stomps into her massive closet. She returns with a purple bag and a wig to match.

"What's that for?"

She passes me the bag first. "There's some extra clothes in there, some food too. Just candy and some energy packs, but it might last you a few days. There's a disposable cred tag in the front pocket with at least five hundred creds on it. It's still loaded with my profile, so if you need to get in somewhere temporarily, you have my permission to use it."

"Thanks." I heave the bag over my shoulder. "But I meant what is the wig for?"

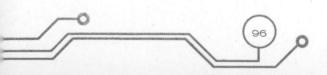

"A disguise. Duh." She moves to arrange the hair on my head but I dodge her.

"You're not putting that thing on me!" It's long and curly and . . . well, purple. "I'll look stupid."

Tellie cocks her head to the side. "Like you aren't ugly on your own?"

I screw up my mouth and narrow my eyes. "Very funny."

She lets out a heavy sigh. "I don't think you have any idea how much trouble you're in."

Hearing someone else talk about it churns my gut like cake batter. I start to explain *why* I'm in trouble, when a scrape sounds from the windowsill. We look over.

The window is open and a bot is standing beside Tellie's bed.

A BOT. IN TELLIE'S BEDROOM.

Tellie lets out a high-pitched squeal and clings to me. I stumble back and ram into the desk.

The bot spreads out his arms. "I mean you no harm. Please, do not be afraid." His voice is quiet and measured, like the lines on a holo ruler.

My heart instantly kangaroos to my head. My knees feel empty, like I'm in zero gravity. And before I know it, I'm shaking all over.

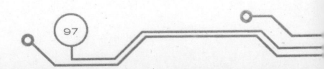

It's been a long time since I've seen a bot up close, so I'm totally geared out *and* super-curious. My nanny, Cleo, was short and boxy, but this bot is tall and skinny, and more human-shaped than any of the old bots I can remember. A few operating lights blink in his neck—blue, then red, then blue again. His head is made of metal, but his eyes look human.

I think instantly of Old New York, of a factory somewhere churning out newer, better bots. Bots that want to be human. This one is even dressed in a real man's clothes: a pair of jeans, a thin jacket, tennis shoes, a baseball cap.

He shifts toward us. "Trout, we need to move quickly."

"Move?" Tellie shrieks.

"He knows my name? He knows my name!"

"Please," he says, "we do not have much time. Patrolmen are here for you."

The intercom crackles behind us and Mr. Rix says, "Tellie? Could you come down here, please? And bring your friend."

Tellie and I look at each other, then at the bot. Patrolmen? Do they know a bot is in the house? Are they here for the bot *and* me?

But how did they know I was here? I have the scrambler—

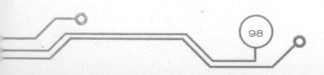

I look down. "No," I mutter when I don't see the outline of the scrambler through my shirt. I pull out the collar and peer inside. It's gone. Even the chain is gone. Which means the ID chip in my heart is sending out its signal right this second.

I am totally notched. I have nowhere to hide! And no way can I outrun the patrolmen now.

My chest goes inferno hot, like the chip is burning through me like a beacon.

And why is there a robot here? To kill us?

The bot inches closer. Tellie and I mash ourselves against the wall, as if we mean to disappear inside it.

"W-why are you here?" Tellie says.

"For Trout." He inclines his head toward me. "He is in danger. Po has already been compromised—"

I straighten. "You know my brother?"

"He is being held at City Hall. I am not certain we will be able to retrieve him at this time."

I recall our last fight. Po telling me to stay quiet and not draw attention. I just thought he was being lame. And now look. For some reason, searching for Dad has caused a lot of trouble.

"Why?" I say to the bot. "Po didn't do anything wrong."

"No," the bot says, his lips moving just like a human's,

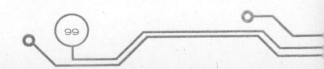

"but the UD government believes your father has. Through Po, they will find your father. They mean to use you both against him."

"Tellie!" Mr. Rix calls again.

My head is spinning like a gyro. The bot knows me, knows Po, knows Dad. How does he know Dad?

"Bots are evil, crazy machines," Tellie whispers to me as she reaches for the doorknob.

"Wait." I grab her wrist. I'm running out of options. I can't go downstairs or the patrolmen will catch me. I can't go out the window because the bot is blocking it.

Footsteps pound up the stairs.

"Please tell me you are not thinking about leaving with that thing." Tellie jabs a finger toward the bot. I look at him out of the corner of my eye.

"I don't know." I take a deep breath. "I don't know what to do!"

The bot whirs. "If you are to leave, now would be the best time."

Tellie wrings her hands in front of her. Her eyebrows pinch together with worry. If you would have told me ten days ago that tonight would find me in Tellie Rix's bedroom with a bot behind me and the police searching for me, I would have laughed in your face.

And I still want to laugh.

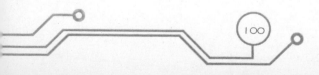

I feel like I've gone completely nuclear.

The footsteps stop outside Tellie's room.

"Tellie?" Mr. Rix says.

The bot charges toward us. We ram back into the door. Someone tries opening it from the other side, but we're pressed so hard into it, we don't budge.

"There is no more time," the bot says. He reaches for me. Tellie tries shoving him away, but she's no match for a bot. He grabs my arm. I have no breath in my lungs to holler.

The bot flings me onto his back as the bedroom door finally bursts open. Tellie stumbles to the floor. Patrolmen flood the room, their guns up.

"Hold on," the bot says to me as he takes two quick strides to the open window and jumps through it.

SIXTEEN

THE WIND PUSHES the hair from my face. The ground rushes toward me. A sling pops out of a narrow compartment in the bot's shoulder and wraps around me, hooking itself into the opposite shoulder. Now I'm hanging there like a baby in a backpack.

Voices shout from Tellie's window.

"Here," the bot says, shoving a pair of goggles in my hands.

I fumble them on as he takes off at jet speeds. The world blurs around me.

I am so notched.

By the time the bot stops running, I've eaten three bugs by accident when they flew in my mouth. The sling unhooks itself and folds away into its compartment, and I thud to the ground.

"I can't feel my legs," I mutter.

"That usually happens the first time a human is transported at such high speeds. It is best if you move around."

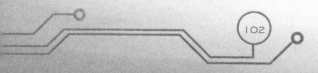

I somehow make it up onto all fours, but sway there for a second before using a nearby tree to climb to my feet. I look around. We're in the middle of the woods. Maybe we've even left 5th District. It smells like pine trees here, and wet earth. There isn't much light except for the moon, which means there isn't anyone around to save me.

I look over at the bot. He stands a few feet away, still as a statue. I freeze.

A robot just kidnapped me.

A ROBOT.

My mind races. How am I supposed to get away from him? Dismantle him? What, with a tree branch? But I don't see anything big enough. Run. I should run.

I push away from the tree and dash into the dark, but my knees are still stiff, and I face-plant on the ground. Dirt grits in my teeth. A fern shivers in the wind, tickling my ear, and I bat it away.

"Are you all right?" the bot asks.

I roll over. "Stay away from me!"

He steps back. "I will not hurt you, Trout."

"Why did you kidnap me?"

"It was not a kidnapping," he says lightly. "It was a rescue."

I lurch to my feet. "That's not how you rescue some-one!"

"I suppose you wrote the handbook on rescue missions?"

"What? No."

A twig snaps behind me. Something mewls in the dark. I skitter in the opposite direction and ram into the bot. He steadies me with his machine hands and I shrink up like a piece of burnt plastic. I wrestle out of his grip, kicking up a cloud of dust as I stumble away.

The bot raises his hands. "I am sorry. I truly meant what I said before. I mean you no harm."

"If you don't want to hurt me, why are we in the middle of the woods?"

"I wanted to find a safe place to allow you to get your bearings. We are in a blind spot." He points at the sky. "There is no satellite coverage here."

My breathing slows. "Tell me why I should trust you. You're a robot, you know. The UD says you're evil machines who want to kill humans."

The bot snorts. "That is the very farthest thing from the truth. And I would hope you would trust I mean you no harm after I risked my life to save you."

"That doesn't mean anything. Especially if you really *did* kidnap me."

"I will do whatever it takes to show my loyalty."

"You said something about my dad. Do you know him?"

He nods. "I do. I consider him a close friend of mine."

I narrow my eyes. "Tell me something about him, something not everyone would know."

The bot thinks for a second. "Your father's favorite hybreed is a wolf monkey."

"That's easy. Give me something else."

"All right." He goes silent, then: "That picture you included in your video, of you, your father, and your brother."

The one from our vacation. "Yeah?"

"Your father told me about the trip to Lake Tahoe, about how you caught seventeen fish, about how proud he was of you. He told me about how your brother lost his Link in the lake, but dove in to try to find it. He told me how happy you all were and how much he wishes he could go back."

My chest gets fuzzy with warmth. Only Dad and Po would know how many fish I caught on that trip. And while I think anyone could figure out we had a good time, only Dad could say for sure how great the trip really was. Because it was our last before everything changed.

"Okay," I say, "so let's say I *do* trust you. Where are we going?"

"We are going to your father."

My eyes get big. "I'm going to see him?" I've waited so long for this, it doesn't even feel real. I want to dance. Or sing. Or throw my arms in the air. But I don't. Because that would be lame.

"Yes, but before we do," the bot adds, "we must address . . ." He looks at my chest.

Somehow I know what he means without him saying it. My ID chip. I lost the scrambler and now the UD can track me wherever I go. Even if the bot rescued me, my time is running out.

"How long before they track me?"

A gear clicks in the bot's neck. "Not long. And the patrolmen who were at your friend's house are the least of your worries. The government officials who originally came to collect you will have better technology than the police. You have less than an hour before they triangulate your location. That is, if we remain here."

Pretty much the only thing I heard him say was: "'Government officials'?"

"Yes. I am afraid this is much bigger than the police."

"What's that mean?"

The bot says nothing and I drop Tellie's bag to the

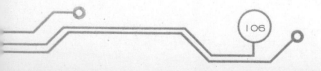

ground with a thump. Frustration and shock make me boil, make me forget the fear. "I wish someone would just tell me what's going on!"

Something in the bot's chest whirs to life and I wonder if it's a coolant fan like we have on the computer to cool the hard drive.

"What is it you would like to know?"

I lean against a skinny tree and the leaves above me shudder. "Why were government officials after me?"

A frog starts croaking in the distance. There must be a pond nearby. It's been a long time since I was out in the woods, or anywhere outside of Brack, for that matter.

"The UD government wants to use you and your brother as bait to lure your father out of hiding."

"Why?"

"Unfortunately, that is an answer best left for your father."

I grumble. "Figures."

"Is there anything else you would like to ask?"

Like I'll get any answers. "No."

The bot points his finger at my heart. "Then we should disengage that, and I am afraid it will not be a pleasant experience."

I cover my chest with a hand. "How unpleasant?"

"That is not something one can measure."

"Do you have to operate on me?"

"No, I will use my scrambler, but it will be a permanent scramble."

"What if it goes wrong?"

"Nothing will go wrong. It will be over before you know it." He takes a few slow, careful steps toward me, as if he thinks I'm a puppy about to dart off. I don't move. Whether he wants to kill me or help me doesn't matter at this point. I've got nowhere to go anyway, and no way to fight back.

I breathe in a deep breath as the bot puts one hand over my heart and the other at the back of my neck. "Close your eyes," he says in that quiet, measured voice of his.

I do as he says. His fingers are warm for being made entirely of metal. My skin starts to crawl. I can't tell if it's because I'm gearing out over the bot or the scrambler, or both.

"I will now begin," he says, and suddenly his hands are burning hot. I try to pull away, but he holds tighter. I feel like I'm being cooked from the inside out, like a hardboiled egg.

The pain grows in my chest where the tracker must be. It grows and wraps around my ribs and then rushes outward, like a flow of hot lava. The pain pools in my feet and I curl my toes, clench my jaw. My knees buckle,

but the bot holds me up as I wish for my brother over and over again. I wish he were here to tell me I'm safe, that he's got my back.

But then the pain is gone with a pop and crackle. My chest still feels warm, but it's nothing I can't handle. I take a few deep breaths trying to stop the achiness in my lungs.

"How do you feel?" the bot asks.

Sweat drips from my forehead. "I'm okay."

He inclines his head. "We should move. If you have a Link, leave it here. The UD can track you through it as well."

I gulp down another rush of air and pull my Link out of my pocket. I've never gone a day without it. The thought of leaving it in the middle of the woods makes me cringe, but I guess I gotta do it. I set it on the ground and pick up the backpack Tellie gave me.

I'm just about to slip it over my shoulder when I stop myself. Tellie's dad works for the UD government. Government officials came to my house to arrest me. Can I trust Tellie?

I see the bag in a whole new light. What if there's a tracker inside?

Doubt wedges into my stomach. I hate this feeling. Like I don't know who is a friend and who isn't.

I dump out the bag's contents and rifle through everything. I pick out the Net-tag and a handful of snacks. Just enough to fit into my pockets. I decide to leave the rest.

"I guess I'm ready," I say.

The bot tells me to climb on his back again and then we're off.

We stop sometime later at a car pool parking lot just off the freeway. The hover rails glow in the distance. Just like before, it takes me a second to straighten myself out when I finally slide off the bot's back. I lean against an old Veemer truck and stretch. I wonder if this is what it feels like riding a horse for the first time, and then make a mental note never to ride a horse.

When I can finally stand upright, I push my hair off my forehead and look out past the parking lot. Only a few scrubby bushes dot the landscape. To my left, lightning flashes through the sky and a rumble of thunder follows. It isn't raining where we are, but the air feels wet.

"We've already missed the storm," the bot says behind me.

"Oh." I turn around. "So will I see my dad tonight?"

The bot stands there and doesn't blink. Thunder rumbles again and it vibrates through the cement. "Hello? Earth to the robo—er . . ."

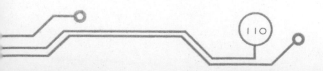

His head swivels toward me and my skin crawls. One minute I feel okay with the bot and then the next minute he does something creepy like that.

My shoulders tense. "What the chop? Why did you do that?"

"Do what?"

"Not answer me and then . . ." I wave my hand around because I'm not really sure what was so creepy about the head swivel except that it wasn't NORMAL. "Never mind."

"I was listening to the news broadcast from Edge Flats."

Edge Flats is a border town about a hundred miles from Bot Territory. I know that because it's where the Super-hero Museum is. Lox and I had plans to go there someday if I could ever get my overprotective brother to let me go.

"You can listen in like that?"

"I can. It seems the UD has been granted clearance from the Texan Council to patrol the border."

"The border?" I say, raising my eyebrows. "As in, the border of Bot Territory?"

"Correct."

"Are we . . . is that where . . ."

"Where we are headed? Yes."

"Whoa. Holy space junk." I thread my hands together

and set them on top of my head. "I'm going to Bot Territory? Lox won't believe it when I tell him." I let my hands drop to my sides. "Is that where my dad is?"

"Yes."

"So, if the UD is patrolling the border, then how are we going to get into Bot Territory?"

"It will have to wait until tomorrow."

My shoulders sink. I've waited forever to see Dad. I'm so close and now I can't go because of the UD, for reasons I don't even know. More secrets. More time to sit around and wait.

Lightning strikes again, turning the dark sky purple for a split second. I feel like I might go nuclear, I'm so impatient, but if Dad taught me anything it was that good things come to those who wait.

"So now what?" I ask.

The bot strides over to a four-door sedan and unlocks it with the press of his index finger.

I hurry to his side. "Are we car-jacking?"

He gives me a look. "Hardly. This is my car. Or, rather, one I planted for our journey." The bot opens the passenger side for me and I slide in as the car's controls flicker on. I notice right away that it's an auto-car, like Lox's mom's car.

When the car doors are shut, the interior temperature

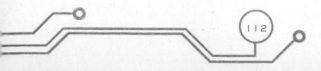

adjusts to a cool seventy degrees, which would normally be fine with me, but since I've been riding on the back of a robot for the last two hours, I'm shivering like a wet dog. I jam at the controls until the screen reads eighty.

"What should I call you anyway?" I ask. "Do you have a name?"

The bot punches in a destination and the car pulls out of the lot. "You may call me LT."

"LT. Okay. So, where are we going, LT?"

"We will stay in Texas tonight and travel to my territory tomorrow. But first we must get past Texan border control."

I once heard my dad say it's easier to get into Texas than it is to get into the UD, but bots aren't allowed in Texas either, because of the treaty agreement. So even if it's easier to go south, there's still a bot in the car with me.

"Are you going to hide in the trunk or something?" I ask.

LT lets out a sound that I'm guessing is supposed to be a laugh, but actually sounds more like sizzling live wires. "Do you know the story of the Underground Railroad?"

"Kind of." I frown. "Well, no."

The car takes an on-ramp and soon we're cruising down the freeway. "It was a network of secret routes and safe houses used by slaves to escape the South back in the nineteenth century. What we have now is similar. We have allies to help us on our way."

"So we're taking a train into Texas?"

LT tilts his head. "Negative."

"That doesn't answer my question."

"Just wait and you will see."

It only takes about fifteen minutes to reach the border. A hovering digital sign flashes bright yellow. *Warning*: *You are now leaving the safety of the United Districts.*

There are huge steel arches over the five lanes that cross into Texas. The arches blaze neon blue in the night, like the rails. Scrolling signs at the top say: *Have your identification ready. Toll to cross border: Seventy-five credits.*

"Lane C3," LT says, and the car chooses the corresponding lane, the one in the middle. There are only two cars ahead of us and three cars in the next lane. The other lanes are closed for the night. Across a field, on my left, is a separate border patrol for people trying to get *inside* the UD. The checkpoint is the same as ours, with five steel arches and lots of digital signage. There are only two cars in line over there.

I start to fidget. What if we're caught? What if they don't let us cross?

I take a deep breath and try to tell myself LT has his railroad, so we'll be fine, but when it's our turn and the

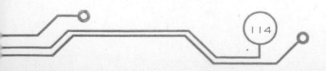

car rolls to a stop at the inspector's booth, I feel like I'm going to barf chunks.

LT presses a finger to the window's controls and the glass slides down. The inspector steps up to the car. He's huge, like a bull, with tiny eyes and ferocious eyebrows. When he hunches and peers inside, his stomach spills over his leather belt.

"Howdy," he says. "What's the nature of your travel?"

"Visiting friends in Edge Flats," LT says.

"Ahh." The inspector chomps on a wad of gum. It smells like grapes and mint. It makes me want to barf even more. "Edge Flats is a fine place to be this time of year. My great-grandmother was born and raised there. I make it back every now and then."

"Fine place indeed," LT says, and hands over a Net-tag. I notice he's careful to keep his hand inside the car and not hang it out the open window where cameras and satellites might see him.

The inspector takes the Net-tag and taps it to a pad attached to his belt. A second later, the pad blinks green and LT gets the Net-tag back. "All right. You're all set. Have a safe trip." The inspector winks at me as LT closes the window.

"That," LT says as the border arches fade behind us, "is our Underground Railroad."

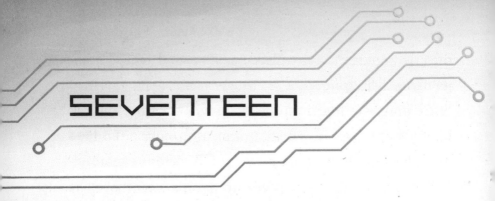

SEVENTEEN

THE CAR ANNOUNCES when we're five miles outside Edge Flats.

As LT listens in on his internal broadcast thingy, I try to picture what the news feed might be saying about me right now. *Boy escapes police. Considered armed and dangerous.*

Have I become an outlaw? Lox would say it's totally wrenched, but that's because he needs his brain thawed. I just hope the news doesn't use Aaron Dekker's nickname and start calling me FishKid in all their vids.

"Did you hear anything?" I ask LT as the car slows for a red light.

"There is a patrol car approximately three blocks to the west, but there has been an incident on the corner of Lemmer and Taylor—a house fire. It would seem most of the city's forces are busy."

When the intersection light flicks to green and the car starts forward again, I peer out the tinted window at

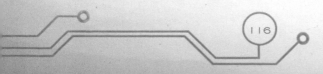

the city known as Edge Flats. I don't know where it got its name, because there's nothing flat about it. The road we're on goes up and down like a roller coaster, and the buildings we pass are so tall, I can barely make out where they end and the sky begins.

But, as we get closer to our destination, the city's skyscrapers disappear behind us. Here, the buildings are short and squat with rounded roofs made entirely of glass. They look like gigantic bubbles glowing in the night.

"Ahh," LT says, "here is our destination."

The car slows and pulls into a crumbling cement driveway. I duck my head to get a better view. There's a three-story building made of red brick in front of us with white decorative brick on the corners. Good climbing bricks. An old holo sign on the roof flickers in and out. *Ft. Worth Firehouse,* it says, but every few seconds, the *H* and *U* fade and it says, *Ft. Wort Firehose.*

I snicker to myself as we get out of the car. "Is this place a fire station?"

"In the past. Now it is a safe house."

When we're nearer the house, I notice little pinpricks of light around the foundation and it takes me a second to realize it's not Christmas lights but a Mozzy Security System. The lights are lasers and they connect to each other forming a perimeter around the house. If someone steps through the lasers . . . well, I don't actually know what happens, but I'm betting it's nothing good.

What kind of house is this?

A cat saunters up to us, her white-tipped tail weaving back and forth like a cobra. I reach down to scratch her between the ears and my knuckles accidentally rap against her head. The sound it makes is a soft *ting-ting*, like metal.

"What the chop?"

"This is Posy," LT says. "She is the perimeter guard."

"Does she have a metal plate in her head or something?"

"No. She is a robot."

Posy meows up at me, her tail going still. She looks like a cat, with fur and whiskers and everything. LT flips up a hidden panel in her back exposing a set of wires and a keypad.

I've never seen anything like that before.

LT inputs a series of numbers and Posy meows again. The perimeter lights wink out. "Come." LT gestures toward a door set in an alcove. "The perimeter shuts off for sixty seconds."

We cross through what used to be the laser line and push open the thick wood door. We enter into a narrow room with a few old coat hooks up on the wall and a framed poster that says: *Rock On, Brother.*

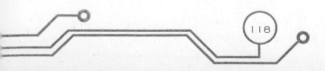

Directly in front of us is a set of stairs. Light spills down from the floor above us. Cyber-tech music pumps from a stereo. LT goes up first, his steps silent, like he knows just where to press to avoid the creaks in the floorboards. I make a ton of noise, hitting all the old joints. They screech beneath my weight. If we were trying to sneak in, we've totally failed.

But when we reach the next floor, we're greeted with a "Whoop-whoop!" like whoever is here is happy we've come. LT is in my way, so I don't see the guy who wraps LT in a big bear hug.

"Dude!" the mystery guy says. "The whole UD is after your metal butt."

The voice sounds familiar. I'm trying to place where I've heard it when LT steps aside.

I gasp. "Aaron Dekker?"

"In the flesh." He grins. "But just call me Dekker."

My brain freezes and I stutter out a few letters but can't form a single word. He comes over to me and gives me a big hug to match LT's. "Dude, that escape was split. SPLIT." He makes a fist and slo-mo hammers it in the air. "They're playing it over and over on the news feed. You rode that hoverboard like a pro."

Dekker is just a little older than Po—twenty-one, according to his Net profile. His hair is dyed in a rainbow of colors. There's a streak of bright yellow at the front, then blue, then green, and lastly red. It sticks up funny, like he didn't bother to brush it after getting out of bed, but I've watched enough Dekker vids to know his hair always looks like that, like he's spent too much time in a wind tunnel. He's wearing black cargo pants and a close-fitting white T-shirt with a gigantic black X on the front. Three separate scramblers hang from a ball chain around his neck.

"Come check it out," he says, and leads me around a big fluffy couch to a wall of desks. I count five computer screens mounted on the wall below a row of windows that overlook the city. The monitors are running various programs, feeds, and vids.

I see myself on the third screen from the left. In the vid, I'm zooming around a street corner on the hoverboard I stole. The vid must have been recorded from the patrol car that was after me. A headline appears and says just what I feared it might.

Twelve-year-old boy—"FishKid"—escapes from police. Suspected bot supporter.

My stomach swims. Being labeled a bot supporter is the same as being called a terrorist.

I drop back into a computer chair and cover my face with my hands. How did everything get so bad? I still

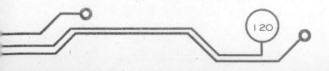

don't know why Po told me to run. Or why the government is after me.

"Little dude," Dekker says, and I peek out from behind my hands. "It's not as bad as it looks. I've been labeled a bot supporter." He nods at LT behind me. "Course, I *am* a bot supporter, but you're just a kid. No one'll hold it against you. Just plaster on an innocent smile and people will love you no matter what."

I sit up and prop my elbow on the desk, pushing aside a line of pens. "It's not that easy. I'm having trouble digesting it all and I just—" Dekker makes this horrified face at me. I go still. "What?"

"I . . . ah . . . the pens . . ." He scoots me away from the desk and lines the pens back up in a neat little row. "Sorry. I just have things in a certain place."

"Dekker has obsessive-compulsive disorder," LT explains.

Dekker grumbles in the back of his throat. "I have an affinity for precision. Not a disorder."

LT says nothing.

"Sorry," I say as I look from LT to Dekker to the pens, and then again at the living room. The place is a mess, if you ask me. There's a ceramic pig on the end table next to an empty flower vase, which is on top of a dictionary, which is on top of a black box. There's a pile of old books

stacked up in the far corner, organized by color so that the spines make a rainbow. A dead plant hangs from a basket near the vid panel, and the couch is so full of mismatched pillows, it looks like a department store threw up on it.

But I guess you could say everything is in its place, whether it's clean or not.

Dekker holds up his hands. "I just ask that if you touch anything, you put it back where you found it."

"Deal."

"Now, what were you saying?" He snaps his fingers. "Right. You were saying you felt like Australian cow dung."

"Umm . . . I don't think I said that."

"Come on." He waves me toward a second set of stairs. "Milk shakes cure anything. Guar-AN-teed. We'll load them up with chocolate and peanut butter. You'll feel better in no time."

"While you are curing this case of Australian cow dung," LT says, "I will go to the roof to listen to the local law enforcement broadcasts. Reception is better up there."

LT follows us to the next floor—the fire station's kitchen—and continues up another set of stairs, disappearing from sight. Dekker tells me to have a seat at the long stainless-steel table in the middle of the room as he whips together the shakes.

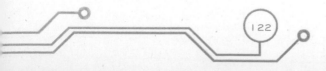

He tosses a couple scoops of ice cream in a blender, then a handful of chocolate chips and two mounded spoons of peanut butter. He taps in a command on the blender's screen and it roars to life.

Once he's poured us each a shake, he rinses out the blender and dismantles it so it'll fit in the dishwasher.

"So, what part of this are you having trouble digesting?" he asks.

I twirl the straw around in the shake. "All of it."

"Let's start from the beginning, then." He hoists himself up on the counter directly across from the table. Dishes are stacked up on shelves behind him. All of them are white. There are enough to serve two armies. It makes me wonder if Dekker's is a safe house for more than just robots.

"When I first saw your vid," he says, "I knew instantly who you were. Robert St. Kroix's son. And I told your friend Tellie I couldn't link to the vid, because I didn't want to draw unnecessary attention to you and your brother. But"—he slurps from the shake and swallows— "then we caught wind of the UD's plot to use you and your brother against your dad, and your dad decided it was better this way. Link the vid, make it viral, and it'd be harder for the UD to grab you without anyone noticing."

If I was having trouble digesting all this before, Dekker

just made it harder. Grab me? Could the UD do that? I guess they could do just about anything if they could get away with it.

I sift through the rest of the information and pick out the important detail. "You know my dad?"

"Course I do. Everyone indirectly or directly involved in the Meta knows your dad."

I crunch into a chunk of chocolate that the blender missed. "What's the Meta?"

"Meta-Rise." Dekker takes the straw out of his glass and tips the cup up to his mouth, draining it in one last gulp. He lets out a satisfied sigh and I silently urge him to tell me more. I can't stand this waiting around.

"The Meta-Rise," Dekker goes on, "is a group of people and bots that came together to support equality and free will and the right to life. We created the bots into something close to human, because we wanted them that way. We wanted them to think and act and be like us. So who says we have the right to cut them down?"

He shrugs and rinses out his glass. I'm so glued to the explanation, I haven't touched my shake in a while. Long enough for it to melt. Condensation runs down the cup.

"Are you part of the Meta-Rise?" I ask. If Po were here, he'd whack me on the back of the head for being so nosy.

Dekker grins. "If the Meta-Rise were a train, I'd be

a station attendant. I help people *reach* the Meta-Rise. And in the meantime, I try to spread word about what's going on in the world that the UD media can't report on because of regulations."

"So why does everyone with the Meta-Rise know my dad?"

"Because . . ." Dekker trails off. I lean forward. A clock ticks behind me. Dekker points at the stairs and then says, "That's a story for another time, little dude. Not my place to go blabbing secrets that aren't mine."

A few seconds later, LT emerges from the stairwell and I conclude that LT, or Dad, doesn't want me to know too much too soon. But it makes me mad all over again.

I just want to hurry up and find Dad so I can finally get the answers I want.

"Is the patrol gone?" Dekker asks LT.

His head swivels a no. "We will rest here for a few hours. By then the patrol will have moved farther south and we will move farther east. If that is all right with you, Dek."

Dekker rubs his hands together. "Me casa is Sue's casa."

LT clears his throat. "Correction. It is *mi casa es su casa*, not Sue's casa . . ."

Dekker grunts. "Whatever, metal brain."

LT gives me a look like he's heard that joke a hundred

times, but I can't help but snicker. Lox would love that one.

"Come, Trout, I will show you to a room," LT says. We go down a hallway. Dekker follows behind. There are a few bedrooms at the end and I'm given the one on the right with a bed twice the size of mine at home.

"There's a vid panel," Dekker says, nodding at the massive screen attached to the wall. "Bathroom there. You need anything, little dude, just call me through the intercom. Or do what the oldies did, and just holler down the hallway. If it works, it works, am I right?" He ruffles my hair just like Po would. It makes me wince because it reminds me in an instant how much I miss my brother.

Dekker leaves, but not before tapping the light switch three times, which makes LT do something close to an eye roll.

I climb on the bed. LT checks the window, making sure it's locked. I see a few pinpricks of light here too. I'm glad Dekker has a ton of security, and I feel safer since LT double-checked it.

Maybe I do trust him after all.

"Your energy is low," LT says once the curtains are in place over the window. "To reach optimum endurance, you would require approximately seven hours and twenty-two minutes of rest, but we may not have that

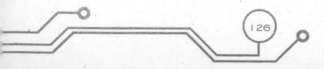

long." He makes his way toward the door in that silent, well-oiled way of his. "Please, get as much rest as you can."

I nod, even though sleep seems the farthest thing from my mind.

I am hours away from seeing Dad.

The milk shake hardens in my gut.

I may be hours away from Dad, but a ton of things stand in our way. Patrolmen. Government officials. And we still somehow have to get through the force field fence that surrounds Bot Territory. I've seen pictures of it on the Net. It's not something you can climb over. It's as tall as a building and, one touch, and it'll bounce you back.

So many things could go wrong.

I collapse against the mountain of pillows. If I can survive the obstacles standing between me and Bot Territory, I'm going to ask Dad all the questions stacking up in my head. I want to know more about the Meta-Rise and I want to know how Dad fits into it.

I'm not going to let him get away with more secrets.

EIGHTEEN

I WAKE UP TO LT staring at me in the dark. "Ahh!" I roll over, fall off the side of the bed, and thump to the floor.

"I apologize," LT says. "I have been trying to wake you for some time. It would seem you sleep, as they say, *like a log*."

"What are you doing staring at me like a space case?"

"Pardon me?"

I straighten my T-shirt. "Never mind."

"The patrol has finally moved south. If we are to cross the border, now would be the time."

After rubbing the sleep out of my eyes, I look over at the clock on the bedside table. The holo numbers say it's just before five in the morning. It feels like I haven't slept at all.

LT leaves and I use the bathroom, splashing cold water on my face to wake me up. Since I don't have a tooth-brush, I just rinse my mouth out and call it good.

When I'm finished, I read the headlines in the news

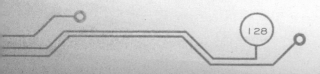

feed that's playing on the screen in the vanity mirror. *More budget woes for the UD. Three-car accident on Interstate 26. UNDC raises application fee.*

Just as I'm about to leave, the fourth headline blinks on and freezes me in place.

Police continue to search for Aidan St. Kroix.

That's my real name. My *real*-real name, and somehow seeing it in the news feed makes the whole thing worse. I've stopped being a cute twelve-year-old dubbed Fish-Kid. Now I'm an official criminal.

Even though I haven't eaten, my stomach feels rotten.

"Little dude," Dekker's voice sounds through the intercom, "I made you a Double Dek breakfast special. Come scarf it down before you hit the dusty trail."

My headline has already disappeared, replaced by a new one about next week's vid con in southern Texas. I flip off the bathroom light, slip into my shoes, and head down the hallway. LT is in the kitchen, standing in the corner still as a boulder.

Dekker notices me staring. "He's recharging. Just a quick pick-me-up."

A charge plate is attached to an outlet in the wall.

"I didn't know bots had to plug themselves in."

"It is not absolutely necessary," LT says, barely moving his lips, "but—"

Dekker butts in. "But a lot of them do. And the extra juice will come in handy if things get hairy."

And by *hairy*, I think he means in case we're ambushed. Great.

I sit down at the table and Dekker slides me a bowl. I frown when I see what's inside. "The Double Dek special is a bowl of cereal?"

"It's special because it was made with love." When I raise my eyebrows, like, *Are you serious?* he adds with a shrug, "Cooking is not one of my strong suits."

"What are you doing up so early, anyway?"

He gestures to an open energy drink on the table. "I drink five of those a day. I never sleep."

As I polish off my food, Dekker empties the dishwasher. He puts the white coffee mugs in line with the others on the shelves, the handles facing out to the right. He even pauses to inspect the distance between them, and then nudges the last just a fraction of a centimeter. When it hits the cup next to it with a clank, he hits them together three more times before moving them apart again.

"Does that drive you nuts?"

He looks at me over a shoulder. "What?"

"Your 'affinity with precision'?" I say, even though we both know it's more than that.

"Ahh. Half the time I don't even notice I'm doing it.

It's just a thing, like someone who chews their fingernails or cracks their knuckles a lot."

"Isn't there medicine or something for that?"

"Sure, but do I look like a guy who has good health insurance?" He goes back to the dishes. "Besides, it could be worse. I figure I got off easy."

By the time LT's finished charging, and his charge plate is back in his torso, my cereal bowl is already in the dishwasher.

Dekker walks us outside. It rained more while I slept, and the everyday grime has been washed away from the hover rails. The driveway is wet and shiny black in the glow.

"Little dude, you've come so far." Dekker wipes away a fake tear before slapping me on the back. "You got a lot of stuff ahead of you, but I think if anyone can deal, it's you. Just . . . promise me you won't go nuclear when you see your dad."

"What's that supposed to mean?"

LT coughs. Since when do robots cough? Cleo never did. Maybe it's a programmed thing, to make him seem more human. I wonder if he sneezes. Or burps.

"We are losing time. If you think you can manage to hold on, I would rather travel by foot at my speed. It would be risky to abandon the car near the border."

131

Groaning, I saunter over. Every muscle in my body aches from holding on to LT yesterday, but I figure he knows better than I do about abandoning cars. And my speed is the speed of a snail compared to his.

When he lowers himself, I climb on his back. The sling pops out and wraps around me. I take the goggles LT offers and slip them over my eyes.

"All right, little dude," Dekker says. "Till we meet again."

I wave as LT takes off.

Before the sun comes up, I see the force field fence flickering in the distance like a dust-filled hologram. It's gigantic, rising over the buildings in the tiny border town of Awaso like an ocean wave.

LT stops at the mouth of an alley in a darkened business section. There isn't another soul in sight. The town is so quiet I can hear the fence humming blocks away.

"Follow me," LT says softly. We go to the end of the alley and LT points to a round metal plate set in the pavement. "This is where we will go underground."

I frown. "Underground?"

"Yes. You did not think we would simply walk into Bot Territory, did you?" LT lifts up the metal plate, expos-

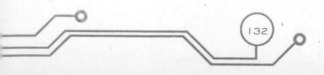

ing a dark hole into nothingness and a ladder that makes its way down into it.

"You will go first," he says to me.

My skin crawls like it's made of bugs. I shake my head. "No way."

One of LT's operating lights blinks once, twice, then winks out. "It is safe. I would know if there was anything down there."

"How?"

"I would detect the body heat. Or hear a heartbeat."

Cleo didn't have sensors like that. It makes me wonder what else LT can do.

My hands shake as I put my feet on the second rung and descend. At first it's not so bad, but once my head is below the opening, the darkness zips up around me. I squeeze my eyes shut and take a deep breath. Po would have no problem doing this. Neither would Lox. So I gotta toughen up. It's the only way I'm getting into Bot Territory to see Dad.

When my feet hit solid ground again, LT closes the metal plate above us. It's like I'm blind. I can't see anything. I stick to the wall, afraid that if I step too far in one direction, I'll fall right off the face of the earth.

I focus on the sound of LT's steps. Even though he's as

quiet as a beetle, it helps. Finally he reaches bottom and flicks on a light hidden beneath a panel in his forehead. It illuminates the tunnel. I see pipes and wires running along the walls and ceilings. The air smells clean and filtered, not at all like a sewer line.

"Where are we?"

"This is a hover rail maintenance line. If you know where you are going, it will lead you straight into Bot Territory."

"And you know where we're going?"

LT takes a step. "I do."

At first I let LT lead the way, because he's the one with the light, but being the last in line freaks me out. I hurry to catch up, putting us side by side. We round a corner, then another. A control panel at one intersection blinks and beeps.

"How long do we travel this line?"

"Approximately twenty-five minutes. We are very close to the border."

"And then how long before we reach my dad?"

"Seventeen and a half minutes."

My chest feels light and fluttery. I wonder if Dad will recognize me. I've grown a lot since I last saw him. I'm taller, for one, and I don't care what Po says, I'm not as scrawny as I used to be.

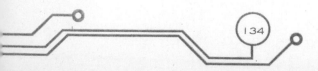

Will Dad be impressed that I made it?

LT stops in the middle of the tunnel and turns toward the brick wall.

"Um . . . what are we doing?" I say, thinking maybe he's officially lost his bolts.

"When I said you could enter Bot Territory if you knew the correct way, I meant the way was hidden from most." He presses a hand to the second brick up from the floor. The brick sinks into the wall. There's a scraping noise from somewhere behind it and suddenly the wall retracts and slides open like the door at a grocery store.

"Whoa," I breathe, when I see the second tunnel on the other side. Cool air sneaks in, like it's air-conditioned. "Is this a maintenance line too?"

"It is the old line that used to connect to Texas's lines. When the wars began and the border was created, the hover rails into Bot Territory were destroyed."

LT steps through the hole in the wall and I follow. Once we're safely on the other side, the door shuts behind us.

The tunnels here are narrower and chunks of concrete dot the floor like land mines. I accidentally kick one and it skitters into the darkness.

"Watch where you step," LT warns too late. "There are chunks taken out of the floor as well. It would be far too easy to twist your ankle." He points his head flashlight in the direction we need to go. "We've maintained this, and other tunnels like it, as best we can, but it is not perfect."

A few cobwebs hang from the pipes above, but for the most part it looks all right.

We head straight down a long hallway, then take three more turns.

"There." LT points to a ladder leading up through the tunnel's ceiling. "That is our entrance to—"

A quiet whirring noise sounds behind me. Then a *tick-tick-tick*.

LT goes quiet. I don't like it when he does that. Because he's a robot, it makes me feel alone. Like I'm the last person left in this tunnel.

Suddenly, he pushes me behind him. "Stay back!"

Something zooms around the corner from the hallway at our right. Tiny ball-shaped things that hover in the air. Lights blink at the front. There are three, from what I can see in the dark, and they come straight toward us.

"We need an alternate exit," LT says, and shoves me the way we came.

"What are they?" I ask as we run.

"Line drones used for inspections, but the UD must be using them to locate us."

We reach the end of the hallway. LT drags me left. My

lungs are burning already. I want to stop running and collapse in a heap and let my brain freeze to a crispy ball. I don't know if I have it in me to keep running. I'm no one special. I'm not smart and stubborn like Tellie. And I'm definitely not as adventurous as Lox or as brave as Po.

"We must hurry," LT says, putting himself between me and the drones.

"I can't." I gasp for air, lose speed.

"Yes you can."

The machines buzz like bees.

"We are moments away from seeing your father," LT yells. "You cannot give up now."

We barrel around another corner. I grit my teeth. Keep going. Po wouldn't give up. Dad wouldn't give up.

Another ladder comes into view.

"There is our alternate exit."

I reach for the ladder when a new machine rips out of a hiding spot on my left. It lights up like a Christmas tree and straightens its crab-like legs. A high-pitched screech fills the tunnel. I slam my hands over my ears, squeeze my eyes shut. The sound hurts so bad, it feels like there's a jackhammer in my skull.

LT says, "That device has an electronic scrambler—" and then collapses to the ground next to me, convulsing. The drones drop a few feet away.

The front of the crab machine flashes red and a voice plays through a speaker. "Remain where you are. You are classified as a criminal. Do not run."

I'm a foot away from the ladder that will take me to my dad. I am *this close*. And I will not let the UD government, or anyone for that matter, tell me I can't see my dad.

I run.

I go down one tunnel. Then another. I find a small room with pipes and boilers and other old machines. I bat away the cobwebs as I go. Near the back, I find a pile of pipes and grab one. Rust scrapes against my hands. I race back to the ladder, my feet pounding in sync with the blood pumping through my veins.

The high-pitched shriek seems worse now, like it's drilling its way deeper into my brain. I hold the pipe like a bat and swing, hitting the machine dead-on. Metal flakes pepper my shirt. I hit again. The shriek cuts out. I hit again and again. The machine loses its boost and plummets to the floor. I whack it a few more times just to be sure and when I'm done it's just a pile of metal and plastic and wires.

LT's fingers twitch. The drones light up. I hop over LT and take out the drones one at a time, like I'm playing Whac-A-Mole at the Brewery Arcade.

I step back, breathing heavy, covered in sweat and pieces of machinery. I did it. I took out the UD machines!

LT sits up and swivels his head back and forth, like he's recalibrating his joints. When he sees the downed machines, he whistles. "You did an impressive job."

I toss the pipe and it clangs as it hits the floor. "A couple of stupid machines weren't going to stop me."

LT makes it to his feet. He tears off his T-shirt, slips out of his jeans. He's one hundred percent robot now with a body made of metal. There are exposed gears at the seams between his torso and his limbs. I think it's more a decorative feature than anything else. A tiny panel in his chest says he's running at ninety-four percent and that he has an internal fluid leak in his left leg.

"Are you okay?" I ask.

"I am fine. A quick tune-up will be all I require." He steps over the smashed machinery and gestures to the ladder. "After you."

I hesitate. "We'll be safe in Bot Territory, right?"

"Of course. The UD government stated explicitly that they would not, under any circumstances, enter our territory. And if they do, the treaty is null and void."

LT taps the ladder with his hand and it *ching-ching-chings* in response. "Shall we?"

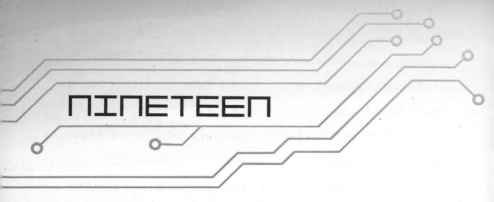

NINETEEN

A T THE TOP of the ladder, we enter a square brick room. There are no doors or windows. Only a tiny light glows from the ceiling. I move into the corner while LT sets the round metal door back in place in the floor.

When he straightens, he flips open a hidden compartment in the wall and reveals one lone red button. He presses it, and the wall makes a *vareeee-juuuu* sound. The bricks in front of me disappear one by one in a flicker of light, like they were never there to begin with.

"It's a holo-barrier," LT explains. "It looks and acts like brick, but there is no brick."

"That's so wrenched," I say.

LT leads the way through the new opening and we emerge into a large room with shelves and tables covered in machine parts and tools. A big engine hangs from a crank in the middle of the room. A length of hover rail is propped up in the corner.

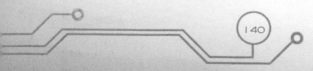

"Where are we?"

"This is the Mech Shop in Line Zero, the city where I live. It belongs to—"

"Number 3498393277-X," someone calls from another room, "but you may call me Scissor."

A bot comes through a doorway and its arm snakes out to greet me. I jump back.

"Scissor," LT scolds.

"What? Oh. Sorry." The arm retracts and snaps into its shoulder socket. "I forget he isn't used to our extraordinary eccentricities."

I think this bot, Scissor, is a girl. Her voice is high-pitched and sweet, and sounds like a flute. She's shorter than LT and her hips and chest plate are rounder. There's a dent in her left thigh and a gash in her right foot where a knot of wires hangs out. Blue paint is splattered on her back like someone pelted her with a paintball and she never bothered to clean it up.

Most of her body is made of some kind of white plastic or composite, except for a diamond-shaped LED panel in her chest. Right now it projects a green plaid pattern, and I wonder if it changes according to Scissor's mood.

"Scissor is Line Zero's mechanic," LT tells me.

"And inventor," she adds. Her arms snake out again and undulate in the air like the tentacles of an octopus. "This is my latest upgrade. What do you think?"

"Is that . . ." I step closer, but not *too* close. "Is that meta-pol?"

"It sure is!"

Meta-pol is a substance that can regenerate with a UV light. If it's smashed or cracked, the meta-pol will liquefy and expand to fill in the cracks. Once it cools, it's soft and rubbery. Lox and I once covered our toilet seat in meta-pol to play a joke on Po, but then I had to use the bathroom before Po got home. That sucked.

"How does it work?" I ask Scissor. "Don't you need a UV light?"

She gestures to her arm sockets. "I have a ring of tiny lights here."

I can see a dozen faint dots of light now that I know where to look. "Wow."

She reins her arms back in. "Did you two have any trouble crossing over?"

LT steps forward. "Line drones at the second west exit, but Trout promptly dismantled them."

Scissor's eyes light up raspberry pink. "That is amazing! And so like your father. Robert St. Kroix is one of the bravest men I've ever met. Heroic, really."

A smile sneaks in. I like being compared to Dad. I like it even more that Scissor thinks of him as a hero.

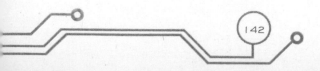

"Took out some drones," Scissor repeats. "That deserves applause!" Cheering fills the room, like there's a grandstand of people hiding beneath the broken bot parts.

"What was that?" I ask.

"Scissor likes to add special effects to everything she does," LT explains. "That includes adding sound effects to conversations."

Scissor raps her knuckles on her chest. "A thousand tracks in here. I have a response for almost anything. Would you like to hear a few more?"

"Umm . . . okay."

Scissor juts out her bottom lip and the crowd goes, "Awwww." Then she widens her eyes and drops open her mouth. The crowd gasps.

"I think that is enough for now," LT says. "I imagine Trout would like to see his father."

Scissor starts swaying back and forth and plays a track of music with violins and piano solos, like my reunion with Dad is some sad-sap movie drama.

"All right, all right," Scissor says when LT starts for the door. To me, she says, "Your father has been patiently . . . err . . . *impatiently* waiting for you all day. So I bid you adieu." She makes her way toward me, hand extended, but trips over a pile of detached robot legs and lands in a clang and clatter on the floor.

The track plays a drawn-out *womp-womp*.

LT sighs and helps Scissor to her feet. There's a new dent in her torso, but overall, she looks all right. We finally shake hands and say good-bye.

LT leads me through a side door on the Mech Shop and when we step onto the front sidewalk, I freeze.

A whole bustling city spreads out in front of me. With bots *and* humans.

This is nothing like the machine wasteland I pictured. There are hovercars. Hoverboards. A hot dog cart. Women in suits. Men in sandals. Families eating ice cream.

A robot tosses a stick for a dog. The dog barks and chases after it into the grass. A woman coos at her baby in its stroller and a bot pauses to coo too.

Around the shopping square, digital advertisements hover on the sidewalks and hang from awnings.

Glitch's Kitchen. Glitch's famous chili on sale today!

Beans, Bolts & Biscotti is running a dinner special! Buy yourself a sandwich combo and treat your bot friend to a free oil change!

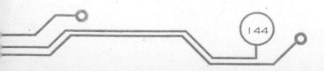

Rewire, Inc. Get your new Krixus
Joint Fittings here.

The UD government used to play military recruitment commercials showing deserted streets in Bot Territory with crumbling buildings and smashed robots lying in the gutters.

It makes me wonder what else they lied about.

"Your father is this way," LT says, pointing to the street that runs between Rewire, Inc. and Line Zero Bakery. "He has a residence on Fourth Street."

I am so close to seeing Dad after so long, I keep thinking something will happen. Like the patrolmen will swoop in and arrest me. Or I'll wake up and realize it was all a dream.

We cross the street, cut through the small park, and stick to the sidewalk when we leave the shopping center behind. Brick buildings line the streets. Flowers burst out of window boxes. Curtains flap in open windows. I wish Po were with me right now. He would totally gear out.

I'm so into the city that when LT stops at Dad's building, I run smack into him.

LT swivels his head around. "Are you all right?"

"Fine. Just . . ."

"Nervous. And perhaps a bit surprised at your sur-

roundings. Understandable. Shall we continue?" He gestures with his hand toward the double glass doors that lead into a lobby.

"My dad lives here?"

"He owns the entire building."

I look up. The building is three stories of super-strong green brick that people use in natural disaster zones, like for earthquakes and hurricanes and stuff. It's supposed to withstand just about anything short of an X-bomb. It's also not cheap. Or at least that's what I heard Lox's dad say once when he was talking about their "standard stick built" house. Whatever that means.

I think of our old ratty house in Brack with the clumpy grass and notched security system and the fridge that clunks around when the motor starts up. How come Dad never came for us? How come he made us sit and wait in the UD while he bought a *building* in Bot Territory?

Calm down, the tiny voice in my head says. *There must be a good explanation.*

I try to push through the doors, but they rattle against a lock.

"Here, allow me." LT steps forward and presses his finger to a port installed in the door. The lock clicks open.

"If you don't have fingerprints, how did that work?"

LT holds up his finger and the metal tip slides away,

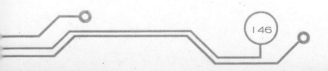

revealing a silicone finger beneath. "I have a print. Or at least one that's unique to me. Bots are programmed into the Central Automaton Database Center in Old New York so we can get through certain security ports."

"Oh." Old New York must be like Bot Territory's capital. The last news feed I watched at home, about the nanny bot that was apprehended, made Old New York sound like a place only for assembling bots. Apparently it's more than that.

We enter into the lobby. Wood floors creak beneath my feet. A vid panel on the wall to my right plays the UD news feed. Big cushy chairs sit empty across from a U-shaped couch.

LT leads me to an elevator hidden in an alcove in the back. When I step inside and the doors shut, my reflection stares at me in the polished steel. LT picks the third floor. The car lurches upward and my knees sink to my toes.

I think it takes all of two seconds to reach the top floor, but in those two seconds, I start buzzing with anticipation. I'm like a firecracker ready to blow. Like a piston ready to pop. Like a . . . like a . . .

The doors rush open and my eyes widen as I try to take in every detail.

Sunlight shines through the leaded glass ceiling. Peo-

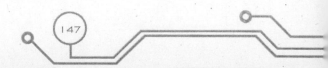

ple and bots buzz around the wide-open room. A gigantic screen on the far wall flashes information about Bot Territory, suspected UD government movements, and weather forecasts. A thin woman with a high ponytail mans a computer in the center of the room.

I scan the faces, searching for Dad. Has he changed so much in two years that I don't even recognize him? Did his hair turn gray? Did he grow a mustache?

People start to notice me standing there. The room goes quiet. A door I didn't notice before squeaks open and a man steps out, his boots thumping on the floor. There's a loft area built above where the man stands, so his face is hidden in shadow.

"Trout?" he says. "Is that you?"

I suck in a breath. My eyes burn with the good kind of tears and I race across the room.

Dad. It's Dad. It's really him.

I am beneath the loft area before I see him. Before I can *really* see him. And when I do, it pulls me to a stop. The goofy, happy smile plastered on my face disappears. Something is wrong.

Dad shifts and the sunlight hits his arm and glares back, making me squint. Metal. Dad's arm is made of metal. He takes a step toward me. My heart bats at my brain and I scan the rest of him.

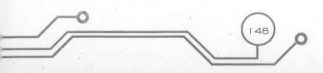

A bolt juts out from his neck. A metal plate makes up half his face and something green glows from beneath his shirt, from the place where his heart should be.

I can't feel my hands or my feet and it's like I've stopped breathing altogether. Like I've officially gone off the edge of the universe. Because this can't be right.

This isn't my dad.

"Trout," he says. Even his voice sounds different now that I listen. It's raspier and it needles at the back of my neck. "Aidan," he tries again, using my real name this time, which means he's being serious.

I take a step back. Then another.

"Wait."

This is not my dad. This is not the guy I crossed into Bot Territory to see. My dad is not a robot!

I stumble over my own feet and slam into the back of the elevator. I jam a finger into the buttons. The bad kind of tears sting my eyes.

"Aidan!" Dad calls.

"You're not my dad!" I shout as the doors whoosh closed.

TWENTY

I RUN. I don't know where I'm going. I just want as much space between Dad and me as I can get.

I grit my teeth. I'm ten nanometers away from gearing out. I want Po more than I've ever wanted him. He'd understand. He'd know what to do. But Po is all the way in Brack being held captive by the UD all because of me. Because of that stupid vid, because I wanted my dad back, and now look.

A traffic light switches to red and I come to a stop at the corner. My chest heaves, I'm breathing so hard. I swipe away the sweat that rolls down my forehead. As I wait for the light to change, for the hovercars to whir past, I notice a park across the street. A big one like Ryder Park back home.

I go there and plop down on a bench between two willow trees. There are kids playing at the top of the hill

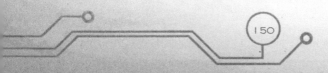

and a group of women jogging around the paved paths, but for the most part, I'm alone.

I curl my knees up, wrapping my arms around them and burying my head so no one will see me cry. I never knew a heart could hurt like this, like it's been ground into dust.

Did Po know about Dad? Why didn't he warn me?

My dad is a robot. MY DAD IS A ROBOT.

As I sit there trying to sniff back the snot running outta my nose, footsteps fall behind me.

"Mind if I sit?"

I look up at Dad, squinting against the sunlight that's shining through the droopy willow branches. I nod my head and he sits on my left side, keeping the part of him that's bot away from me. I'm glad for that, even if it makes me feel like a crummy person.

The wood bench creaks as Dad settles in. I hold my knees up tight. I don't know what to say. I don't know what to think. I'm like a ball of space junk floating through the ether.

We sit in silence for what seems like forever. I keep my eyes trained straight ahead watching the group of kids playing at the top of the hill.

Finally, Dad takes a deep breath. "I was injured pretty

badly in the war," he says, and leans back, draping an arm over the bench. "I thought for sure I was dead. LT and another bot, Ratch, they found me and dragged me to safety. Scissor fixed me up, but . . ." Dad raps his knuckles against the metal plate on the side of his face. *Ting. Ting. Ting.* "Obviously I'm not quite what I used to be."

I let go of my knees and my feet drop to the ground. I sniff. Wipe my eyes. Sniff again. Thing is, sitting here next to Dad—it's the only thing I've wanted for forever. And when I don't think about the parts of him that are metal, he sounds just like the Dad who left me and Po two years ago.

The very same person I've been fighting for and worrying and wondering about every night since.

And if LT hadn't found him . . .

My chest squeezes real tight as I lean over and collapse against Dad. I can't help it, I start crying again. Shoulder-shaking, lip-quivering baby sobs.

Dad is alive. And he's sitting right next to me, and that's all that should matter. He's still my dad. Just . . . with a robotic arm. And a half-machine face. And his heart . . .

"If you don't have a human heart, are you still the

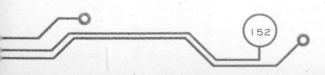

same? I mean, can you . . ." I trail off, because I'm afraid to ask what I want to ask.

"Can I still love you guys?" Dad says.

"Well, yeah, I guess."

"Of course I can." Dad pats my back with his real arm. "Nothing has changed. None of the things that matter, anyway."

I wipe my face with the sleeve of my shirt and look over at Dad. His eyes are still the same shade of brown, just like mine, like river mud. There's the scar above his right eyebrow where a framed family photo fell on his head when he was cleaning out a closet.

He smiles at me, and while the side of his mouth that's on the side with the metal plate doesn't move the same, it's still Dad's easy grin.

"If you cross a man with a bot, what do you get?" he asks.

This is the game we used to play. We would try to come up with the best, most wrenched, most hilarious hy-breed. I hold the winning title so far with koala parrot. Everything is better in rainbow colors. I bet Dekker would say so too.

"A man-bot?" I guess.

"No, silly. A ro-man."

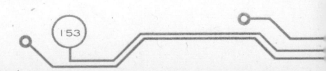

Dad and I laugh. It's like we're back in Brack at the kitchen table drawing pretend hy-breeds on an old tab-pad. I wish we really were back there, before the war, before everything got so jammed.

"You grew up on me, ya know?" Dad says.

I snort. "Po says I'm still a little squirt."

"That's because he's afraid you'll end up bigger than him."

I can't help but smile at that one. "Paybacks."

"Exactly."

The kids on the hill drop onto their backs and roll down to the bottom. It's been a while since I hung out with Lox and did stupid stuff like that. Will I ever get to hang out with him now that I'm considered a criminal?

"Come on." Dad squeezes my shoulder. "I bet you're starving, and I have one of the best cooks in the city. We can finish talking over food."

I rise to my feet and Dad stands next to me. For being made partly of metal, he moves quickly, just like LT. I wonder what other pieces of him had to be replaced with machinery. I wonder if he runs faster now.

"I'm glad you're here, son," he says as we head toward his building. "I've missed you. More than you'll ever know."

He puts his arm around my shoulders and it feels just like it used to.

On the walk back, I find out that everyone calls Dad's building the Fort and that he spent over a year fixing it up. It was falling apart on the inside ever since the Bot Wars started, and its owner—a banker—abandoned it when the UD recommended people flee to the safer districts in the north.

"And every time I completed a project," Dad says as we cross the lobby, "I thought about what you and your brother would want in the place if you were finally able to escape the UD safely."

"I'd want a pool," I say. "Is there one?"

Dad blows out a puff of air. "I knew I forgot something." The elevator opens on the second floor. "But I promise, this floor might make up for it."

"What's on this floor?"

"Living quarters. Kitchen. And a media room, courtesy of Scissor."

My eyes light up. That's wrenched.

We exit the elevator and step into an open kitchen. Sunshine pours through a wall of windows and makes the glossy white floor shine. Another loft area stretches over the mile-long dining table. Bookshelves line the wall up there. A couple of kids toss foam balls over the railing and "bomb" the enemy. The enemy is made up of various adults, bots, and a few people Po's age. A short man sets the table while an equally short bot preps the food. It's like a bustling city in here too. Instantly I like it. I'm used to being home by myself with nothing more than the sound of the TV to keep me company.

Dad introduces me to Merril, the bot who is the Fort's head cook. He's a big robot, as tall as Dad, with shoulders as wide as an eagle's wingspan. His voice is deep, and dark, like molasses, and he has a laugh that starts way down in his belly. When he sees me, he wipes his hands on a yellow apron and leaves behind a streak of flour.

"Well now." He shakes his head. "You look just like Mr. St. Kroix. Right down to the distance between your eyes and the pinched bridge of your nose." He squints at me, then: "Ahh ya, and the left ear is lower than the right. Just like your pops."

Automatically, I tug at my ears and look at Dad. "What the chop? How come no one told me my ears were different?"

"Probably only a millimeter off," Dad says. "Not noticeable. Trust me."

I'm trying to catch my reflection in the window to

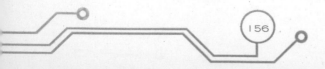

check my ears when Dad pulls me away. He introduces me to everyone. I meet a string of people, men and woman who Dad says are "part of the security tech." They don't say much. Mostly *Nice to meet you*. And *Hi*.

It's the bots that seem the most friendly, but every time I shake their hands, I'm reminded that Dad has an arm just like that. So when the food finally comes, I'm more than happy to plop down at the table and dig in.

Merril made biscuits, fried up some bacon, toasted a whole loaf of bread, and scrambled a big pan of eggs. I'd been up for so long, traveling so far, that I'd forgotten it was only breakfast time. I'm so hungry, though, I'd eat just about anything.

The kid who sits next to me—Jared or Dave or something—informs me that Merril's the best cook around and that "he takes cooking more seriously than programming."

Dad cracks open a canned drink and starts chugging. I realize he doesn't have a plate in front of him. "You're not eating?"

He shakes his head. "I can't. My stomach was damaged when I was wounded."

I stop chewing. "And?"

"And now I don't have one."

My eyes widen. "Really? So like, you can't eat? At all?"

Dad holds up his drink. The can says LIFE WATER on the side in big, spindly letters. #1 DRINK AMONGST ROBOTS. "This is it. And I take supplemental shots, so I get the necessary nutrients and calories for the parts of me that are human."

"Wow. That's notched."

Dad raises an eyebrow. "Is that what you kids are saying nowadays? Notched?"

"Dad," I moan, which makes him chuckle real hard.

When breakfast is done, I'm so stuffed, I can barely move. Merril and a few other people clean up the table. Everyone else disappears from the room.

"So," Dad starts, "we have a lot more to talk about. Where should I begin?"

I try to think of the biggest, most important question I've been harboring, but they *all* seem big and important. "Did you know about any of this when you signed up for the war?"

A pot bangs against the counter in the kitchen. Merril inspects the new dent and tsks. Dad leans back in his chair across from me.

"I knew a little about what was going on." He takes a breath. "Remember when your brother came home from the war? How badly his leg was injured?" I nod. "We

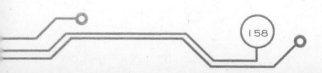

told you it was the Deeta disease because I didn't want to worry you. But that wasn't what happened."

I frown. "What happened, then?"

"Po was on a routine border check with his unit when they came across a dismantled bot on the side of the road. Po pulled over when the bot tried waving them down. At first he meant to smash it, and fry out its operating system only because it didn't have legs or much of a torso anyway. There was nothing left."

I sit forward. I had no idea about any of this and I'm feeling guilty for ever thinking Po's real story—that he was injured in the Bot Wars—was a jacked-up lie just to impress girls.

"But when your brother got out there, the bot told him there were humans and bots in the woods who needed his help. The bot said people were being injured by army officials, not just men, but women and children too."

Dad folds his hands in front of him. "When Po and his unit entered the woods, what they found was a base camp with people and bots held prisoner in little more than cages. And when Po tried to let the women and children go, the officials running the camp fought back."

Dad looks right at me when he says, "Your brother got

caught in a force field blast. And that's how he lost his leg."

"What?" I breathe; even though I heard every word he said, I'm still not sure I heard him right. "A bomb? His leg got . . ." My stomach flip-flops as I think about what Po must have gone through. I squeeze my eyes shut and try to shake off the image.

He must have geared out when he realized his leg was totally gone.

I reach for my glass of water, my mouth suddenly dry. I guzzle the rest and the water swims in my stomach.

Dad goes on. "Po faked amnesia and was honorably discharged. When he told me what happened . . ." Dad runs his hand through his overgrown hair. Flecks of silver strands stand out amongst the darker ones. "I knew I had to do something. So I volunteered. Gut instinct told me there was something bigger going on."

When I look around the kitchen and dining room, I realize we're alone. Merril is gone. Still, I lean closer and whisper just to be sure. "Was it the Meta-Rise?"

An AC vent clicks to life. Cold air rushes into the room. Gooseflesh runs down my arms. Dad leans back so his chair tips on two legs. He used to yell at Po and me for that. *You'll fall over and break the chair,* he used to say. *And your head.*

"Where did you hear about the Meta-Rise?" he asks.

I open my mouth to tell him what Dekker told me, but decide to keep that a secret. I don't want Dekker getting in trouble. Instead, I shrug all nonchalant, and say, "I just heard some people talking about it."

Dad frowns, like he's onto me, but he doesn't push. "The Meta-Rise is near and dear to me. It's more than just a group of bot supporters. It's people and bots fighting for the truth. Fighting for opportunity and freedom and above all else, fairness. The UD is light on all fronts. They banned robots because they were scared, but what's next? What if they don't stop with bots? They already control what goes on the Net through the UNDC. Their regulations are turning the country into a dictatorship. The Meta-Rise wants to change that."

A couple of kids laugh somewhere down the hall. Cyber-tech music blares through speakers. The *tick-tick-whoom* of the music vibrates through the floor.

"Are *you* part of the Meta-Rise?" I ask.

Dad doesn't even skip a beat. "I am."

"Can I be?"

"Absolutely not."

"Dad!"

"Trout!" he singsongs back. "Being part of the Rise is more than just believing in something. It's putting your

life at risk and I will not allow my twelve-year-old son to risk his life. You've already done enough just by getting here."

I cross my arms in front of myself. "You're just gearing out because you think I'm still a kid. You and Po both. I'm not a kid anymore."

A sigh wheezes past Dad's lips. "I know, but that doesn't mean I want you putting yourself in danger for something you might not understand yet. I've gone to great lengths to make sure you and Po are not labeled bot supporters and enemies of the Districts. I only wish that could have remained."

I tighten my hands into fists. "What you mean is you wish I was still living my fake life in the Districts thinking you were dead."

Dad shakes his head. "That's not what I meant."

"Everything back there was totally notched, Dad. I hated every single day of my life." I let out a breath. An inferno builds in my throat, like I might start spewing fire at any second. I'm just so frustrated with everyone treating me like a little kid. And I'm annoyed that anyone would think keeping me in the dark was a good thing. Because it's not. Because it's totally cracked. I hate liars. And I hate lies. And I hate people thinking I'm not old enough to do important stuff.

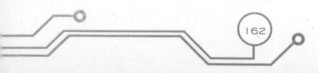

A beeping noise sounds from Dad's chest. He looks down at the glowing light where his heart should be. "I have to go. Have to charge up. LT will show you to your room." He comes around the table and wraps an arm around my neck from behind. He gives me a half hug and kisses the top of my head like he used to when I really *was* a little kid.

Now it just makes me feel lame and silly.

"I'm glad you're here." He pats my shoulder. "I've missed you."

But not enough, I think, as his footsteps thud away. If he missed me, he should have done everything in his power to come get me.

TWENTY-ONE

T SHOWS UP exactly 1.3 seconds after Dad leaves the dining room. And as soon as he sees me hunched in my chair, arms crossed, eyes narrowed, he says, "Is it safe to assume the conversation did not go as you planned?"

I shove my chair away. "Dad still thinks I'm a baby."

"I highly doubt that is the case, considering you do not wear diapers and eat from a bottle."

I start to laugh, and then remember I'm mad. It turns into a snort instead. "It's just stupid." I follow LT down a hallway, through a living room, and down another hallway. We don't cross paths with a single person. It's like everyone just up and disappeared.

"Are you part of the Meta-Rise?" I ask when LT finally stops at a closed door.

He turns to face me. "I suppose in some respects I am. Though I do not serve on the front lines of the movement."

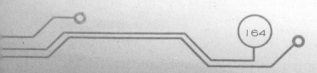

"So what *do* you do?"

LT pushes open the door. "Right now I am in charge of you. Your friend, should you need one."

I frown. "*Babysitter* is what you mean."

"Hardly. I would consider myself more of a body-guard."

I shove my hands in my pants pockets and wander into the room LT revealed behind the closed door. "I'm not sure *bodyguard* is any better. It's like a word used in place of *babysitter*."

"Tanner Waylon uses bodyguards and they serve a very good purpose."

I turn around and face LT still standing in the door-way. "The pop star? He's a drain—"

"Clogger," LT finishes for me. "So I have heard."

I finally look at the room we're in. It's located in a tower in the back of the building, so the room is a half circle with windows overlooking the tiny backyard. A bed takes up one wall and a vid panel hangs across from it. There's a vid controller on the nightstand.

I do a circle in the middle of the room, taking it all in. "Wow. This is bigger than my room at home. Like twice the size."

"It is the best room in the building. It was your father's. When he heard you were on your way here,

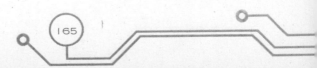

165

he moved into a smaller room to give you this one."

I stop. "Really?"

"Yes." LT glides forward. "Your father is very happy you are here. I know it might be hard to believe that, considering all the secrecy and the concerns for your safety, but he is only being a father."

There's a big bench beneath the row of windows, so I go there and climb up on my knees, looking out at the city. The sun blazes from its high perch in the sky. The hover rails look almost silver in the daylight. This place is different than Brack, but it's the same too, in some ways. My dad lives here, which makes it automatically feel like home. I can see myself staying here for good. Knowing what I know about Bot Territory and the United Districts, I'm not sure I'd ever want to live there again.

They were lying to us about the bots, but why?

"Hey LT, were you alive when the Bot Wars started?"

"I was."

"I know what the UD wants me to believe, but why do you think it started?"

"I know precisely why it started. There is no contemplation or speculation about it."

"Then why?"

"In its infancy, it was a labor dispute. After the government created the Machinery Tax and Labor Law, robots

were worked until broken because the more they worked, the more product a manufacturer had, and the more taxes the government collected on machine labor. So you see, robot owners were benefitting, the government was benefitting, but the machines themselves became workhorses with no rights at all."

He looks over at me with his almost-human eyes. "Have you heard of the ThinkChip?"

I nod. "We learned about them in history class last year. They were made by some scientist and put into all robots so they could feel and understand human emotions."

"That is correct. Humans made us more like them, but when we became *too much* like them, they realized it was not what they wanted after all.

"We eventually went on strike and asked for more rights. The government countered. They said they would agree to fairer labor laws if all ThinkChips were removed. We may be made of metal, but we are not stupid. We knew the chips were our only link to human emotion and organic thought. So when we resisted, the government twisted the facts around so that it appeared we were turning against our owners and plotting a takeover. From there, it spiraled out of control."

LT looks down and shakes his head. "That was not our intention at all. We just wanted to be treated fairly.

"We are not simply machines anymore. We are so much more than that."

All the robots I've met so far have been totally different, like humans, each with their own personalities and opinions. They all look different too. I believe what LT says.

I turn around and sit on my butt on the bench. "The UD has been exaggerating the evil robots conspiracy this whole time."

LT holds up his hand. "Well, yes, but for the most part, I understand their fear. We are treading on new ground and no one knows what to expect. A war is a war, no matter who is fighting it. It is human nature to protect what is theirs and to keep their loved ones safe."

I set my chin in my hand. I know that all too well. Po is always so protective, nagging me all the time. But deep down, we'd do anything for each other. Anything.

And I think LT would too. He risked his life to save me in the UD. That's major.

"I'm glad you still have your ThinkChip," I say, and rap my knuckles against his arm. "I like you this way, metal brain."

LT sighs. "You were with Dekker approximately five hours and have already adopted his ridiculous sense of humor." His head swivels back and forth. "I will leave

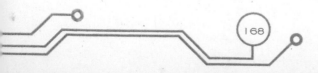

you now, but if you need anything, feel free to call me on the intercom."

Just before he walks out the door I yell out to him. "Hey, LT!" He turns around. "I really do like you. You're totally wrenched."

He goes still as he looks the word up on his database. "*Wrenched* is modern slang for *cool* or *awesome* or *swell*. I will take it. Thank you. You are totally wrenched too."

He shuts the door behind him and I'm left there trying to remember a time when people said "swell" instead of "wrenched."

TWENTY-TWO

I FIND THE MEDIA room the next morning on my way up to the third floor. It's this big room with exposed ducts and pipes in the ceiling. There's a gigantic vid panel and full media center in front of a U-shaped couch. Beanbags sit in front of the couch, the centers mashed down from whoever sat in them last.

I crane my neck and look up, and then nearly fall over at what I see. There are rope bridges running all over in a maze. One bridge runs to a landing backed by a row of windows. Another bridge disappears through a doorway. Yet another bridge leads to an iron landing where comfy-looking chairs are pushed against the wall.

This place looks more and more like a true fort every day.

I decide to come back later and hurry to the elevators. When I finally arrive at the command center, the light in Dad's chest is glowing blue and blinking like the navi lights on an airplane.

"There he is," Dad says, and lets out a sigh. "I was just about to send LT on a search and rescue. Where were you?"

"I got lost."

"There's an intercom in every room."

"Sorry." I shrug. I guess some things never change. I still get yelled at. And Dad still does the yelling. "I didn't think about calling. Po and I don't have intercoms, you know. We just shout through the house."

LT comes forward. "Of course, we knew you were safe. The house registered your presence. Unfortunately, it had no idea where you were. A terrible side effect of the recent accidental pulsar blast. The sensors are out of sync." He looks across the room at Scissor, who pretends to push buttons in her arm panel while whistling innocently.

Just behind Dad, I notice a few people and a bot I haven't met yet. Dad introduces them one by one. Jules. Parker. Ratch. Cole.

Cole isn't much older than Po, but he looks nothing like my brother. His muscles are bigger than my head, and tattoos wind up and around his arms. Three horizontal laser implants glow beneath the skin at the bridge of his nose. I wouldn't mess with him even if you paid me.

Jules is Dad's age, I think. She's the thin woman I saw manning the central computer yesterday. Her eyes are big and blue and her skin is shimmery copper brown, like she's glowing from the inside out.

She's wearing a black tank top and black jeans and laced black combat boots. A set of military tags hangs from a ball chain around her neck along with a scrambler. Her high ponytail swings behind her as she shakes my hand.

Parker stands near enough to Dad that I instantly think bodyguard or best friend. If it's bodyguard, I don't think he'll make a very good one. He's the smallest guy in the room, both in height and weight. Like you could knock him over with a burp. A swoop of bright red hair sticks up from his forehead and a silver stud pierces his left eyebrow.

And then the robot.

He's nothing like the other bots I've met. He's as tall as LT with a face of clear silicone and a glowing orange band where his eyes should be. The rest of him is made of a flat black metal that seems to absorb the light instead of reflect it.

"Ratch," he says, and offers me his hand.

I stare at it for probably too long. LT's hands look like hands but are made of metal. Ratch's hands are just long

spindly fingers of gears and bars. Like he once had an exterior layer that he ripped off.

"Pleasure to meet you." He smiles and his silicone mouth stretches over a jaw of metal.

He's totally wrenched. And scary. And I can't decide if I should like him or run away screaming.

I finally shake his hand. "Nice to meet you too. You're the other bot that saved my dad, right?"

He nods. "I am."

"Well, thanks. Thanks for saving him."

"No need to thank me." He steps back, putting him shoulder to shoulder with Cole.

"I consider these people my closest friends," Dad says. "And that includes LT, Scissor, and Ratch."

Scissor's LED panel lights up bright red and her audience cheers.

Cole shakes his head.

"All right." Dad crosses his arms over his chest. "LT, you have a report for us?"

LT steps forward. "While in Fifth District, I gathered as much information as I could. Po is being held at the moment in City Hall. I do not believe they plan to move him. At least not yet. And secondly, I believe the UD is planning an attack. I wasn't able to decipher when or where, exactly."

Dad swears and turns away from us, running his robotic hand through his hair. "Parker, what chance do we have of retrieving Po?"

Parker squares his shoulders. "We can get into the UD easily enough. It's getting into the building that'll be the hard part."

"I know how we get in," Ratch says. "Blow a hole in the side of the building."

Dad sighs as he turns back around. "While that may be effective, it's not going to help our cause. And we risk harming innocent people."

"No one in that building is innocent."

I think of Tanith, the woman in the Heart Office. She's nice. And she doesn't deserve to get hurt.

"Let's not be rash. Parker, can you start working on a route?"

Parker says, "I'm on it," and disappears inside the office below the loft.

Dad puts his hands on the edge of the central desk and leans over. "What else do we have?"

I clear my throat and everyone looks at me. "Um . . . I don't know if it will help or anything, but Po called me right before I bolted. He called to warn me and someone was there with him."

"It's worth taking a look." Dad glances at Jules.

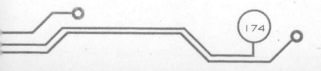

"I don't have my Link anymore," I say.

"That's all right." Jules drops into a computer chair. "I can hack into the system and replay your last phone call."

"You can do that?"

"Don't repeat this," Dad says, "but Jules is one of the best hackers on the planet."

"One of the best?" Jules says over a shoulder. "*The* Best. Better than Dekker. Even though he'd probably argue that." She hits a few more commands on the board and cues up my last call on the big screen. An image of Po blinks on, his face frozen in pause mode. A lump of guilt wedges in my chest. I was a total lame-o to him right before he left that day.

With his face blown up to fit the screen, I see he was sweating big-time and his eyes were bloodshot when he called. I don't know if that means he was angry, or that he'd been crying. I don't want to know.

The call replays. I watch it closely, looking for any clues I didn't notice the first time around when things went nuclear.

"RUN!" Po says, and his words dig into my bones like splinters. I cringe but can't look away. Something crunches. The table slams against the floor. Po lashes out. My hands tighten into fists and an arm comes into view on the screen—the arm of Po's attacker.

And that's when I notice it. The watch on the man's arm, a watch I know I've seen before.

"That's Tellie Rix's dad," I say. "The night I left the UD, he was wearing an Ionex watch with a bronze band. I don't know why I didn't figure it out then." Maybe because I was geared out of my mind.

"Rix." Cole snaps his fingers. "That the congressman?"

My stomach plummets to my toes as I nod. I feel sick. My mouth goes dry as sandpaper. Mr. Rix saw me in his house just hours after attacking my brother.

Does Tellie know what her dad did?

The call ends and the screen blackens. I lean against one of the support columns and tip my head back. Did Tellie betray me? Did the patrolmen show up so fast because she called them? Or maybe her parents called?

I try to think of all the ways she's helped me. If it hadn't been for that vid, I wouldn't be here with Dad. And Tellie was the one who packed me a bag and tried to help me escape. That had to count for something.

"Hey." Dad comes over. "You all right?"

I'm ten million shades away from all right. I want my brother back. I want everyone safe.

"Scissor?" Dad calls. "Why don't you show Trout around town? Take him to Janolli's. Put it on my tab."

"I'm not leaving," I say.

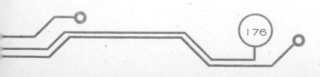

"We've got some stuff to work out. It's pretty boring stuff." He gives me his best Dad look, which is a combination of frowny eyes and a be-a-good-sport head tilt. "Besides, you look like you could use a break, and Janolli's makes the best ice cream in town."

"Ooooh," Scissor's audience track says. *"Ahhh."*

"Scissor?" Cole says, craning his big neck around. "Is that really necessary?"

Scissor ignores Cole and sidles up next to me. "We will have barrels full of fun, Trout. That is my promise to you."

Ice cream. Like ice cream will somehow make it better. Well, it won't. It didn't make things better when Dad was missing, when my worst fear was that he was dead. And it won't help now that my brother is in trouble.

But then Dad says, in a quiet but serious voice, "Please, kiddo? Take a break and come back later with a clear head. We need all the fresh brain power we can get."

I sigh. I don't want to admit it, but he's right. I need to come up with a new plan, some way to get Po back without anyone getting hurt. My vid worked for finding Dad. Maybe not the way I thought, but it still worked.

"Fine," I mutter, and push off the support column with a foot. Scissor trails behind me, her audience cheering the whole way.

TWENTY-THREE

I GET ICE CREAM at Janolli's, and Scissor buys a round of oil. "For my joints," she says, like I don't know. There's no Bot-N-Bolts here, so I take a leap and try something new. Raspberry Hairy Coco Hut ice cream. And holy jet smoke is it good. It's this weird combination of raspberry ice cream threaded with coconut flakes and topped with donut "hair." Basically it's just a doughnut made into strings.

I don't come up for air until my bowl is empty. When it is, I sit back in the booth and pat my stomach. "That was mega."

A group of bots file inside and line up across from us, their backs to the wall. They go still as sentries, hands at their sides.

"Umm, what are they doing?" I whisper.

Scissor looks up from her can of oil. "They're charging. See the black strips in the wall? Those are charge docks. A bot just needs to be near enough for their battery to connect." She pours more oil in a spigot at her shoulder. A second later, it leaks out her elbow. "Jam." She sops up the mess with a napkin.

"How is it you're still running when you have live wires sticking out of weird places and oil leaking out your elbow? Shouldn't you be backfiring and farting blue smoke or something?"

Scissor gives me an are-you-serious look. "Blue smoke? Please, Trout. Give me more credit than that." A smile spreads across her face. "I fart confetti, of course."

I roll my eyes but can't bury the laugh that knocks its way outta my throat. Anyway, it feels good to laugh.

When we're done at Janolli's, we walk east and stop in the park where I had my major nuclear meltdown yesterday when I found out Dad was part bot. The park isn't super-busy, but there are more people than I saw the day before.

Two bots look after a group of kids running circles around the playground kicking up woodchips as they go. A gray-haired man rides an oldie bike with the kind of pedals you have to move yourself. Lox's mom said those were "making a comeback." I guess she was right.

I haven't been on a playground in a kajillion years, and I get the sudden urge to run around too. I start with the monkey bars. The healing cut on my hand from the fountain climb burns a little, but it's nothing I can't deal with. I swing from one rung to the next.

I leave the monkey bars and climb up the giant metal dome made out of thin linking bars. I make it to the top without breaking a sweat. Propping my feet on one bar, and my butt on another, I kinda hang there at the top, letting the wind push through my hair. If I close my eyes, it almost feels like I'm on a hoverboard, like I'm weightless.

"Hey you."

My eyes snap open. There's a girl only inches away from my face. I gasp, lean back, lose my balance, and slip through one of the gaps in the dome. At the last second, I scramble for another bar, catching myself before I plummet to the ground.

The girl pokes her head through a gap and laughs. "Didn't mean to scare ya."

"I could have broken my neck!"

"Nah. Scissor woulda caught you with her stretch arms. Besides, it's not that far of a drop."

"Far enough." I latch on to the bar with my other hand and get my body swinging like I'm an acrobat at the circus. When I have enough momentum, I arch my back, kick, and wrap my legs around another bar. From there it's easy. I push up, duck beneath one bar, pop my head

out the top of the structure. Then it's just a matter of pulling myself into a sitting position.

"Impressive," the girl says.

As I catch my breath, I take a good look at her. She's nothing like the girls in Brack. Her hair is spiked at the top, but shaved on the sides, and long down the back. And when she shifts, and the sunlight catches her at a different angle, her hair changes color. It's gone from pink to purple to blue in a matter of seconds. The only word I can think to describe it is iridescent, like pearls or something.

Her skin is rich and golden, and her eyes are wide, but pinched at the outer corners like a cat's. I can't tell if it's a natural thing, like from her heritage, maybe, or if it's an illusion from some wrenched makeup that I don't know about.

"Hi," she says. "I'm Veronica, but everyone calls me Vee. You're Trout." She squints, and looks me up and down. "And you are just as small in person."

"You know me?"

"Sure. Your face has been plastered all over the news feed."

Oh, right. I forgot that everyone here probably saw the feed where I was declared an Official Criminal. "Sorry to disappoint you with my shortness."

Vee giggles. "It's okay. Anyway, my dad sent me to

check on you. How are ya? You getting into trouble?"

I narrow my eyes, ignoring the dig, and say, "Who's your dad?"

"Parker Dade."

The tiny guy, Dad's friend or bodyguard. Now that I know the connection, I see similarities between the girl and Parker. The brown eyes, for one. And they both have this wiry kind of energy like they could spring on you at any moment. Maybe Parker would make a good bodyguard after all. There's more to defense than just muscle. You have to move quickly, and think quickly too.

"I met him." I wipe the sweat from my forehead. "So I guess you've checked on me, then. You don't have to stay."

Vee waves her hand around. "Ain't like I have anything else to do."

A dog Scissor was petting darts away and barks at a squirrel. Scissor calls after him. "Here, boy! I'm friendly! I scratch ears better than squirrels!"

Vee guffaws. "Scissor is so hilarious." She watches as the bot disappears in a grove of trees, trailing the dog by a foot or two.

"Yeah. She's pretty awesome. LT too."

Vee turns to me and readjusts her position on one of the bars beneath her. "So my dad says you're here to stay?"

I shrug. "I guess. I mean, no one's really saying what's going on."

"What's it like in the Districts? I have family up there, but they don't talk much about it."

"Umm . . ." I trail off, because I'm not sure what I'm allowed to say. But then, if Dad trusts Vee's dad, then maybe that means I can trust Vee.

"I don't know. Lame. Bots are nonexistent. My brother and I were always broke. He's always complaining about parking taxes. Says everything is regulated and restricted in the Districts. I try not to pay attention."

Vee pushes a wisp of now dark green hair behind one ear. "I can't picture a place without bots. I grew up around here. I can even kinda remember when people called this place Louisiana, instead of clumping the entire southern and eastern coasts into Bot Territory."

The area where I live used to be Colorado. They teach us in history class what the states in 5th District used to be, so we never forget where our country came from. Our teacher even made a mnemonic for it: Serious Nations Knit Classy Orders. SNKCO=South Dakota, Nebraska, Kansas, Colorado, Oklahoma.

Lox and I couldn't stop laughing at the image of President Callo knitting anything, let alone his orders for Congress, but it really did work for a memory tool. I got that question right on the test. I think that might have been one of the *only* questions I got right. I'm not very good at history.

"What was it like around here? When the Bot Wars started?" I ask.

"Split chaos. People geared out and left their houses empty. Lots of them jetted north."

"Why did you guys stay?"

Vee picks a pebble out of the bottom of her shoe and flings it to the ground. "My dad comes from a family of believers. Like in fate and spiritual messages and stuff. He said he had a bad feeling about moving north, so we stayed." She snickers. "Don't tell him I told you that, though. He keeps that stuff to himself. Says no one takes a religious man seriously anymore."

"I don't know. He seems pretty tough if you ask me."

"And definitely don't tell him that! He thinks he's so jammed as it is!" She laughs, tilts her head back, and her hair shines golden.

"If a bunch of people ran north, where did all *these* people come from?" I ask.

Vee shrugs. "Some of them just stayed, like us. Some of them are soldiers who fled the war when they stopped believin' in what the UD was doing. It's just a mixture of a lot of people."

I guess that's true, because, like Vee, everyone looks so different down here, like they were born of a dozen different cultures. I like it. Everyone looks the same in Brack.

"I didn't know some of the missing soldiers were down here in Bot Territory the whole time."

Vee nods. "The UD probably knows, but doesn't want to admit it. They don't want people thinking this place is inhabitable, probably."

I look around at the park and the city beyond it. "The UD always made it sound like Bot Territory was a machine wasteland."

"A load of nuke waste. They've been lying through their fat teeth. The only place that got hit real bad was northern Mississippi because it's close to the military zone. And I think some of the East Coast got it too." She scrunches the top of her hair, like she's trying to make it stand straighter. "We're pretty much untouched here."

Scissor runs past us down on the ground, still chasing after the dog. "Doggie! Doggie!"

We're quiet for a second as we watch her. Then Vee says, "You think you're gonna join the Meta-Rise if they let ya?"

I snap my attention back to her. "You know about the Meta-Rise?"

"Course I do. Everyone knows about it."

My cheeks flame red. It's like I've been living under a rock this whole time. "I don't," I admit, because I want answers and I think it's the only way I'll get them. "What is it?"

Vee leans back on her hands, propping herself up on a bar. "It's people and bots, a big group of 'em, fighting for rights and fairness, ya know? Bots want their rights. And people want choice. I heard my dad saying the Districts are turning into a regulated rat maze. I don't know if that's true, but I do know people want the Districts to return to a democracy. And if they don't, they want the UD to declare Bot Territory a separate country so they can have their freedom."

I lick my lips, my mouth suddenly dry. This is big. Maybe bigger than I thought.

"I'm gonna join it one day," Vee adds. "As soon as I'm old enough."

Even though I just got here, I think I want to join it too. "Who's the leader?"

Vee lets out a tiny little laugh, more a grunt and a breath disguised as a laugh. "You mean you don't know?"

I wrinkle my nose. "Um . . . no. If I knew, I wouldn't have asked."

"It's your dad, you nutter. Robert St. Kroix is the leader."

I can't feel my face on account of the numbness running through me. I nearly fall over again, but catch myself at the last second and lean forward for balance.

Vee snorts. "You're not gonna gear out, are ya? You're lookin' a little toothpasty."

I gulp down some air. Dad is the leader of the Meta-Rise? Course, it all makes sense now. The reason Po kept all those secrets from me was because he knew how dangerous it was being Robert St. Kroix's son. It's why the government wanted to use Po and me as bait, to get Dad to turn himself in.

They know he's up to something. And apparently they're up to something too.

I should be angry—it's just one more secret that everyone has been keeping from me—but all I can think is, Holy. Space. Junk. My dad is the leader of the Meta-Rise.

It's beyond wrenched. I want to tell Lox ASAP. I want to shout about it from the rooftops.

"You sure you're okay?" Vee asks.

I ignore the question. "How did he become the leader? Did he start the Meta-Rise?"

Vee pushes her long hair off her shoulder. "He was part of the founding, yeah. Everyone nominated him as leader. I think it had to do with him being the first human with bot parts. People could relate to him as a man, and bots could relate to him as a machine."

It's weird hearing someone refer to Dad as a machine, but I guess it's half true. He doesn't even have a normal heart anymore. I don't know if I'll ever get used to that.

"How do you become a part of the Meta-Rise?" I picture stacks of applications and big red stamps that say REJECTED or RECRUITED. And I'll do anything to get a RECRUITED stamp.

"I don't know. I think you just have to have the same beliefs as everyone else, ya know, so you're fighting for the same thing. Also, I'm bettin' it helps if your dad isn't Parker Dade and wants to protect you At All Costs."

I snicker. "It's a good thing my dad isn't Parker Dade, then."

"Yeah." Vee rolls her eyes. "My dad doesn't let me do anything. *Ever*. At this rate, you'll be a Meta member eight decades before I am. And you just got here."

Scissor runs past again, but this time it's the dog chasing her.

"Hey," Vee says, "there's a big thing here tonight. You should come."

The dog barks as Scissor climbs the playground structure shaped like a pirate ship. She clings to the pointy bow looking down at the dog.

"What kind of thing?"

"A party. You'll learn we're big on parties and get-togethers here. It's a southern thing. But I promise it'll be fun."

I narrow my eyes. "Your dad didn't ask you to ask me, did he?"

"No. My dad doesn't decide everything I do." I must look skeptical, because she adds, "Besides, I like you so far. So it doesn't really matter whose idea it was."

A perma-grin spreads across my face. She likes me? No girl has ever said that to me before. Back in Brack, I was the lame-o with lame pants and lame gadgets and lameness stamped across my lame face. Here, I'm Trout, son of the leader of the Meta-Rise. I like the sound of that.

"Yeah, I'll probably come," I say, all cool-like. That's how Po'd say it.

Vee slides down the structure. "You ever been on a hoverboard?"

I lean over. "A couple of times. Why?"

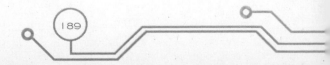

She hops to the ground. "Tonight. At the park. I'll show you the southern version of a hoverboard. You'll love it."

"What, do they go faster or something?"

She walks backward. "You'll just have to come to find out!"

TWENTY-FOUR

WHEN I RETURN to the park later that night with LT in tow, I'm overwhelmed with everything. There are a ton of people and rows and rows of food. Flickering lights hover around the park on tiny little pods. They look like candles, but I think they're holo lights.

"Scissor's invention," LT says when I ask. "She may be physically clumsy, but she is a genius when it comes to creating. I suspect you will love her hoversuits."

"Her what?"

LT starts to explain when Vee runs up, grabs me by the hand, and wrenches me in the opposite direction. "I'll see you later, LT!" I shout as I stumble after Vee.

A group of grown-ups are clustered around a holo-fire. The night air is so warm and balmy that I doubt the heat feature is on. Crickets and bugs chirp and snap and croak in the dark.

Vee nods at a food table set up below a large white canopy. "You hungry?"

"I'm always hungry."

A bot named Wen6 serves us taco pops and I cover mine in cheese. We make the trek up the big hill in the middle of the park and plop down in the grass. From here we can see the entire north side of the park and a good chunk of the city too. I can just make out the leaded glass ceiling of the Fort. The entire thing is lit amber with lights. When I left, Dad was still working, but said he'd try to come later.

Vee picks a diced tomato from her taco and flicks it down the hill. "Tell me the story with your brother. I heard my dad talking about him."

Po.

No one has heard from him. He might not even be at City Hall anymore, for all we know. And here I am at a party. But I have to remind myself that Dad and his team are on it. Po WILL come back. I just know it.

I tell Vee what happened right before I bolted from home. She listens as she finishes off her taco. "Basically, my brother sacrificed himself for me," I say. "So the guilt is turning into nuclear waste in my gut. I just wish there was something I could do to help him."

Vee nods. "I get that. If I were you, I'd go after him."

I blink. Look over at her. "How the chop would I get him out of a government building?"

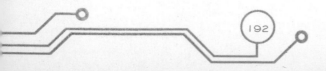

"There are ways. You just gotta think on it. Your dad said you were massive smart."

"He did?"

"Course. Never stopped talking about you and Po. Sometimes I felt like I already knew you, even though I'd never met ya."

I let her words sink in. I spent so much of my time feeling sorry for myself because I was alone in Brack, but I never really thought about Dad being here without any family. Was he lonely too?

"Hey, so, ya wanna see our version of the hoverboard?" Vee says, pulling my head outta my thoughts.

"Sure."

We toss the sticks from our tacos into a nearby garbage can and start off toward the patch of woods. A gravel path winds through the trees. A few hovering lights keep us from tripping over our own feet.

When we emerge on the other side of the park, I see Scissor surrounded by a group of kids. "Ahhh! Trout!" she shouts when she sees me. Her front panel is black tonight with little glowing polka dots. It looks like the night sky. "Come on. I saved a set for you and Vee."

"A set of what?"

Two of the hovering lights hang just over Scissor's shoulder, shedding some light on what she's passing out.

"These are hoversuits." She shows me a thin black strap. "You get four of these. They go on your knees and elbows." She presses something on the strap and it hums to life, glowing blue in the center. She takes my arm and winds the strap around my elbow. "It's like a hoverboard, but made for your entire body. The blue here"—she points at the glowing button—"that's just like the hoverpoints on a hoverboard. Works the same. You just use your entire body to hover."

When I look over at Vee to ask her if this is for real, I find her fully suited up. There are straps at both elbows, at both knees, and two shoe-shaped boards on the bottom of her boots.

"Come on, Trout! You're gonna love this!" She runs and jumps across the sidewalk into the street like she's diving into the deep end of a pool. The hover rails catch her before she hits the ground and she finishes the move with a somersault.

A few other kids strap up. They follow Vee's lead, running, jumping, hovering, skating down the street.

Scissor straps me in and turns on the hoverpoints. My entire body vibrates with the energy. "What if the rails don't catch me and I go splat?" I ask.

"Never happened," Scissor answers as she helps a tiny kid with his shoe plates.

"That's it? Just 'never happened' is your answer? There's a first time for everything."

As Scissor turns to me, the joint in her neck squeaks. She winces, then: "Statistically, you're more likely to go splat from a plane crash than you are from my hoversuits."

"What about traffic?"

"We have the next six blocks sectioned off for tonight so the kids can ride safely, but if you're not comfortable using the suits, that's quite all right."

I watch the kids skating back and forth in the street. Vee leaps and twists and dances as she waits, the blue glow of the rails making her hair look purple.

Not only have I spent almost zero time on a hoverboard, but the hoversuits look ten times harder to ride. Still, I'm not about to give up. If I can outrun the UD government and cross into Bot Territory, then I can do anything. Or at least that's what I tell myself when I jog toward the street.

Once I hit the sidewalk, I leap over the rails into the force field. It catches me and I hover there for a second before I totally lose my balance and slide around like I'm on ice. My feet go out from beneath me and I fall back, bouncing against the force field. I lie there suspended in midair looking straight up at the sky.

A second later, Vee's face pops into view with a smirk curling her lips. "Not bad for a first-timer."

I grimace as she holds out her hand and helps me up. It takes me a second to find my balance again, and Vee holds on to my elbow the whole time. Everyone stares at me and I have to bite down the urge to run into the trees and hide.

A kid half my age skates past and yells, "Hey, bolt sniffer. Bet you can't catch me!"

Vee scowls. "Knock it off!"

The kid laughs as he zooms around the corner.

"Maybe I should just take them off," I say, holding my arms out straight for balance.

"Nu-uh." Vee pushes a hunk of hair behind her ear. "No one's good the first time. Just pretend you're skating—"

"I've never been skating."

"Then pretend you're pushing off the ground, like you're running a race and you're poised at the start line. Try that."

I slip around once, twice. It's like I've been thrown into a vat of butter. Finally, I steady myself. I put one foot behind me, feel the force field push back. With my other foot, I take a step and rush forward. I'm not ready for it and trip over my own feet, pitching forward onto my stomach.

"If it wasn't for the rails," Vee shouts behind me, "you'd be eating grass right now!"

I sigh. "I told you I wasn't any good at this."

"One more try." She helps me up. A couple of girls soar past and giggle, watching me over their shoulder. I shake my head. Vee clucks and tells me to stay focused.

I push back again, but this time, my first step is slow, like I'm a baby learning to walk for the first time. I feel the force vibrate through my legs and I skitter forward. Hold out my arms. Find my balance. Take another step. And another. Whatever I'm doing, it looks pretty close to what the other kids are doing, even if I'm going at the pace of a rusted bot.

"Corner!" Vee calls. "Lean into the corner."

When the street curves to the left, I lean. Vee speeds past me. I keep at a slower pace, but try to mimic the way her feet slice through the air.

The road straightens. I push faster, harder. Pretty soon I'm zooming down the street, arms swinging. A hill rises in front of me. I bend at the knees like Vee, lean forward, and when we slide down the other side, it's like we're on a roller coaster. We blaze past shops. Past people. *Thwip. Thwip. Thwip.*

Everything is a blur and a smear of color.

Vee twists in front of me and skates backward, waving

her arms in the air. Her laughter reaches me in clips of sound. She swings back around, dances, bopping up and down.

"Wooo!" she shouts.

I'm doing everything I can just to stay on track. So I don't notice when Vee yells, "We're near the end of the street. Lean back!"

She digs in her feet, slows, and I barrel right on by.

Buildings spring up in front of me. I scramble to the left. The park comes into view, but there are people and bots crowding around.

"Trout!" Vee shouts. "Back! Back! Lean back!"

I start to lean back, but it's too late. The street ends abruptly at the park's side entrance. I barrel over the top of the rails. The force field cuts out and I'm soaring through nothing but air.

"Hooooollly jet smooooke!" I shout as I sail straight into the willow tree. Leaves whip me in the face and I scrabble for something to hold on to, finally catching a branch. My hands slide, tearing away leaves. I tighten my grip and manage to stop myself, only to have the branch bounce back. I lose my grip. Thud to the ground. Pain shoots up my spine. My chest aches, like I've been run over by a bull.

I squeeze my eyes shut and lights blink behind my closed lids.

"That's not how you're supposed to do it," Vee says, an edge of concern in her voice.

I peer up at her. "Yeah, I kinda figured that out."

"Trout?" LT kneels beside me. A red light blinks in his neck. "Hold still."

It takes me a second to figure out he's scanning my body. "Heart rate is accelerated, but that is to be expected. No broken bones. Ribs are fine. No internal bleeding. No swelling of the organs. I suspect tomorrow morning you will have a few bruises, and perhaps many sore spots, but overall you are well."

With his help, I make it to my feet and brush the dirt and leaves from my hair. A crowd has gathered around. Some of the other kids are trying real hard not to laugh.

Vee walks with me to the park entrance. "Maybe it'll go better next time."

I rub at a sore spot on the back of my neck. "I don't think there will be a next time."

"Don't say that! That was totally split, what you did back there, ya know? Nobody takes to it the first time, not like you did."

"Really?"

"Really. You just have to learn how to brake," she adds with a laugh.

"Ha. Ha."

"Perhaps it is best if we retire to the Fort," LT says. "You should rest."

"Yeah. Okay." I turn to Vee. "Thanks for inviting me tonight."

"You're welcome. Feel better." She slaps my back before jetting off and I wince from the pain.

"Perhaps some rest *and* a medi-patch," LT adds as he walks me out. "You will be better in no time."

I can only hope he's right.

When we're back in the Fort, Merril tells me Dad wants to see me, so I can't crash into bed just yet. After LT applies a medi-patch to my back, he gives me directions to Dad's workshop in the basement (which I didn't even know existed, and have to take the stairs to reach).

"Hey," Dad says after he downs a can of Life Water. "I'm just giving myself a tune-up. Come talk to me."

I anchor my feet just over the threshold because while I'm okay with Dad being part robot, I don't know if I'm ready to watch him give himself a tune-up. Whatever that means.

"Trout," Dad says, when he realizes I haven't moved. "Come sit down."

With a cringe, I slide onto the stool next to him as he crumples the can of Life Water in his machine hand. The

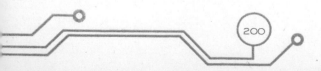

can is nothing but a ball of aluminum when he's done. He tosses it in the recycling bin.

The workshop is pretty big, and I can tell Dad has made it into his personal space. There's a row of hy-breed posters on the opposite wall, like the ones I have in my bedroom in Brack. On the shelf below the posters are real books with old hardback covers. Dad is a huge fan of sci-fi, aliens and stuff like that, and he likes real books even though the stores stopped selling those before I was even born.

Behind me is a cabinet and next to it is a washtub. The counter we're sitting at goes from the doorway all the way to the back corner. There are shelves here too, but not as neat as the ones across the room. Glass jars of nuts and bolts and gears line the shelf, along with tools and several boxes of meta-pol.

When I turn back to Dad, I realize he has his shirt off, and my breath knocks around in my throat like a beemer ball when I get a good look at him. I didn't know how bad Dad's injuries were until now, until I could see every-thing. There's the glowing orb where his heart should be, surrounded by a metal box. From there, black rubber tubes branch off and disappear beneath his skin, sinking into him until they disappear completely.

His left side is an exposed rib cage of molded metal

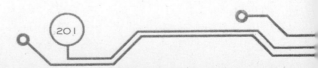

that connects to a robotic shoulder that connects to his robotic arm.

"Pretty gruesome, huh?"

I look up. "I . . . um . . . didn't know there was so much."

Dad nods. "I should have died. It's a miracle I didn't."

"I guess LT, Ratch, and Scissor did a good job of saving you."

"They sure did." Dad gestures to the counter. "Can you grab me that screwdriver?"

I find the one he wants and hand it over. He unscrews the front plate of his ex-heart, placing the screws carefully on the counter, before finally pulling the plate off and revealing what's inside. The orb is bigger and deeper than what you can see on the surface. The tubes that branch off it merge into one big tube that's hooked directly into the orb. Dad unscrews that tube and says to me, "I gotta be quick with this part. Will you help me?"

"Yeah. Sure. What do I do?"

"In the cabinet, there are bottles of what's called D-T Epocks. I need one bottle."

The bottles are on the second shelf in the cabinet and they're filled with goo the same color as Dad's glowing orb. I grab one and hurry back with it.

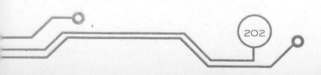

Dad opens a tiny port on his orb and the old goo starts draining into a can he holds beneath it. It only takes a minute to empty, and when it is, the orb is nothing but a black dome.

With the port now closed, Dad opens a metal spigot buried in the depths of his heart contraption. "Okay, hand me the Epocks." I thrust the bottle into his hand and he upends it, clicking the thin tip into the metal spigot. The goo starts glug-glugging into the orb. I watch as it fills up.

"What is that stuff?" I ask.

"Think of it as blood."

"The blood of a robot?"

Dad smiles. "Exactly."

When the bottle of Epocks is empty, Dad tosses it in the trash, closes the spigot, and reconnects the tubing. It only takes him a second to screw the plate back down.

Dad raises his eyebrows. "Help me with one more thing?"

"Sure."

He taps his left side. "One of my ribs is loose. I need you to tighten it."

"Umm . . ." I lick my lips. "Okay."

I take the screwdriver Dad says I'll need and carefully, and maybe a bit too slowly, unscrew the cover that is per-

fectly molded to his ribs. When it swings open on a set of hinges, I see more of the inner workings: a tangle of wires, and gears and screws, more rubber tubes.

"The third rib down, that's the one that's loose. There's a screw in the back that's used to adjust it. Do you see it?"

I move behind him, where the plate hangs open by its hinges. The ribs disappear here inside another metal plate, connecting to the part of him that's real, I guess. I find the screw and go in—*inside Dad*—with the screwdriver. I twist it clockwise a fraction of a micrometer and Dad chuckles, which makes his insides jerk up and down.

I snatch my hand back. "Dad!"

"Sorry." He gets control of himself. "You don't have to be so careful. Give the screw a full rotation, at the very least."

I go back in and twist till I feel the screw tighten. "Is that better?"

Dad tests the rib in question, checking it to make sure it doesn't rock. "Much better. Thank you."

When the plate is screwed shut, Dad finally puts his T-shirt on and I exhale with relief. He cracks open another can of Life Water. "I heard you had a little accident at the park." He eyes me over the can as he takes a drink.

I grumble. "How did you find out already?"

"You'll learn, around here, there's nothing I don't know." He straightens his shoulders. "I'm glad you're hanging out with some of the kids here in town, but just be careful, okay? The kids here, they . . ."

He pauses, so I try to fill in the blank. "Do crazy things that no kid in Brack would do because either a) the UD wouldn't let them, or b) everyone is afraid of every little thing? Which makes the kids here totally wrenched compared to the kids in Brack?"

Dad raises his eyebrows and tilts his head toward me in that Dadly kind of way. "That's not what I was going to say but . . . yes. They are a bit adventurous down here."

I shrug. "So is Lox, and you never had a problem with him."

"I don't have a problem with the kids down here either." He spreads his arms out innocently as a smile creeps onto his face. "I'm just being a dad, kiddo. My job is to worry about you."

"You sound like Po."

The can of Life Water crinkles in Dad's bot hand. "How's your brother, anyway? He have a girlfriend yet?"

"Nah. He likes a girl, but he's chicken."

"Who?"

"Marsi Olsen."

Dad squints. "That name sounds familiar. Not placing a face, though."

"She's pretty, I guess." I lift a shoulder. "Po takes me to Smoothie Shack all the time because she works there, so I guess I get something out of it at least."

"You boys." Dad chuckles, but his eyes look watery and he goes quiet real quick.

"How come you never came and got us?"

Dad leans back and props the heels of his boots on the bottom rung of the stool. "It's complicated."

"Yeah. Of course it is."

"I don't expect you to understand. Someday when you have kids, you will. You do what you think is best at the time. Might turn out it wasn't, but you go with your gut and hope everything turns out."

Vee said her dad says the same thing, that you have to go with your gut. Maybe it's a cheesy adult thing, but I guess I kinda get it.

"Are we going to save Po?"

The can of water lets out a big *ca-rump* as the sides cave in Dad's hand. The spot where his heart should be glows bright orange, from the water or his anger, I don't know which. "I'm going to do everything in my power to bring your brother here safe and sound."

I swallow. "Can I help?"

Dad shakes his head so fast, I worry the bolt in his neck might twist loose. "Did you not hear a word I just said? About keeping you safe?"

I hop off the stool and my entire body twinges with pain. "Come on, Dad. Please!"

"No. Trout. NO." He sets the can down. "Promise me you will stay out of this."

I purse my lips together and say nothing.

"Trout." Dad draws my name out in a warning.

"Fine," I say, crossing my fingers behind my back. "I promise."

"Good." He ruffles my hair. "Now go to bed and get some rest. There's a gathering in the town square tomorrow afternoon and I'd like you to come."

"What kind of gathering?"

"A rally. People getting together, supporting the same things."

I raise an eyebrow. "Is it the Meta-Rise?"

Dad frowns. "I'm not answering that."

"So obviously yes."

Dad shoos me away. "Go on, get to bed."

I start for the stairwell.

"Oh, and hey?" he says. "Next time, use the brakes."

His chuckle follows me as I creak my way up the stairs.

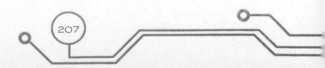

TWENTY-FIVE

MERRIL MAKES BLUEBERRY oatmeal special for me the next morning. "Because of your accident," he says with a wink. After my stomach is full, I feel a ton better. I spend the rest of the morning before the rally watching a sci-fi movie with Vee in the media room.

Dad leaves early with LT and the rest of his group to get everything ready in the town center. Vee goes home just after lunch to change and promises to meet me later, so I walk down to the rally with Ratch and Scissor.

The streets are filled with people, and everyone is walking in the same direction. About two blocks away from the town center, I start seeing holo posters plastered over every open surface. Posters of my dad.

In one, he's waving with his machine hand at some unseen person. The message at the bottom appears, then flashes bright green. *Robert St. Kroix is our future*, it says.

Across the street, three identical posters are taped on

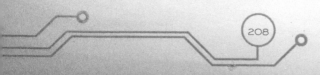

the brick wall of a hoverboard repair shop. The holo image starts out with President Callo, then it crumbles and a 3-D rendition of Dad stands from the rubble along with the words *Rise from the Heap*.

It isn't until I see this poster that I realize how Dad must look to everyone else, with his machine parts, how strong and wrenched he is.

"People really believe in my dad, don't they?" I ask.

Scissor is passing out flags that let off holo fireworks, so she doesn't hear me. It's Ratch who answers.

"Humans need something to believe in, some greater power. Without it, they're lost."

I look up at him. The band of orange where his eyes should be glows in the shade as we walk beneath a store's awning. "You don't sound like you agree with that, believing in something bigger."

Ratch tilts his head. A flash of sunlight appears behind him, blinding me. "I believe in power, but not when it's in the wrong hands."

"What's that mean?"

"It means you should be careful who you give your power to."

I want to tell him that I'm just a kid, and that I don't really have any power to give, but by then we're in the town center, and I'm swept into the throng of people.

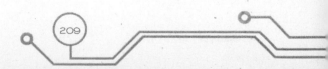

209

The first thing I notice is a robot that stands out from the crowd by at least three feet, which would put him nearly nine feet tall. His arms are massive, like tree branches, and one lone eye glows in the center of his wide, squat head.

A little girl giggles and yells at him. "Pick me up, Jamper!" And the bot scoops her up with one hand and settles her into the crook between his head and the disc-like armor jutting out of his shoulder.

I can't stop staring at him until Scissor nudges me forward. "They're about to start!" she says, and nods to a stage that's been constructed on the small block of grass right between two massive oak trees dripping with Spanish moss. Flutter-flies dart through the air, trailing banners behind them that say RISE FROM THE HEAP in big, block letters. I'm beginning to wonder if that's the Meta-Rise's slogan, and decide to ask Vee later.

The air is a mixture of smells: roasting peanuts and baked pretzels and burning sparklers.

We move through the assembled audience, trying to get a good spot. "There are a lot of robots here," I say, looking around.

Ratch nods his head once. "Robots outnumber humans four to one."

"In Bot Territory?"

He looks away. "No, in the world."

Dad takes the stage and a hush zips through the streets. When Dad speaks, his voice is broadcast over the top of the crowd.

"Afternoon, everyone," he says. No one utters a sound. "I'm so glad you could all be here."

I look across the audience and it's like I'm the only one not glued on Dad. Everyone else can't seem to tear their eyes away. As I stand there, taking it all in, my insides fill with awe. These people are here for my dad. And they're looking at him like he's a wrenched hero, bigger than life.

I see it too.

"As you all know," Dad goes on, "I believe in doing the right thing, not making trouble if it can be avoided, and following the law. But two days ago, the UD attacked my family, my sons, Mason and Aidan. Aidan got away with the help of our beloved LT." Dad pauses as the crowd cheers and hollers. They all turn to LT, who's standing just behind Dad.

Next to me, Scissor's audience track hoots and her LED panel flashes bright yellow.

"But," Dad starts, and the crowd quiets again, "the UD got hold of my older boy, Mason. A veteran of the Bot

Wars, a hero in his own right." Dad takes a deep breath. "And I am the reason they took him. Because the UD looks at me like a terrorist. And why? Because I support bots?

"Robots are not the problem." Dad clenches his machine hand into a fist and raises it in the air. "Robots gave me this and in doing so, they gave me another chance at life, the ability to see the world through their eyes. And let me tell you, it's a good view to have."

Ratch crosses his arms over his chest, rocks his shoulders back, and sweeps the crowd with his band of eyes.

The audience hollers their support. Goose bumps crawl over my arms. There's so much energy here, it's like it's running through my veins.

"The UD is naïve to think our nation would be better without robots," Dad says. "We can exist together. And if the UD can't agree with that, then we, Bot Territory, want our freedom.

"Enough of living in the UD's shadow. We are our own nation. A nation of robot supporters and we are proud of that!"

The crowd explodes in cheers. Dad stands center stage, his machine hand still raised in the air, his metal face plate blazing in the light of holo fireworks going off all around him.

My chest swells with a warm, fuzzy feeling, and I don't care if that's totally lame. I'm so proud of my dad, my eyes sting. This is why he had to stay here. To the humans and robots in Bot Territory, he's more than just my dad. He's their leader, silently as the head of the Meta-Rise, and out in the open as a half-man, half-robot hero.

I want to race to the stage and hug my dad real tight. I want to tell him how proud I am.

When the crowd quiets again, Dad continues. "I am promising you, all of you, human and bot alike, that I will not stop until robots are given their rights, or until Bot Territory has its freedom."

More cheers and applause. Dad lowers his hand. "If you're wondering what you can do for Bot Territory, there are booths all over the town center. There are many ways to lend support, and no effort is too small. Now, everyone, enjoy yourselves. There's plenty of food to go around!"

Dad exits the stage amid a riot of noise. Parker, Jules, and LT follow behind him.

I have a big smile plastered on my face as I make my way over to Dad, pushing through the masses. I'm just feet away when Cole, the big tattooed guy from the Fort, hurries up to Dad and whispers something in his ear.

Dad's face falls. He searches the crowd till he finds me

squeezed between a woman with a crying baby in her arms and a man letting off fireworks.

Dad doesn't move, or try to say anything, but I know instantly what Cole whispered in his ear.

Po. It's something about my brother.

I shove through till I'm standing right next to Dad. "What's going on?" I ask.

Dad takes a deep breath. "We just got word. The UD is allowing your brother to call home."

"Under no circumstance will you be present during a phone call with the UD government," Dad says once we're back at the Fort.

"But, he's my brother! I want to talk to him."

Dad shakes his head as he and Parker enter the elevator. "You're to stay out of sight. Do you understand me? I don't want the UD knowing for certain that you're here. At least not yet." Dad looks at LT, who's standing behind me. "I'll call you up when we're done. I don't want to expose all of you to this if I can help it."

LT nods. Ratch shifts next to me, like he's itching to go up to command center just as badly as I am. Jules and Cole plop down at the table with a box of doughnuts between them. "Good luck," Cole says around a long John.

The elevator slides closed.

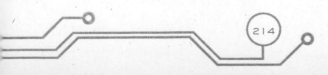

"Pssst," Vee whispers in my ear.

I nearly lurch outta my skin. I didn't know she was here, let alone right behind me.

She wiggles a finger. "Come on."

"Where are you two going?" LT asks.

"Back to the rally," Vee answers. "They just opened the virtual Mars tent."

LT thinks for a second, and I can tell he's trying to figure out if Vee is lying or not. I don't even know if she is, but she must pass LT's test, because he says, "All right. I will call you if we hear anything."

Vee tugs me toward the stairwell, but once we're out of sight, she veers left toward the media room.

"What are we doing?" I whisper.

"You want to listen in on that call with your brother, don't you?"

"Well, yeah . . ."

Vee leads me up to the rope bridges, past the sitting area, through a supply closet, up a metal ladder, and through a hatch in the roof. Wind blasts me in the face and I suck in a breath.

"Climb out," she instructs, so I hop onto the roof. Gravel and old tar grits beneath my shoes. Vee shuts the hatch behind us, and together we scuttle across the roof.

Command center's leaded glass ceiling glows in

the fading light in front of me. I can hear the distant sounds of the rally several blocks away. The pop of fireworks. The cheer of the crowd. Music blasting from a band.

We crouch at the corner of the glass ceiling and look down into the Fort. Dad and Parker stand in the middle of the room, waiting. The screen on the wall is dark, so Po must not have called yet.

Vee grabs a screwdriver that was tucked in a vent and quietly, carefully, slides open one of the ceiling's vent panels.

"I take it you've done this before?" I say, nodding at the screwdriver in her hand.

"You could say that."

"How did you even know how to get up here?"

She flashes me a grin. "If you need to get somewhere, I'm usually the girl to ask. There aren't many places I can't reach."

I shake my head, in awe. "Anyone ever tell you you're wrenched, Vee?"

She shrugs. "It's no big deal."

Something buzzes in the room down below. Vee and I get in close to the open panel and listen.

Parker looks at Dad. "You ready?"

Dad sets his hands on his hips. "As ready as I can be."

Parker taps something on a control board, ending the buzzing noise.

"Hey, Dad," Po says as he appears on the giant screen. The instant I hear his voice, my chest crackles with hope.

I lean closer to the vent and press my face against the glass above it. I'm so happy to see my brother, I want to shout. But then I get a good look at him and everything inside of me sinks. The skin beneath his left eye is bruised and swollen. Blood is crusted to the corner of his mouth. He looks tired, more than anything. He doesn't look scared, though. Po isn't afraid of anything.

"It's nice to see you," Po says to Dad. "You got older, though, since the last time."

Dad chuckles. "I could say the same for you." Dad clears his throat. "How they treating you?"

Po shrugs. "It's not an island vacation, but I'm surviving."

Beard appears on-screen next to Po, her brown hair sprayed into submission. It's poofy behind her ears, flat at the top of her head. One lone hunk of hair has been gelled to the side of her face. It looks like a stalagmite.

"Unfortunately, gentlemen, this isn't a reunion. We've a message to relay." She nudges Po's shoulder. "Go on."

Po looks at the ground, cracks a knuckle, then takes a deep breath. "They say they'll let me go if you turn yourself in. And if you don't . . ." He winces when he moves just a sliver of an inch, like he has more bruises than the ones that are visible. "I'll be sentenced as a person affiliated with known bot supporters."

Vee and I share a look. I don't know what that kind of sentence is, but it can't be good.

"Mr. St. Kroix," Beard says, "I'm sure you're aware of the mandatory sentencing for a person affiliated with bot supporters."

Dad takes a step toward the screen. The expression on his face reminds me of that look Po got once when he had the flu, right before he puked all over the place. Even Dad's metal face plate looks green. "That punishment is taking it a bit far, don't you think?" he says.

"It's the law, Mr. St. Kroix."

"What's the sentencing?" I whisper to Vee. "What's it mean?"

She looks pained as she tells me. "Immediate execution."

"What?" I start to shout, but Vee clamps her hand over my mouth, cutting me off. I breathe through my nose as she says, "Shhhh!"

Down on the street, a bunch of kids laugh and screech. A second later, a firecracker snaps and hisses.

Beard holds up a SimPad, prompts the screen with a

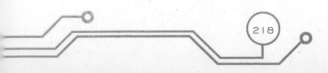

finger, and looks back at Dad. "Let's move on, shall we? I want to talk about the people you have working for you." She reads from the Sim. "Jules Montgomery. Once a decorated Air Force computer programmer, now a wanted hacker, responsible for the crash of Tak-On Corp, who fled during the height of the wars. Cole Vincent, a military colonel wanted for the heinous crime of breaking free an entire prison of robots and robot supporters during the war." Beard tsks and shakes her head. "And the robot known as LT who illegally crossed into UD territory and kidnapped a minor."

"A minor *you* were planning to kidnap," Dad says, his voice low and throaty. "My son. An innocent child."

"Not innocent," Beard insists. She swings her attention finally to Vee's dad. "And Parker Dade, a genius cartographer. You're the whole reason so many people and bots have been able to successfully cross from Bot Territory into the UD and vice versa."

Parker leans against the corner of a desk and props the heels of his hands on the edge. He doesn't say a word.

"What's this all about?" Dad asks.

"These are the people I demand in exchange for your son's freedom."

Dad holds up his machine hand. "You're demanding people who aren't even involved in my family's issues."

"This isn't about you and your family, Mr. St. Kroix. This is about the safety of the people of the United Districts. This is about you helping to harbor criminals. As long as you're free, the entire UD is in danger. You don't think we know what you're planning? You and your Meta-Rise and Old New York? There's no telling how far people will go when they're acting on their beliefs, fighting for power they think is rightly theirs." She shakes her head, but her hair stays firmly in place. "We are only protecting our country and our citizens."

"You can't expect these people to turn themselves in, in exchange for only Po," Dad argues.

"No," Beard says, "I don't." She comes closer to the camera, so her face takes up the entire screen and I lose sight of Po. "What I do expect is that a father will do whatever it takes to rescue his son. Including turning on his own friends."

"I'll go," Parker says. "Me and Robert. That's it. In exchange for Po."

Vee lunges to her feet, and now it's my turn to stop her from shouting. I move to cover her mouth with a hand, but she bats me away. I stagger back and clip the edge of the vent panel with my elbow. The glass rattles.

Vee and I hit the ground, me on my back, her on her

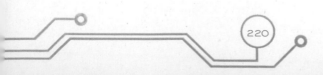

stomach. She arches a brow as if to say, *Now look what you did!*

I squeeze my eyes shut and listen real hard. I can still hear Beard's voice filtering through the vent and I breathe a sigh of relief that we went unnoticed.

"This isn't a negotiation," Beard says. "I've given you my terms. You have until three o'clock two days from now. Turn yourself in to the police station in Edge Flats, Texas. We know that's your unofficial headquarters on this side of the border. You have safe houses all over the city, don't you?"

Dad doesn't answer, but since I know Dekker's is a safe house, and that he can't possibly be the only one, I'm betting Beard is right.

"If you're missing even one of your cohorts," Beard goes on, "your son will enter the court system at three oh two p.m. Good day."

I pop up and peek through the glass, willing to risk being caught to see my brother again. I catch one final glimpse of him as he waves good-bye to Dad, raising both his cuffed hands, just before the vid cuts out. I stare at the screen, hoping it'll come back on, that I'll get just a few more minutes.

"Three o'clock, two days from now." Parker pushes

away from the desk, but his boots are silent on the concrete floor. "You think it's a trap?"

Dad turns away and bows his head. "Could be."

The elevator opens and Jules, Cole, Ratch, and LT step out.

"We watched the feed downstairs," Jules says. "But we only heard what Hopper said, obviously. God, that woman is a snake."

"A perfect metaphor," LT says.

"I'm not sure *snake* is the word I would use," Ratch says.

Cole drops into his desk chair and turns to Dad. "I guess it's no longer a secret that you got the baddest dudes working with you. I'm kinda honored she included me in the mix."

Jules laughs. "I'm sure that was some sort of mistake. What could they possibly want with a wimpy ex-military colonel?"

Cole curls his mouth in a sneer. "You find yourself so funny, don't you?"

"I do."

"Parker," Dad says, ignoring the jokes, "we got a safe route into the UD yet? Can we snatch Po back without risk to anyone?"

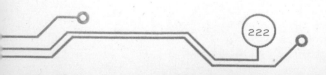

Parker looks to Jules. "Bring up the diagram?"

Jules slips into her chair and types in two quick commands. A blueprint of Brack and City Hall comes up on the screen. Parker slides a thin rubber glove on his right hand with tiny white dots that run down his fingers. When he points, his hand is projected on the screen.

"Cravley Street is our best bet. Less camera points. We enter City Hall here." He points to a side entrance. "But we'll need a Net-tag to get in. A regular citizen tag would work." He paces to the left. "We run into trouble in the stairwell, where a series of security checkpoints stall our progress."

"I'm working on that," Cole says. "I'll see what I can come up with."

Parker strips off the glove. "In the meantime, I'll work out an exit strategy."

Dad nods. "Thanks." He starts for the elevator. "I think I need a few minutes alone. You okay for a bit?"

"Sure." Parker tosses his glove aside. "Hey, Rob?"

Dad turns around. "Yeah?"

"Don't mention this around Vee, ya? I don't want her to know."

Next to me, Vee's hands tighten into fists. Her teeth grit.

"You have my word," Dad answers. "Same goes for Trout. Everyone." His team goes still as they listen. "Don't tell the kids what we're up against."

Cole and Jules give one quick nod of their heads. Ratch and LT agree to stay quiet.

As Dad passes beneath Vee and me, I hear him whisper, almost beneath his breath, "God help us," right before he enters the elevator.

Vee and I meet eyes. Hers are tight and watery, like she's not sure if she should burst into tears or growl in rage. I feel the same way. The UD is forcing my dad to choose between his freedom or Po's, and I'm pretty sure I know what he'll choose.

"I can't let my dad turn himself in," Vee says.

"I know. You think we can do anything about it?"

"You got all the way here, didn't you?"

"With LT's help."

"And now you have my help."

I look past her across the city. I like this place. I like Bot Territory and Line Zero, but it's nothing to me if Dad's not here.

"I don't want to lose my dad *or* my brother."

"And I *can't* lose my dad." Vee gets this scrunched-up look on her face, like she's trying real hard not to cry. "I

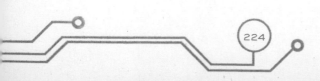

don't have anyone left besides him. At least not in Bot Territory."

"There's no way they'll make it into Brack and into City Hall undetected," I say. "Everyone will be looking for them."

"So now what?" Vee says.

"I don't know. But we need to figure something out. And quick."

TWENTY-SIX

THAT NIGHT I lie in bed staring at the ceiling, doing everything but sleeping. So when Vee calls me the next morning to go for a tour of the city, I almost say no. But then she adds, "Come on, Trout. Seeing the sun might help clear our heads."

She's probably right.

She meets me at the park twenty minutes later. Her hair looks bright pink in the early-morning sun, and the longer section in back is twisted up in a bird's nest at the top of her head.

"Here," she says, and hands me a backpack.

I take it from her and whatever's inside clanks together. "What is it?"

"Scavenger hunt pods. We have a scavenger hunt once a week and since I'm a Dade"—she flashes a half grin—"I'm the one who plots the route and plants the pods. I usually love doing this, but jam, I sure don't feel like it today."

"Yeah." I shuffle my feet. "I don't feel like doing anything but melting into a pile of space junk."

She starts forward. "Anyway, we have a lot of ground to cover, so we should get moving."

We reach an intersection and stop for traffic. Vee brings out her Link. It looks like nothing more than a sheet of glass with rubber corners.

I gape and drool over her shoulder. "That thing is wrenched."

"Thanks. My dad got it for me for my last birthday. It's the new LinkQ."

The light changes and we cross to Water Street. The hoverboard lane is packed with kids and adults flying down the street with thin goggles covering their eyes, their clothes flapping behind them. The billboards on top of the surrounding buildings play ads for cupcake shops and clothing stores and repair shops, but not one of them flashes a warning about robots.

Over a week ago, when Po took me to the Heart Office, I saw a bot warning on a Brack billboard and I was instantly zeeved out. Probably because the UD made bots look like evil killing machines. I don't feel that way now.

Vee stops at a metal door stuck between a bakery and a Link provider. She flips up the door's handle and it pops

open. Behind it, there's a scrolling track installed in the ceiling that moves a series of lockers round and round in a circle.

"What is this?" I ask.

"A hoverboard garage." Vee pushes a button to the left of the doorway and the track cranks to life. The lockers zoom forward. Several of them are full and the hoverboards inside are locked in place by something that looks like a mini-length of hover rail. They even glow neon blue.

Vee releases the button when a free locker appears. She presses her finger to a black screen on the side and the interior light flickers on.

"Pod, please." She waggles her fingers at me and I fetch a pod from the backpack. She places it in the bottom of the locker, turns it on, and a holo emblem appears. It's a triangular design with a bolt and gear in the center.

"What's the emblem stand for?"

"That's the symbol on our new flag. Some designer came up with it back when the war began and the UD started calling us Bot Territory. My dad said we might as well embrace it."

"Our flag was changed too. It now has thirteen blue and white stripes and a line of six red stars for each district."

"It's totally jammed, isn't it? How much has changed?" Vee shuts the door on the garage.

At the next corner, two bots are reenacting one of Tanner Waylon's dance routines, and his latest song, "Wrenched and Sideways," blasts from the tall, lean bot on the left.

We stop for a second to watch. They move in perfect unison, arms flailing, feet tapping, hips shaking. When the routine ends, the shorter bot takes a bow.

"Bravo!" Vee and I clap.

The bots start a different routine, this one to the bass beats of Junction Box.

I want to stay and watch, but Vee drags me off. "We have eleven more pods to place and lots more to see. Come on."

Our next stop is at a place called Willow Café, and the bot behind the counter gives us six free cookies. They are the best cookies I've ever tasted in my whole entire life.

Next, we go to the aquarium, where, on one side of the place you can see the real animals and on the other you can see robotic animals that were created to resemble prehistoric marine animals. There's this massive tylosaurus that swims back and forth past the glass. And this weird scorpion lobster thing. Dad and I should come back here. It's like our hy-breed animal game come to life.

We leave the aquarium somewhere around noon and make our way back toward the Fort, stopping at a small pond surrounded by big oak trees that are covered in thick green moss.

Vee takes me to her school next. "Where are we leaving the pod?" I ask, digging one out.

"On the football field." We walk around the brick building and slowly, the field and bleachers come into view. It isn't until we're closer that I realize the field is ringed in hover rails.

Vee tells me football around here is played wearing hoversuits. And I've never been big on sports, but that sounds like the coolest thing yet.

We make a few more stops, then finally our last one. It's a three-story shop with a big hovering holo sign out front that says: *Get your robot upgrade today! Leave here with a bionic limb! Or an optical chip! Get the St. Kroix special!*

"The St. Kroix special?" I ask.

Vee smirks. "Your dad has a fan club. People want to be like him."

I frown. "Wait. *People*?"

Vee crosses the street. I hurry after her. Cyber rock plays through the shop's speaker system. We go down a

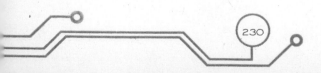

wide hall where posters hang on the wall showing the latest and greatest upgrades.

The hall opens to a circular atrium that rises up the full three stories, so no matter which floor you're on, you can look down on the ground floor.

"Whoa." I make a full turn before stopping at the base of a huge holo display in the center of the atrium. The display is my dad. "What the . . ."

"Pretty rad, right?" Vee says.

The holo image changes rapidly. There's one of my dad, hands on his hips, his robotic arm shining in the light. It flicks to an image of my dad's face with his metal plate and the bolt sticking out of his neck.

Do you want to be more like our esteemed leader, Robert St. Kroix? the display reads at the base. *Get the St. Kroix special today. In one week you will have a robotic arm and an indestructible face plate for just 25,000 creds. Schedule an appointment with one of our upgrade technicians today.*

I look around at the customers and realize there isn't a single robot inside.

"People really want to be part bot?" I ask.

"Sure do. Your dad is a hero down here. People respect him." Vee's voice gets real quiet, so I have to lean closer to hear her. "It's probably why the UD wants him so bad.

They know people will listen to him. Maybe one day he'll change the minds of the UD citizens, and then he'll have the entire nation on his side."

I look over at her. Out of the sun, her hair looks dark purple, almost brown. "I'm sorry that your dad is mixed up in this mess. It's all my family's fault."

Vee shakes her head. "My dad has a choice, ya know? No one is forcing him to be part of the Meta-Rise, and if I had a choice, I'd be a part of it too. I just . . ." She gets this far-off look in her eyes. "I wish things were different. I got no one left after my dad."

I want to tell her everything will be all right, but we both know it won't. Instead, I say, "When we get back to the Fort, we should start brainstorming heavy. Figure out a plan."

She nods and smiles. "You got it."

We plant our last scavenger hunt pod in the office of a tall woman named Mrs. Kipper. She seems excited to be the last stop on the hunt and gives us each a package of voice changers, which are these little stickers no bigger than a pebble. You put it on your tongue and swallow it, and it changes your voice for a few hours.

Vee and I take one each right away.

"How can a clam cram in a clean cream can?" she says

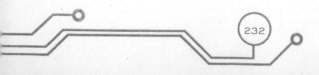

in a smokier version of her own voice. It sounds like she's been shouting for weeks.

"How *can* he cram in a can?" I answer, and bust out laughing. My voice is so deep, it's like my chest is the Grand Canyon and my voice is thunder booming through it. "I love these things!"

Vee grins. "Pretty jammed, right?"

"Totally jammed." I pocket the rest of the stickers as we head home.

TWENTY-SEVEN

I SIT ON THE bench in my room with an old tabpad in my lap, a mess of notes written on the screen. Vee disappeared fifteen minutes ago in search of food. I don't want to eat. All I want to do is brainstorm. Tellie made me write down my plan for our vid on a SimPad, so I tackle Operation: Rescue Po Without Losing My Dad or Parker or Anyone Else the same way.

I'm staring at the tabpad, thinking, when LT glides into the room. I power down the pad so he can't see what I've written.

"What are you doing?" he asks.

"Nothing." My voice cracks and I clear my throat. The voice sticker wore off an hour ago and left my throat all scratchy.

LT comes closer. "Are you all right?"

"Yeah." I lift a shoulder. "I'm fine."

"I would not call myself a lie detector, by any means, but I would suspect you are not, in fact, fine, considering the low, uneven pitch of your voice."

I sigh and lean against the wall. I don't know how LT does it, but he can figure out what I'm thinking without me actually saying anything. "It's nothing important," I lie.

If LT had eyebrows, I think he would be arching one right now. He just stares at me. Finally, I cave.

"I hate what the UD is doing to my dad and brother."

"I hate it as well," he says.

I sit forward again. "I mean, did you see Dad at the rally? The people here like him. How come the UD thinks he's a bad guy?"

"He is different now that he is no longer fully human and under their control." LT comes closer. "The UD is simply afraid of the unknown."

"I just . . . I don't want my dad to give up so easily."

"Giving up would imply he has done, and plans to do, nothing. I think I know your father well enough to know inaction is not in his nature."

I slide off the bench. "What about me? Dad's the only parent I have left. If he's dead, I'm an orphan. And Vee faces the same jam."

One of LT's operating lights in his neck blinks twice. "The other option is to lose your brother. Your father would never allow that to happen."

"It's not fair. No one should have to decide between their family members."

"I agree, but without clearance into the city building, we stand no chance of rescuing your brother without others endangering their lives. The UD government buildings have some of the best security features anywhere and—"

I'm only half listening to what he says, because something has lit a bulb in my brain.

Without clearance.

I cut him off. "But what if we *did* have clearance?"

"Well, we do not."

"Hippothetically."

"You mean hypothetically."

"Whatever. Yeah."

LT tilts his head to the side and brings up a hand, like he's thinking. "Well . . . if we had clearance, if the route was well thought out, and we could enter the UD and the building undetected, then yes, I would assume we would be able to rescue your brother. You would also have to consider escape, however. The issue is not simply

entering the building and finding Po, it will also involve escaping the building undetected with a prisoner."

Yes. Yes! Excitement does a backflip in my chest.

"Say you had a temp Net-tag that once belonged to the daughter of a big important congressman, would that Net-tag have a higher level of clearance into the building?"

LT gives me the robot version of a look that says *don't even go there*. "You are speaking of Tellie Rix?"

I don't answer. I'd be an idiot to answer.

LT paces the room without making a single sound. "Most government officials give their family members greater clearance capacity in case of an emergency. So yes, I would have to say Tellie Rix has a higher clearance in City Hall than you would, for example. But I highly doubt that clearance would get you all the way to where Po is being kept."

I start for the door. I've already heard what I need to hear and it's enough to convince me.

LT follows me out. "Where are you going?"

"I'm just gonna go find Vee. I'm . . . uh . . . hungry!"

"Why do I have a feeling you are, how does it go? You are about to do something stupid."

It's not stupid if it's saving my family.

I hurry out of the room before LT can use his robot voodoo on me. 'Cuz if he did, he might realize he helped me figure out my plan to break into City Hall and steal my brother back.

I find Vee in the kitchen digging through the cupboards. Merril is at the stove whistling over a pot of boiling *something*. It smells salty, whatever it is.

Vee comes up with a handful of granola and pops a chunk in her mouth. "Can I talk to you?" I ask.

We find a quiet corner far in the depths of the Fort's second floor and I fill her in on what I think might be the ultimate, mega plan of all plans.

"That might actually work," she says. "Now I just gotta figure out how we'll get out of Bot Territory. I can either a) steal my dad's plots, or b) create my own."

I start backing up. "Whatever you do, can you do it like, now?"

She wipes granola crumbs from her hands. "Already on it."

I make my way back to my room to take care of one last thing.

I call Lox.

He answers on the third ring, and when he sees it's me on the other end, he sputters and bolts for his bedroom.

"Dude, what the chop?" he says, bouncing back on his bed. "No warning? You got the whole UD looking for you. You're a regular line jumper." He gives me a sly grin. "How did you get so wrenched? I've been gone a few weeks and I come back to your face plastered all over every Link within a hundred miles. You've gone from a lame oil licker to a level-ten lens-cracker."

Lens-cracker is Lox's way of saying someone is hot, or totally wrenched. And I'm hoping he means I'm wrenched and not hot, because that would be level-ten weird.

"I have more important things to talk about. So focus for a milosecond."

Lox sets his Link in its port, propping it up. Hands free now, he crosses one leg over the other and curls his fingers around the side of his face, elbow on his knee. He screws up his mouth in a serious frown. "I am as focused as a monkey on a banana."

I shake my head. "Do you remember that one time we talked about going to your aunt's for a visit and then we'd go to that one place near there?"

He curls his upper lip. "Ehhh. That one time we talked about that one place. Oh right, that one place!" He narrows his eyes. "What place was that again?"

I sigh. "You know! The place with the costumes."

"Oh. The Superh—"

"Wait, don't say it! I don't know if this line is secure. Better safe than sorry. Just . . . do you remember what it was?"

"Yeah."

"Can you meet me there?"

Lox and I had this plan where we'd go to his aunt's in Dallas, Texas, for a weekend and then go to the Superhero Museum in Edge Flats for a day.

Since Dekker's location is secret, I figure this is as close as I can bring Lox. Vee and I will meet him there and then we'll drive to Dek's.

It was simple, except for the one little issue of Lox getting permission to take the auto-car all the way to Texas on such short notice.

Lox leans back. "And why would we be going to That One Place at a time like this?"

"That's just the meeting spot. I'll fill you in when you get there."

He shakes his head. "The things I do for you, bolt sniffer. I should be awarded a medal."

"I can award you one after this is over."

"So if I meet you at That One Place, where are we going after that?"

"That's a secret too."

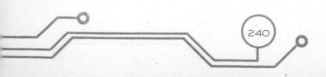

"Will it be wrenched?"

"Yeah." I laugh. "Totally."

"Well, why didn't you say so? I'm in!"

"Okay. I'll call you later about when to meet, but is it possible you could make it tonight?"

"Yeah. I'll just tell my mom and dad I'm visiting Aunt Mary. She's been howling lately about how I never come down, so my mom will be happy I'm going."

"Thanks, Lox. I owe you big-time."

"I know. I know." He stands up and unjacks the Link. "I'll be awaiting your super-secret call."

"I'll let you know as soon as I can."

We say good-bye and hang up.

Now Vee has to work her magic and this level-ten secret mission will be on.

TWENTY-EIGHT

I SHOVEL DOWN MY dinner. I'm thinking about the plan more than eating. I have a way into the City Hall building. I have a way to get from Texas to Brack. Vee is working on a route out of Bot Territory. And we've already agreed to head straight to Dekker's as soon as we're in Texas so we can beg him for help in crossing the UD/Texas border. It might take some sweet talking on our part, but I'm sure he'll cave.

So there's just one big problem I haven't solved yet: *How the chop am I gonna get out of the government building once I rescue Po?*

Like LT said, I'm not gonna waltz right out the front door with Po in tow. And despite all the action movies I've watched, I don't think crawling out an air-conditioning vent is going to work either.

"Trout? Earth to Trout?"

I look up. Dad is trying to hand me a glass of ice water. "Oh, um, thanks," I say, and take the drink.

The big table in the Fort's dining room is full of people. Some of them I recognize from the command room, others are new, but I'm pretty sure they're all part of the Meta-Rise. Merril told me Dad extended an open invitation to all of his workers, and their families, to join in for meals at the Fort.

Voices and laughter tangle together like fishing line. Three chairs down Vee smashes a baked potato with her fork, then douses it in butter. Her dad is at the other end of the table trying to show one of the littler kids how to program the salt and pepper shaker so you get the perfect amount of both.

"How's the food, y'all?" Merril asks, wiping his big boxy hands on a dishcloth. "Made everything special for y'all tonight."

I've realized every meal is special to Merril. I'm not complaining. "Potatoes are perfect," I say.

"Hey, kids!" Scissor bursts into the room. "Who's in for the rail scavenger hunt after dinner? I'm supposed to get a head count and I forgot!"

"Scissor!" Vee groans.

A couple of the older kids raise their hands. The tall kid sitting next to me must think I'm clueless, because he leans over and says, "A rail race is a race through town on the hoversuits."

243

"Yeah, I know."

"Well, are you gonna enter?"

"I don't know. Maybe," I lie. I have better things to do. Like plot a rescue mission.

"Just make sure you put on the brakes this time, hey?" the kid says with a chuckle. "Wouldn't want you flying into another tree."

"Ha. Ha. Ha." I roll my eyes. But that's when it hits me. And despite the fact that Giant McGiant Pants was making fun of me, I'm really glad he did.

Wouldn't want you flying into another tree. Flying. Hoversuits. They work on any of the hover rails, so they should work on the rails in Brack. If Vee and I strap the suits on, we could jump from City Hall and the rails would catch us.

"You know what," I say to Scissor, "I think I'll sign up for the race."

Vee catches my eye down the length of the table. I jerk my head, trying to give her a hint as to what I'm thinking. She catches on real quick.

"Make sure you bring a few extra hoversuits, Scissor," she says. "I'll ride with Trout to make sure he doesn't lose it on the rails."

"That's cheating!" McGiant Pants says. "You know the route!"

"I won't help him on the hunt, you nutter. Besides, do you really think that scrawny fish butt will win?"

The other kids laugh. I just shake my head and grin big. Because Vee and I both know we won't be around long enough to even start the scavenger hunt. Once we score a hoversuit, we're gone.

"Hey, Trout," Vee says after the dinner table is cleared. "Come help me with something real quick?"

Dad slaps me on the back. "I'm headed back up to the command room. Have fun on the scavenger hunt."

"Thanks. How late do you think you'll be?"

Dad's expression softens and he exhales real slow. "Probably a while. Don't wait up, okay?"

"Sure." Since this is the last time I will see Dad before heading into the UD, I give him a big hug. He hesitates at first, and then leans over, wrapping me up tight with his real arm *and* his robot arm. "Love you, Dad."

He chuckles and the sound reverberates through the metal in his side. "Love you too."

I pull away before the stinging in my eyes turns into real tears. Vee leads me into the media room and up the rope bridges. We settle into a pair of the comfy chairs on the metal rafter. A lamp glows on the table between us.

"So, are you thinking what I'm thinking?" she says.

Down below, a few of the kids are watching a movie on the giant vid panel. It's a futuristic movie about deep space travel. The sound effects are so loud, there's no way they can hear us.

I raise my eyebrows. "Hoversuits?"

"You got it."

"Now we have to deal with our dads. They're going to know we're gone."

There's an explosion from the speakers down below. One of the kids cheers.

"My dad always comes home late," Vee says. "And I bet it'll be even later tonight because of the thing with Po. So that will buy us a few hours. But I know my dad uses our apartment's security system to check on me before he goes to bed. Your dad will probably do the same thing."

I huff in frustration. "Once they realize we're gone, they'll come after us. Or send someone to stop us."

"Unless we can trick them until morning. By then we'll be in the UD."

I frown. "How are we going to do that?"

Her smile widens. "Thankfully, I have experience with this kind of thing. You think I've never snuck out for the night?"

"I don't know? Maybe?"

She cocks her head. "The answer is yes, FishKid."

"I wish everyone would stop calling me that."

"Yeah, and I wish I had ten million creds." She starts for the rope bridge. "Call Lox and tell him we're ready. Meet me in your room in twenty minutes."

TWENTY-NINE

"**H**ERE'S WHAT YOU need to know about the house's security system." Vee drops onto my bed and slides her backpack off her shoulder. "The system is the same as the one at our apartment. It uses thermal to scan every room, looking for a heat register where it should or shouldn't be. Your dad probably has you programmed in for your room, so if you're not there, it'll send a ping back to him."

I sit on the bench, propping my elbows on my knees. "Okay. How are we going to beat that?"

Vee digs in her bag and pulls out a long, thin wire with plastic discs every five inches or so. "This is an internal heating link. They're used to line winter coats and snowpants in the north."

She climbs off my bed and pulls back my blanket. "I'm gonna need at least one more pillow."

I know exactly where to find one. Merril showed me the closet with extra sheets and blankets and stuff my first day here in case I ever needed something. It's the fourth door on the left across from my room. I go there, grab a pillow and an extra blanket just in case, and jog back.

"Here." I hand everything to Vee.

The heating link and its control pad is stretched out on my bed, from the head to the foot. Vee lines the pillows over the top of it and presses a finger to the control to turn it on. "Help me spread the blankets over the pillows."

We use my blanket, plus the extra I brought. "Can't hurt," Vee says with a shrug. "The more layers, the more heat that will be trapped inside."

When we're finished, we stand back to assess our work. There's a lumpy me-sized shape in the bed. Vee clicks off the light and in the dark, it looks even less like a mountain of pillows.

"Wrenched," I say.

"The heating link will warm the pillows to a temp close to your body temp."

"You're a genius, Vee."

We go quiet for a full minute, then I say, "Are we really doing this?"

Vee meets my eyes. "I can't lose my dad for good."

"I can't either."

"And I'm tired of him thinking I'm too young to do

anything important. I want to show him I can be part of the Meta-Rise."

I take in a deep breath. "Then I guess we're doing this."

"I guess so."

"Rules!" Scissor calls over the group of us waiting in the park. "Please listen to the rules!"

Everyone quiets. The wind picks up. The branches of the willow tree behind Scissor sway back and forth like a pendulum.

"As soon as you receive your list of items, the hunt begins. There's to be no tampering with the pods. No fouls! No sabotaging whatsoever. Are we all in agreement?"

Around us, everyone nods.

"All right." Scissor's meta-pol arms grow by a foot and she claps her hands above her head. "Everyone is suited up?"

More nods. I have all the straps on. Elbows. Knees. Foot plates.

"Take your places!" Scissor says.

Vee and I hurry to the street. The others line up next to us. Some of the bigger kids push the littler ones back like they already forgot about the rules.

Links start beeping as they receive the list of clues Vee

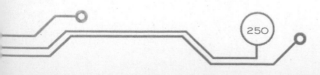

created. The bigger kids take off at a sprint. Everyone else follows. Since we're supposed to be doing the scavenger hunt, Vee and I disappear in the same direction, but as soon as we're out of sight, we dodge left, back toward the center of town, toward Scissor's repair shop.

We make it in record time, even though I had a near run-in with a street cleaner and fell on my face at the sharp curve on Emerald Street. Which made Vee laugh her fool head off, which lost us even more time.

"Can we go now?" I say, fixing my shirt.

Vee wipes the tears streaming down her face. "Yeah. Yeah. Okay. I'm ready." But then she laughs all the way to Scissor's.

Once inside, we are all business. As we tiptoe to the back of the shop, my heart tha-dums in my ears. I'm so nervous, there's sweat pooling beneath my nose. I show Vee the wall where LT and I came through a few days ago.

She frowns. "It's a blank wall."

"It's a holo-barrier. LT pressed a button or something on the other side and the wall disappeared . . ."

"You didn't tell me there was a secret way to get in! This is something I could have worked on if I'd known about it."

"Sorry! I wasn't exactly thinking about it. I was thinking more about my brother, ya know? And breaking into City Hall . . ."

Vee runs her hand down the wall. "It feels solid. There must be a button on this side somewhere. Start looking—"

She's cut off by someone clearing their throat.

We whirl around. Ratch stands in the doorway between the back room and the shop. His strip of eyes glows in the muted light. "Am I interrupting something?"

I swallow loudly. "Umm . . ."

Our rescue operation is over before it even began.

"Just looking for an extra part," Vee starts. "Something Scissor asked us to get."

Ratch comes closer. "I don't think you'll find what you're looking for in a brick wall." He takes another step and twists around. We take two steps back. "You aren't trying to escape, are you?"

"N-no," I stutter.

Vee shakes her head.

"Because if you were . . ."

"We're not," I say.

Ratch reaches around us. Vee and I shrink away. He taps the shelf just above our heads.

Something clicks. I hear that familiar *vareeee-juuuu* sound I heard the day LT led me into Scissor's shop. The

bricks flicker and disappear again, one by one. The tiny room on the other side comes into view.

Vee and I stare at the exit. "That is split," Vee whispers.

"If you were looking for an escape," Ratch says, "all you had to do was ask."

The shop goes super, mega silent. Vee and I jam into each other. Is he serious?

"You're not going to tell on us?" Vee finally asks.

Ratch shakes his head once. "What you're doing is admirable. If one of my own was in trouble, I would do whatever I needed to save him or her. I'll cover for you as long as I can. I suspect LT will catch on relatively quickly, however. So you best hurry."

We look at each other, then back at Ratch. He's always kinda geared me out, but in a good way. He's like the popular kid at school who you want to hang out with, but you know you can't because you're not wrenched enough to breathe the same air as him.

Right now I want to hug him. But I know that would be lame.

"Thanks," I say.

"You're welcome. Now go." He shoos us on.

We clamber through. Ratch salutes us and hits the button on his side. The bricks flicker on and Scissor's shop disappears. We're sealed inside.

"That was jammed," Vee says.

"Yeah. I can't believe he helped us."

"Me neither."

"You think he was telling the truth when he said he'd cover for us?"

Vee shrugs. "I don't know, but I'm not gonna stick around to find out." She points at the hatch in the floor. "I take it we go down?"

"Yup." I turn the lever in the door and it pops open with a hiss. "Who goes first?"

Vee shrugs. "I'll go."

When she reaches the bottom, I go in, pulling the door closed, plunging us into the dark. I forgot how cave-like the tunnel felt. I only brought my bag with Tellie's Net-tag, some food, and a bottle of water. Fresh out of flash-lights.

Vee didn't even bring a bag.

"I can't see a thing," I complain.

Vee pulls out her Link and activates it. The screen illuminates the tunnel. "This will have to do."

We take off the hoversuits and shove them in my bag. Vee pulls out a second suit that she stuffed inside her gray vest. "For Po," she says.

"Oh, I didn't even think of that."

"I figured. That's why you got me." She taps in a few

254

commands on her Link and shows me a blueprint of the maintenance lines. "We need to go south. It'll take us to an old line that will connect back west to the line that'll take us straight to Dekker's."

"Why not take the same way me and LT did?"

"'Cuz I'm sure the UD is watching those lines. Duh."

"Right."

"Anyway, this route will be faster. There's just one minuscule little problem."

"What?"

She raises her eyebrows. "Well, we might have to cross through an underground tunnel that might be a known secret route for a few uppity members of Congress to get from the UD to Texas without crossing the border out in the open. And the floor may or may not be riddled with tacky pods. So basically it might be hard to cross but not impossible."

I'm frowning so hard, I feel like my eyebrows are trying to swallow my eyes. "First of all, what are tacky pods? And second of all, are you kidding me?"

"Tacky pods are like giant glue dots. And no, I'm not kidding you. Quit gearing out, FishKid. I have a plan."

"Isn't there another way?"

"Not one that'll get us there tonight."

I sigh. "Fine. Lead the way."

THIRTY

"**STEP ON ONE** of those," Vee whispers as we stare at the floor glistening with tacky pods, "and you're instantly glued in place until someone comes to fetch you."

"Great," I mutter.

There are tiny lights installed in the wall every four feet here, so I can see everything just fine. This tunnel is three times as big as the others and it's extremely, extremely white. White floor. White painted brick. And it smells different. Like plastic. Like a beach ball fresh out of the package.

We got here by slithering down a tiny return-air tunnel, pushing through a grate, bursting from a boiler room, and finally into a small alcove that met the tunnel. I have no idea how Vee figured this all out, but I'm glad she did.

Vee points at the ceiling in the main tunnel. "See the pipes up there?"

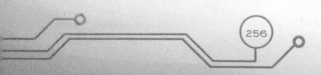

There's a big blue pipe, hugged by two smaller red pipes and lastly, a thin white pipe. "Yeah?"

"We're going to climb on them."

"How? They're like ten feet away."

She pulls a little circular object from her pocket. "With this. It's a frog whipper."

There's nothing special about it, whatever it is. It's no bigger than a slice of cucumber. The color of dirt. The center glows green.

"Okay, so what's it do?"

"Watch." Vee presses the object between her thumb and index finger and then runs. When she reaches the end of the alcove, she leaps, whips her arm forward like she's bowling, and the little object *zings*. A glowing green line flies out of it, wraps around the big blue pipe, and ties itself up.

Vee swings back and forth, holding on to the line with just one hand as she grins down at me. "And then," she says quietly, "you just press the button again." The line retracts, hoisting her up until she's close enough to the pipe to pull herself on.

"Where did you get that thing?"

"Scissor. It's just like her arms, but miniature. Here." She tosses me the object and I fumble for it, almost fall-

ing off the ledge of the alcove and into the field of tacky pods.

"Awww, come on!" I whisper-shout. "What if I didn't catch it?"

"But ya did. Now get a running start and don't forget to press the center with your thumb. That's what activates it."

I return to the back of the alcove. I hold the object— the frog whipper—in my open palm. This seems like a crazy idea. But then, so does breaking into City Hall and stealing my brother from the UD government.

"Here goes," I whisper, and push off the wall.

I get a good, fast start. When I reach the alcove's ledge, I press the whipper so hard I feel like I might mash it into pieces. I leap, copy Vee's movements, swing my arm out.

Zing. The line sails through the air, ties itself up, but in an instant, I can tell there's too much slack. Instead of swinging in the air, I'm falling to the ground, and fast.

"Trout!" Vee leans over the edge of the pipe. "Stop pressing the center!"

I do as she says. The line finally snaps back. I'm two inches from the floor and a glimmering tacky pod. It emits a faint humming sound, like the hover rails but ten times quieter. Deadlier.

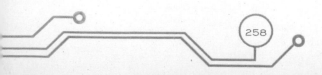

I'm upside-down, dangling like a spider with one leg wrapped around the line. "What the chop?"

Vee winces as she leans over the pipe, her single earring dangling like a knot of Spanish moss. "I forgot to tell you to press once, ya know, to get enough line out. Sorry!"

"That would have been nice to know!"

"Yeah. Yeah. Now press the center again to retract it."

Sweat rolls from my forehead and drips straight down to the floor. The droplets hit a tacky pod and the humming noise powers up to a full-on *whummmp*. The sweat beads tremble, like they're trying to dissolve into a puddle, but can't.

And then, the *whummmp* goes silent and the sweat flattens out. I blink. I'm trying to figure out what that means when two male voices carry down the hall.

It means the tacky pods have been deactivated.

"Retract!" Vee whispers. "Retract!"

I fumble with the device, jamming my finger into it until I realize it's the wrong side I'm trying to activate. The voices get closer. A drop of sweat rolls into the corner of my eye and burns. My arms start to shake. My head is pounding from all the blood rushing to it.

I twist the whipper around and mash my thumb into

it. The line grows hot and retracts. I untangle my leg as the line lurches toward the ceiling. When I reach the pipe, Vee grabs my arm, hauls me back, and presses a finger to her lips. I nod, clamping my mouth shut even though I'm breathing so hard I feel like I'm suffocating.

The men round the corner. I can just make out the tops of their heads through the gaps in the pipework. One man is short and dark-haired and wearing a blue jacket. The other is tall, blond, with a booming voice.

I know that voice. It's Mr. Rix! Tellie's dad.

I freeze every muscle, praying they don't look up. Vee is sprawled over the blue pipe and one of the smaller red ones. Will the red one hold her?

"You have to admit," the shorter man says, "Sandra's tactics may be brutal at times, but they're effective. Why do you think Callo made her Head of Congress?"

Sandra Hopper. That's Beard's real name. The same woman who wants my dad to turn himself in.

"The greater population of the UD loves her," the man continues. "She looks as innocent as a kitten."

"I don't care what the population thinks of her," Mr. Rix says. "I'm not sure I agree with her planned attack simply to launch a new war campaign."

"Congress and the lower District councils won't approve it without a little push, and we can't sit idly

anymore. The Meta-Rise is real, Wesson. We know that group of renegade bots in Old New York are planning something, and the longer we keep our heads in the sand, the worse it'll be. The bigger the war will be. This is the best option." He scratches the back of his neck. "We never should have implemented the ThinkChip in the first place. None of this would have happened. We'd still have cheap bot labor all over the country and pockets lined with Machinery Tax money. The war has run us dry and our economy is tanking. As soon as we have an agreement from all Districts, we can strike quickly and this whole thing will be over. And you know what that means?"

Mr. Rix sighs and massages the bridge of his nose. "Yeah, I know."

"We put bots back where they belong," the other man answers anyway. "They belong in boiler rooms and factories and grocery stores and toll booths. Unthinking, unfeeling machines. Because that's what they are."

Mr. Rix shakes his head. "Let's stop talking about this. I'm starting to get a headache and I haven't had a drink in four hours."

The other man chuckles. "Fair enough. I heard the Tralon has a new kind of Irish liquor, imported daily. Rich, throaty kind of stuff that'll . . ."

Their voices fade away when they round another corner and disappear from sight.

Vee and I share a look.

"Did you hear that?" I say.

Vee's eyes tighten with suspicion. "Sounds like they want to start Bot Wars part two."

"Are they planning on attacking those renegade bots? In New York?"

Vee thinks for a second. "Maybe."

"Do you know anything about them?"

"Not really. I've heard my dad mention them, but nothing about them being renegades. That's kind of a funny word, when you say it out loud."

"Someone should warn them if they're going to be attacked."

Vee nods. "We have a while, at least. Sounds like Beard needs Congress and District approval first, and she's got her mind on other things right now."

I snort. "Yeah, like ruining my family."

I make a mental note to tell Dad later, after Po is rescued. Right now, I need to get out of this tunnel.

Vee slinks off like a slug and I slink off after her.

We make it out of the sterile white tunnel by following

the pipes into another maintenance room. Vee points at a set of metal rungs that rise upward through the ceiling to a hatch.

"That'll take us to ground level. We'll be two blocks away from that museum you told Lox to meet us at."

I breathe with relief. "Great. Because I'm tired. And hungry."

Vee rolls her eyes. "You're not a very good adventurer, are you?"

I glower at her. She snickers and we head up the ladder cemented straight into the wall. At the top, I turn a circular handle on the hatch and it glides open easily. Cool, fresh air rushes down the shaft and I suck it in.

I'm the first to climb out of the ground into a park. A fountain gurgles somewhere behind us. The wooden benches are empty this time of night and the lampposts create pools of light on the cement. In the distance, the hover rails glow in the dark.

Vee taps her Link and holds it in front of us. It displays an image of the city with directions telling us how to reach the Superhero Museum.

Go straight. Then left, then right.

I get excited, thinking about seeing Lox after a few weeks. I miss the wrenchhead. Not that I'll tell him that.

Vee and I stick close together. We turn the final corner and a large, sand-colored brick building comes into view. "That's it," Vee says.

Two holo banners hang from the roof of the museum. One is a 3-D rendition of last year's Batman movie costume. The other is a 2-D announcement of the newest Trakor Comics installment opening next Tuesday.

Too bad I'm not here to actually see the museum's displays. Maybe next time, I tell myself. If there *is* a next time.

Vee points at the parking lot on the side of the building and the lone car parked there. "Is that Lox?"

"Yeah, that's him!" I jog across the street and pound on his window, making him jump sky high.

I blow into a riot of laughter and Lox narrows his eyes as he climbs out.

"Geez, oil licker! Don't do that to me." He clutches at his chest. "I could have had an involuntary heart attack."

Vee frowns. "Because there's such a thing as a voluntary heart attack?"

Lox smoothes back his crazy blond hair and looks from Vee to me. "Who's she?"

My laughter trails off. "This is Vee. She's a friend. So that means be nice."

"Pssssh. Nice is my seventh sense."

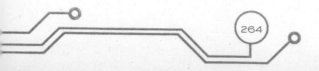

I shake my head and say to Vee, "You'll get used to him eventually."

"I doubt that."

"What's up with your hair?" Lox says. "A second ago it was red. Now it's blue."

"It's transive dye."

"Transie . . . I don't get it."

I skirt around the front of the car to the passenger side. "Can we go?"

Lox opens the back door and bows. "After you, milady."

Vee arches an eyebrow before climbing in.

It isn't until I settle into the wide, cushy seat next to Lox and he commands the car to play "something wrenched and jamming but with soul and beat" that I realize just *how* much I missed him.

The car pulls out of the parking lot and I tell it to head east, to Mercury Street. I only vaguely remember how to get to Dekker's. What I do know is it's somewhere around Mercury Street. I'm hoping I'll see something familiar once we're in the neighborhood.

Lox leans over and slaps my back. "What took you guys so long? I was starting to get worried about you."

"We got hung up," I say.

"Well, *Trout* got hung up," Vee adds, and I can practically hear the smirk in her voice.

265

Lox pops a piece of gum in his mouth, but doesn't bother to offer us any. "I need to hear this story."

"No way!" I tell the car to turn right. "It's a boring story anyway."

Vee snorts.

"So where are we going?" Lox asks. "I thought we were going to the museum."

"It's closed. And this isn't a vacation. It's a mission."

The houses are starting to look familiar and I tell the car to turn left. As soon as we're on Tunston Street, I see the outline of the old fire station up ahead.

"There it is." I point through the windshield and both Lox and Vee lean forward for a better look.

Lox chomps on his gum. "Whose house is that?"

Since he's a huge fan of Dekker's, I don't want to spoil the surprise just yet.

"Wait and see."

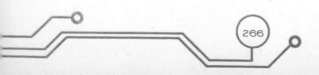

THIRTY-ONE

"**A**ARON DEKKER?" Lox screeches after I introduce everyone once we're safely inside Dekker's living room.

Dekker must be used to this kind of reaction by now, being as famous as he is. He ignores Lox, shoves his hands in his pants pockets, and leans against the back of the couch. "Please tell me there is a good reason for your being here, little dude. Without LT *or* your dad."

"Umm . . ."

"Aaron Dekker! Is that really him?" Lox's eyes get bigger and his jaw sags lower.

Dekker pats his stomach. "Yeah, I'm pretty sure it's me." He's wearing a baggy navy blue T-shirt and a pair of jeans with holes torn in the knees. Thin copper wire runs back and forth through the holes, suturing them closed. I read on the Net that soldiers on the front lines used crazy things to repair their clothing when nothing else was available. Some big fashion designer in 1st District took the idea and made it popular. I would climb Mt. Hood for a pair. They're too expensive for me to ever buy on my own.

"So tell me again why you're here?" Dekker asks.

Lox gets control of himself, but not his curiosity. He circles the room, picking up random things as he goes. Dekker hurries behind him, fixing whatever Lox moves out of place.

"We need your help getting back into the UD," I say, hoping he's too preoccupied with picking up after Lox to fully digest what I'm asking.

No such luck.

"Whoa, whoa, little dude. Repeat that?"

"Err . . . we need your help—"

"Yeah, I heard you, and the answer is why would I do that?"

"That's not an answer, it's a question," Vee points out, and Dekker shoots her an annoyed look.

I take a deep breath. "Because I want to rescue my brother. And my dad and Vee's dad are going to turn themselves in in order to get Po back, so if I rescue him first, they won't have to and we'll win."

Lox picks up a long, thin remote control and starts tapping at the screen. Dekker snatches it out of his hand and puts it back on the table, then taps it three times.

"I'm all for a hero's mission, but do you have any idea what your dad will do to me if he realizes I helped you?"

No, I hadn't thought about that. I hadn't thought about a lot of things other than The Plan. Because now that I see Lox here, all the way in Texas in the house of Aaron Dekker planning to drive me to Brack to commit a crime, I realize how much non-thinking I've done.

What if we get caught? What if Lox is punished because of me? And what about Vee?

My shoulders sink. Maybe this is a bad idea. Maybe we should go back to Bot Territory and let the adults take care of everything like they said they would.

And what if your dad turns himself in, a voice in my head says, *and you really really never see him again?*

What if the UD doesn't honor the bargain and they arrest Dad and *keep Po?*

My throat constricts like a tightly coiled snake. I'd be alone. Alone for the rest of my lame life. I don't have any grandparents. I know I've got an aunt in London, but I've never met her, and she's never shown any interest in getting to know me and Po. So why would she want to take me in?

I've got no one.

I have to do this, but I have to protect my friends too. As best I can.

"Dad won't know you helped me," I say to Dekker. "I won't tell him if you don't."

"He'll know either way," Vee says quietly.

"I'll tell him I called Tellie and asked for her help. She may be the enemy's daughter, but she's still my friend. Dad might buy it." I take a step forward and straighten my spine so I'm an inch taller at least. "Besides, if we rescue Po, it's not going to matter. Dad will be so geared out, he'll totally forget about everything else."

I press my hands together like I'm praying. "Please, Dek. Please? This is life or death."

He sighs and runs a hand through his rainbow hair. "Little dude, you know how to pull on the heartstrings, don't you?"

"He's got that innocent yet adorable look," Vee says.

I scowl at her. Nothing adorable about that.

"Fine," Dekker says. "When do you need to leave?"

"Well, trying to break into a government building at night would be risky." I pace the room. "Even though it'll be dark, and there will be less people, there's probably more security in place."

Dekker nods. "Go on."

"So, that means we should leave early in the morning so we can get into Brack and break in to save Po soon after the building opens."

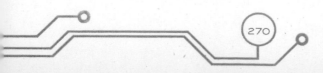

"And how do you plan to break in?" Dekker asks.

Everyone is looking at me again. Well, except Lox, who is staring at a metal pelican sculpture on one of Dekker's shelves like he's trying to decide if it's really a sculpture or a robot in disguise.

I dig in my bag and pull out Tellie's Net-tag. "With this. It has extra clearance on it. It belonged to a friend whose dad is a congressman."

"You mean Tellie," Lox says, still staring at the pelican.

"Yeah. Tellie."

Dekker folds his arms across his chest. "Aren't you worried about getting your friend in trouble?"

I shake my head. "Tellie is clever. She'll just say I stole it and everyone will buy it, considering what I've done lately. Or, what I'm about to do."

"What if the tag doesn't work anymore?" he asks.

"It does. She said it did."

"She could have been lying. She is the daughter of a congressman, after all."

"It's a risk I have to take."

Lox whistles. "What's my job in this cracked plan of yours?"

"Drive us into Brack and then back to Texas."

"Boring."

"I don't want you getting caught in this," I argue.

Dekker wags his finger at Lox. "A good point. This is serious stuff, man. If you get caught, there's no talking your way out of it."

"Fine." Lox huffs and plops into one of the chairs. "But next time you go on a grand mission of Jupiter proportions, I get to be more than the wheelman, you get me?"

I agree, but there won't *be* another grand mission. At least I hope not.

THIRTY-TWO

I CAN'T SLEEP. Neither can anyone else. Which is why we're in Dekker's workshop in the basement at four a.m. discussing strategy.

"All right, so . . ." Dekker claps his hands. "You'll need some good disguises, considering there's a wanted post on every major billboard, Net site, and Link across the entire country. I've got you covered there. And I'll see if I can hook you up with some useful James Bond toys."

Lox, Vee, and I share a look. "Who's James Bond?" Vee asks.

"Wahaha? You don't know who James Bond is? He's only the greatest spy of all time! Double-O Seven ring a bell? *Smoking Gears*? *The Meta Gun*?"

"That would be a negative," Lox says. "But . . . The Meta Gun, now that sounds like my kind of toy."

"It's not a toy." Dekker grumbles. "It's a movie title."

"Oh. Then it sounds like my kind of movie."

Once Dekker has recovered enough not to pass out

from shock, he takes us to a separate room farther back. Here, there are jackets and shoes and bookcases lined with wigs and sunglasses and other things. Dekker opens a metal cabinet stuck behind the door. He pulls out three poly masks.

Vee gasps. "Where did you get those?"

"I have my sources, little missy dude." He hands each of us a mask. It's made of flimsy poly, so it jiggles when I take it. I know what these things are, but I've never seen one in person. They're mostly used on movie sets to age a character or to save money by having one actor play multiple characters.

Vee puts the mask to her face and instantly the thing suctions to her skin. The angles and humps and ridges form to her face so that she kinda looks like Vee, but only because I know it's her. She looks three years older.

"Dude, that is wrenched," Lox breathes. "It's like it knows you."

I turn a circle in the room. "Why do you have all this stuff?"

Dekker shoves his hands in his jeans pockets and hunches his shoulders. "I get recognized a lot. I mean, I don't want to brag or anything, but if I go into town, I'm stopped eighty billion times for an autograph or a photo.

Sometimes a famous dude just needs a little peace and privacy. You get me?"

Lox snaps his fingers and points at Dek. "I get you, bro. I get you."

Vee rolls her eyes.

We spend the next hour picking out masks and wigs to go with our new faces. We grab three extra sets too, after Dekker warns we may need them to escape the UD, or if one of our masks detaches and we can't get it back on.

"Careful not to get too hot," he adds. "They tend to lose suction if you're sweating."

Great. Because that's exactly what I'll be doing when I break into City Hall. Sweating like a hog.

When we're in full gear, Dekker stands back to survey his work. "Perfect."

But Lox can't stop laughing at my face.

"It's just . . . haaa . . . you look like . . . haahauuu . . . a gorilla with blond hair."

I check my reflection in the mirror screwed into the wall. My nose got fatter at the base. My lips are thinner, like two slices of pepperoni. The blond wig covers up the rest of my hair, but pokes at my ears. It's a good disguise, so I can't complain.

Vee's wig is black as a burnt-out hover rail and reaches

past her shoulder blades. She looks like a princess from some cold, mountainous foreign country. She even holds her neck real high and straight like she thinks she's royalty.

Lox looks like a cross between a monkey and a potato. His cheeks are big and puffy, his nose wide and knobby. His new eyebrows curl at the end. "It's like I'm an evil scientist," he decides. "Call me Dr. Fluton from now on."

"You are such a nutter," Vee says.

Lox turns to her and squints one eye. "Oh, and what do we have here? What a fine saucy lass! Do you wish to be my diabolical assistant in my secret laboratory?"

He says laboratory like la-BORA-tory.

"Is your brain jammed?" Vee asks. "Because something about you isn't right."

Dekker snaps his fingers. "Oh, a few more things." He hurries out to the workroom. We find him rummaging through a toolbox, shoving aside metal things that *cling-clank* together.

"Ah-ha." He grabs a handful of something and then replaces everything he took out in a slow, deliberate way, like there was a certain order to the chaos.

When he's finished, he holds out his hand to reveal a cluster of tiny worm-like devices. They're all identical with a button on top, a red eye at one end, and a clear lens

on the other. "They're recording devices. I figure if you're going into enemy territory, you might as well plant one of these buggers and see what we can get."

Vee says, "How does it work?"

Dekker puts one worm up to his eye, like a binocular. "You look through the clear lens side, press the button once to zero in on a person or object, press it again to lock on them." He locks it on to Lox and twelve spindly legs sprout from the worm's lower half. "That's how it moves," Dekker explains when we all shrink back. He sets the device on the counter. Immediately, its body changes color and texture to mimic the worn wood of the countertop and disappears. "Virtually undetectable."

"Whoa." I take a step closer. I know the spot where the worm was a second ago, but I can't see anything. Even the red eye and clear lens are gone.

"Lox could walk into the other room," Dekker explains, "and the worm would follow him. It'll follow anywhere and record video and audio."

"So how do you retrieve it if you can't see it?" Vee asks, flicking a lock of her new black hair away from her face.

"You don't. They're programmed to record for six hours. Everything is uploaded to one of my online shell-boxes, where I can either watch it live or retrieve it later. The device itself will self-destruct immediately after its

time is up." He spreads out his hands. "Like I said, little dudes, virtually undetectable."

"I'll take a dozen," Lox says.

"Well, you already have one," Vee points out.

We look around, trying to spot the worm, even though it's pointless.

"That thing is going to follow me around for six hours?" Lox says.

Dekker pats Lox on the shoulder. "Don't worry. You won't even know it's there. Anyway, it'll give me a way to keep an eye on you while you're gone."

I carefully tuck a device into the front pocket of my pack. "Oh, wait," I say. "Do you have a scrambler? I figure Po will need it to block out the signal of his ID chip once we escape City Hall."

"Good thinking." Dekker pulls open a drawer filled with scramblers strung up on ball chains. "There you go."

"Thanks." I slide it in next to the worm device. "I guess we're ready, then?" Vee and Lox nod. Dekker leads us out to the street, where the sun has yet to peek over the treetops. The air is already warm, but not sweltering like a sauna.

Lox slides in the car and invites Vee to take shotgun, even though I always get shotgun. I try not to whine. Both he and Vee are doing me big favors today.

At the back door, Dekker wraps me in a loose hug and slaps my back. "And we part again. No worries, little dude, I'm like . . . ninety-seven percent sure we'll meet again."

I frown. "What about that other three percent?"

He shrugs. "You have to account for earthquakes and accidents and zombie apocalypses."

I raise an eyebrow. "And getting caught by the UD government?"

"Well, there's that too." He slicks back his hair again and the bright yellow strip flops over the blue. "Oh wait, one more thing. Your way into the UD."

In the excitement of trying on new disguises and seeing the worm device, I'd forgotten the whole reason we'd come here in the first place.

"When you get to the border, go to the second toll booth from the right, but only between six a.m. and six thirty-seven a.m. The guard will say, 'A beautiful day today, isn't it?' and you will reply, 'Beautiful as a field of daisies.' Pay the toll with this." He hands me a temporary Net-tag with the name Peter Gunter stamped on the front. "You'll be good to go."

I slip the Net-tag into my pocket. "Thanks, Dekker. Really. I can't thank you enough."

He hooks an arm around my neck and gives me a bolt

burn, just like Po always does. My insides dance when I realize I'm only hours away from seeing my brother.

"Good luck, little dude. Now get out of here." He shoves me toward the car. "And don't gear out! Secret agents keep their cool under pressure."

"Got it." I slip into the backseat as Lox programs the car to take us to the Texas/UD border. The computer system says in a cool male voice that we have approximately two hours and thirty-six minutes of travel time.

After waving good-bye to Dekker out the back window, I slouch in my seat and the easy lull of the car finally puts me to sleep. I burst awake sometime later when the car rams on its brakes and I go slamming into the seat in front of me.

I sit up, eyes all squinty, and look through the windshield. "What the chop?"

"Um . . ." Lox nods at the two figures standing in our headlights in the middle of the road. All around us is flat, prairie land. There isn't another car or house for miles.

"Clanking robots!" Lox says, his voice squeaky. "We're dead!"

THIRTY-THREE

INSTANTLY, I KNOW who the bots are. I know it by the way the lights flicker in the bot's neck, the one on the right. I know it by the way the eyes glow orange on the other one.

"It's LT and Ratch," I say. "I guess he didn't cover for us after all."

"Jam it," Vee mutters.

I climb out. A warm wind blows across the flat land, making the dry grass rattle. The sky has changed to a shade of lavender since I fell asleep. The sun will be up soon. It's probably almost 6:00. We're running out of time if we want to make it to the border before six thirty-seven a.m.

I start to say something, a jumble of pleas, mostly, but LT cuts me off with the raise of his hand.

"I wish not to hear excuses, Trout. I am merely here to take you home."

"My dad knows I'm gone, then?"

LT shakes his head. "He has a lot on his mind now. I had hoped to locate you and bring you back without anyone noticing. It would spare you punishment."

"How did you even know I was gone?" I look at Ratch. "Did you tell him?"

Ratch cocks his head to the side. "I gave you my word that I would cover for you."

"He is not to blame." LT raises a finger. "What was it . . . ahh yes, I am your babysitter. Correct? You said so yourself. I am in charge of you. It is my duty to check on you every four hours, as scheduled. I discovered you were gone an hour and fifty-seven minutes ago."

"So how did you find me?"

"I traced your Link. Also, Dekker called me."

I sigh. Of course he did. I guess he agreed to the whole thing a little too easily.

And it was stupid of us not to leave our Links behind. Mine's just a temporary one Dad gave me, but all Links have tracking devices in them, even if they're not the fancier models that are connected to your Net-tag or your heart chips, if you have one.

LT takes a step closer. "Are you . . . Why do you look different?"

I touch my face and remember I'm wearing one of Dekker's masks. "It's a disguise. To get into Brack."

"I see. Well, there will be no need for it now. We will return home immediately. If we hurry, your father will never know you were gone. I will keep this to myself as long as you agree never to do something as senseless as this ever again."

I straighten. "No."

LT goes still. "Pardon me?"

I grit my teeth as I look up at him. "I can't, LT. I have to do this. I know I can do this! Either my brother will die or my dad will be taken by the UD! I can't let that happen."

"And what is your plan, exactly?" he asks. "Do you even know how you will get your brother out of the building? A government building, might I add? A building that has numerous cameras and security guards? I suppose you plan to climb out an air-conditioning vent?"

I snort. "No. Hoversuits." And I explain how I mean to use them. It's like I can see the gears twisting backward as he changes his mind.

"It could work," Ratch says, and gets in close to LT's side. "Think about it. Is this not what we've wanted to do from the very beginning? Show the UD that their security and their brick buildings are no match for us?"

A light in LT's neck blinks to green. "But this way? Putting Trout and the others at risk?"

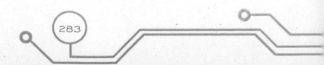

Ratch makes a fist with his spindly machine hand. "We can do this, brother."

LT looks away. The light in his neck flickers, then glows steadily. "I will admit, this could work. Nevertheless"—he turns to me—"you are risking your life—"

"I'm willing to do that." A gust of wind crosses the field. My wig shudders and a lock of hair falls over my forehead. I kinda feel squirrelly in this disguise, but I'm doing my best not to let it bother me. I bat the hair away. "Please, LT. I can't sit around doing nothing."

"Your father would have me dismantled for this, and every human instinct and emotion programmed and learned is telling me I should not allow it."

My arms hang at my sides. I have nothing left to argue with except for the obvious. "He's my brother. And I can't lose my dad. I just got him back."

If a robot can sigh dramatically, that's the sound LT makes right before he says, "Yes, fine. All right."

"Yes!" I shake my hands in the air.

A crow caws overhead. LT glides away on his silent joints and slides in the car. Ratch follows behind.

I guess they're *both* coming with us.

We arrive at the Texas/UD border at six twenty-two a.m. and make it through using Dekker's instructions. The

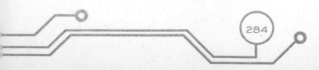

security guard smiles a big smile when I say "Beautiful as a field of daisies."

"Yes indeed," he adds with a wink. "You all have a good day. Be safe, now."

It seems like it's been forever since I was inside the city of Brack. And even though it's only been a week or so, an aster-ton of stuff has changed for me, so Brack doesn't even feel the same anymore.

Lox programs the car to head toward City Hall. Billboards on every corner flash pictures of Dad, Po, and me, along with a warning that says: *Known terrorists! Robot supporters! If you see these terrorists, please call 5511.*

I shiver and shrink away from the windows. Even though I'm in disguise, and the car's glass is tinted dark, I feel like there's a spotlight trained on me.

The billboard changes and an ad for an improved Verto hoverboard comes on followed by another routine UD warning that says: *Robots are our ENEMIES! If you see a robot, call the hotline!*

"This is totally cracked," Vee breathes as she practically sticks her nose to the window. "Does everyone hate bots?"

"Yes," Ratch says.

LT gives his friend a look and Ratch ignores it. "*Hate* is a strong word," LT answers. "I like to believe they have merely been misled about our kind."

Ratch snorts.

They're both wearing clothes, hats, boots, and gloves after we stopped at a twenty-four-hour department store outside of Brack. LT made it clear he was following us into City Hall. I pointed out that there was no way we'd be able to disguise his robot face, but Lox admitted we had extra poly masks, and that ended that argument.

Ratch didn't say what he planned to do, but he asked for a set of clothing and a mask anyway.

LT elbows me in the side. "Are you all right?"

I tense up. "Yes. Fine. Why?"

"Your heart is racing."

"LT!" I squeak.

"What?"

Thanks for telling everyone, I think. My heart feels like it wants to leap right outta my chest and take off for the Fort, where everything is safe and fine. And as we turn the corner toward City Hall, my stomach drops out like I'm riding the rails.

I collapse against the plush seat and take a deep breath. Sweat gathers beneath my mask. *Don't sweat,* I think, remembering Dek's warning. *Don't sweat. Don't sweat.*

Lox commands the car to pull over to the side of the street. A guy zooms past us on a hoverboard. On the side-

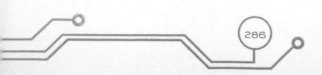

walk, a woman in a business suit sips from a canister of coffee while chatting with someone on her Link.

The sun has barely made it past the tops of the buildings, but the light reflects off the metal and glass, making it hard to look up without sunglasses.

Lox turns around in his seat. "So now what?"

I lick my lips and start digging in my bag. I come up with one of the extra masks and wigs and hand them to LT.

He looks at the two objects like they're alien dog turds. "How does one use these items?"

Vee leans between the front seats to help. "Just put the mask on, lining it up with your eyes and mouth. It'll do the rest."

Sure enough, as soon as it's in place, the thing suctions to LT's face. Next, the wig goes on and when LT turns to me, all my nerves fizzle out and I burst into laughter. So does Lox.

"What is the matter?" LT asks, which makes me laugh harder.

"Your hair is huge!" I say. "You look like a poodle!"

Ratch shakes his head.

"Shut up, you two." Vee thumps Lox on the arm. "We have a mission! Stop acting like a bunch of nutters."

My laughter dies away and I'm serious in an instant. "Okay, so Vee, LT, and I will make our way to City Hall." I swallow back the lump bobbing in my throat, hoping that Ratch doesn't say he wants to come too. He doesn't, so I surge on. "Lox and Ratch, you'll wait a block away, on the other side of the diner."

"Got it," Lox says. "Don't get your face melted off." He twists back around.

"Vee, we should leave our Links in the car." LT was able to trace my Link when he located us in Texas. I don't want to risk the same thing here. We put our Links in the center console.

"Last chance, FishKid," Vee says. "We doing this?"

I look out the window at Brack, at the only place I've ever known. Po and I walked this way every time we came to the Heart Office. Dad used to take me to the little vid shop on the corner across the street. If we had enough money, he'd buy me a new map pack for the vid game *Trane Maze*. But this isn't home anymore. It can't be home if none of my family is safe here.

I want to go back to Bot Territory more than anything, and I want to take Po with me.

"We're doing this," I say, and step out of the vehicle.

THIRTY-FOUR

WE SNEAK AROUND to a side entrance, hoping to bypass the people who might be hanging around out front. As I stick Tellie's temp Net-tag in the ID reader, footsteps shuffle up behind us.

I whirl around. There's a dude with a lumpy nose jumping around on the balls of his feet, shaking out his hands like he's getting ready for a sprint. A taller dude in a trench coat stands behind him.

Adrenaline spikes through my veins.

"What are you doing?" Vee says.

It's Lox and Ratch in disguise. The breath I was holding bursts out in a puff. "Lox! Geez!"

"Sorry. Didn't mean to scare you."

"You're supposed to wait in the car."

He hops around some more. "I parked and we sat there for a long time—"

"And we decided," Ratch fills in, sunglasses hiding his band of orange eyes, "that perhaps it would be best if

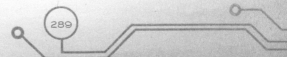

we stuck together. You might need a distraction, which I would be more than willing to provide."

"Only if it is needed," LT adds. "You must assure me you will not deliberately make a scene."

Ratch tilts his head. "You have my word."

The ID reader beeps and I pull out the Net-tag. The lock clicks and the door rushes open. Now or never.

We enter into a long hallway and directly in front of us are narrow stairs hidden behind a curve in the wall. We go there, hurrying across the hall before anyone has the chance to get a good look at us.

Even though I've changed a jet ton since I was last here, the building still smells the same. Like leather shoes and lemons. It still feels the same too, like there are cameras watching our every move.

I'm not sure if that's true here, in the stairwell. I look at the corners up near the ceiling and find them empty. That doesn't mean anything, though. Cameras could be embedded in the wall and I'd never see them.

I'm the first to make it to the second floor, where another ID reader waits for us next to a thick steel door. I push the fake blond hair out of my eyes so I can see better.

Please let this work.

The others group behind me. I can hear their breath,

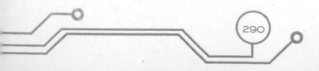

the whir of LT's and Ratch's internal mechanisms. I readjust the backpack on my shoulder, where all our gear is stored, and stick the Net-tag in the little black slot.

My teeth grit. My muscles tighten. I'm ready to run if an alarm goes off.

But the red light blinks to green, the door unlocks, and we're in.

We enter single-file into another hallway. It splits off from here, like an L.

"Which way?" I whisper.

LT says, "Po is still being held on the fourth floor."

"Do we go straight, or right?"

"Straight."

We nearly run down the hall. LT guides us, telling us when to turn. We pass a supply closet, a line of offices, and a closed cafeteria. We turn the last corner and I see the next ID reader, the next locked door.

But then it's opening and someone is stepping out and we're going to be caught.

I stop. Lox slams into me. Vee slams into Lox.

We need a place to hide.

There's a watercooler right behind me. I go there and fill a paper cup with water. The others follow my lead, grouping around like we're all so choppin' thirsty.

The cup trembles in my hand. The water sloshes

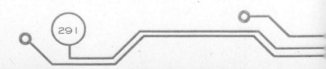

around inside. I squeeze my eyes shut as the person passes us, carrying on a conversation with someone on his Link.

The door glides closed and I rush forward, sticking a foot in the way, catching it at the last second.

Lox crushes his empty cup in his hand and tosses it in the garbage. "We are like ninjas, bolt sniffer!"

"Shhh!" I say as he pushes past me into the next stairwell.

"If he gets us arrested," Vee says once we're on the other side of the checkpoint, "I'll kill him."

Lox turns just enough to grin. "Is that code for 'kissing'?"

Vee grits her teeth.

"I think she likes me." Lox nudges me with an elbow. "Huh? Huh? She likes me."

I ignore him and hurry after Vee. We're so close, I can taste it.

We come to the next ID checkpoint and I slip the Nettag inside. The light doesn't turn green. The reader makes an *annnnt* sound and I know right away what that means. We don't have clearance for this floor.

"What now?" Vee says. "Should we—"

She goes zip-quiet when voices reach us from the next hall over. And not just any voice. Beard Hopper's voice.

"Chop!" Lox squeals. "Go! Go!"

We backtrack, scrambling for a second like we're a bunch of bumper cars. I turn about three circles before I know which way I'm going.

"This way, come," LT says, and leads us to a janitor's closet.

We cram inside, pushing the brooms and vacuums and dusters out of our faces. It's dark and stuffy and hot in an instant. Only a sliver of light glows from the crack beneath the door. Vee moves to get comfortable and jabs me in the ribs. I bite back a cry.

The footsteps in the hallway get closer. The voices are clearer than they were a second ago. I can hear everything Beard says even over the ramming of my heart against my rib cage.

"I'm not interested in your opinion," Beard argues. Her high heels clip-clop over the floor. "These people are not innocent if they support trafficking between the UD and Bot Territory. They must be taught a lesson."

"We have to think about the consequences of our actions," a man says. That's Mr. Rix! "And the thousands of lives we harm by attacking."

Next to me, Ratch goes rigidly still. His eye band brightens.

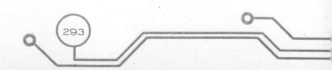

Is Beard talking about the attack on Old New York?

Their voices fade away. I want to know more. I *need* to know more.

For a second, I think about chasing after them, slinking along the hallway, but I'd be caught for sure.

And then it hits me. The worm device! The little worm Dekker gave me can lock on to people. I drop my bag to the floor, pushing away a mop bucket to make room. I fetch the worm and move to open the door, when Vee grabs my wrist.

"What are you doing?" she says.

"That information could be important," I whisper. She holds on for another millisecond and then nods. I crack open the door. With the worm device in hand, I point it at Beard. A laser light appears on her navy blue skirt suit. I press the button twice. The legs appear. I crouch and set it on the floor. It instantly camouflages itself and I lose sight of it.

I slip back inside the closet. "I think it worked."

"So now what?" Vee says.

"We don't need a Net-tag to gain access to the fourth floor," Ratch says. "LT and I are strong enough to arm our way through the doors."

"No," LT says. "There would not be enough time to

reach Po before we would alert the guards to our presence. That would put the kids at risk."

"Then what do you suggest?" Ratch says. "Ask someone nicely if we can borrow their Net-tag? I'm sure that will go over well. Perhaps we can ask Sandra Hopper."

LT's expression tightens into pure robot annoyance. He starts to say something, but I cut him off.

"No, wait, Ratch has a point." Ratch looks down at me. "The only way we're getting to the next level is with a Net-tag. At least if we make it to the third floor, we're one step closer to Po. If we have to smash through a door once we're there, well, then, I guess we have to smash through a door. We might be able to make it at that point. Don't you think, LT?"

He sighs. "It would still be risky—"

"But not impossible?"

"No."

"Then it's settled."

Vee says, "So how are we getting to the third floor?"

"Leave that to me," I say, and dart out of the closet before anyone can stop me.

THIRTY-FIVE

HE ONLY THING running through my head as I hurry down the hallway is chop chop chop chop what am I doing I am so jet smoked.

I take the same turns we made to get to the third-floor checkpoint and then burst from the stairwell onto the main floor. My shoes squeak on the freshly polished marble as I cross through the lobby, trying real hard not to look at the two guards stationed at the main, grand staircase or the slick glasses covering their eyes.

And because I'm trying to act normal, I thump the shoulder of the statue of President Callo as I pass him on my way to the Heart Office.

Wish me luck, Callo.

When I round into the office, I stop for a second to catch my breath. Tanith looks up. "Good morning. How can I help you?"

I swallow. Breathe deep. "Umm . . . I ah . . ."

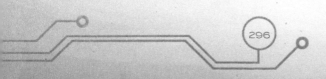

She rises from her chair. Her dark wavy hair is pulled back in a ponytail and it swings behind her. "Yes?"

The fact that she doesn't recognize me says how good my mask is. "Do you have a tabpad?"

She frowns, but nods and slides a tabpad onto the counter. I pull its pen from the holder on the side and write *I'm Trout St. Kroix.* I slide it around so she can see.

When she reads my sloppy handwriting on the screen, she looks up, eyes wide, lips parted like she wants to say something but doesn't know what.

Please don't gear out, I think.

She clears the pad's screen and leans closer, her ponytail curling around her neck. "What are you doing here?"

"Please help me," I whisper. "I need your Net-tag. Please."

Her eyes pinch at the corners. She knows what I mean to do with the tag without explaining.

"I don't have access that high."

My shoulders sink. I should have known. She's just a clerk. Not a high-level congressman.

We are jammed.

I purse my lips, give her one quick nod, and turn to the door. Po isn't getting out of here. And my dad is going to turn himself in. I couldn't save them.

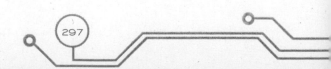

"Wait," Tanith calls. I stop in the doorway. "I'll be right back."

She disappears down a hallway to her left. "Mrs. Dawson?" she says to someone I can't see. "Can I borrow your Net-tag for a minute? I went into the supply closet for some bar codes and left my tag in there."

A woman chuckles. "It's embarrassing how often I lock my tag in weird, inconspicuous places. Here."

"Thanks." Tanith rounds the corner out of the hallway and gestures to me to follow her. We leave the Heart Office. I follow her down the hall and into an empty conference room. "No cameras in here," she says, then thrusts the borrowed Net-tag into my hands.

The picture on the card is of an older woman with poofy gray hair and thin, bright red lips. *Edith Dawson,* I read. She must be some higher-up employee. "Mrs. Dawson will know the tag is missing when you come back without it," I say.

Tanith shakes her head. "I'll give her my tag for now, just so she thinks I returned it. She's not very observant. She'll never know. At least, not until you're long gone."

"But . . ." I look down at the tag, at the one thing that'll get me to my brother, and I can't help but think about what'll happen to Tanith if I use it. "I don't want you to get in trouble."

"I don't want you to lose your brother," she counters. She hunches over so we're staring each other straight in the face. Her breath smells like sweet tea. "Sometimes, the right thing looks an awful lot like the wrong thing. And in this case, I *know* it's right. I don't care what comes because of it. Let me deal with the consequences."

My lower lip trembles in a dumb, happy way. I bite it. "Thank you," I finally say. "You have no idea how much this means to me."

She winks. "I think I can guess."

I start for the door. "Oh, Trout?" she says, and I pause. "Yeah?"

"*Rise from the heap.*"

My mouth drops open. Tanith smiles and waves me on. "Now go save your brother."

Somehow I manage to cross the lobby without barfing or totally gearing out. I make it up the stairwell, through the second-floor checkpoint, down one, two, then three hallways. Sweat collects at the back of my neck and my skin itches beneath the mask. I scrunch up my nose. The mask sags around my eyes.

No. No. No. Don't fall off.

I'm almost there.

I cut around the next corner.

And that's when I run into Beard.

Seriously run into her.

I bounce back with an umph. "Excuse me," she hisses.

"Umm . . . s-s-sorry."

She tugs on the hem of her suit coat to straighten it. "Watch where you're going. Are you—" She draws back, her thin eyebrows sinking in a frown. "You're just a child. What are you doing on the second floor?"

Sweat pools beneath my nose. The mask droops from my chin.

"I'm . . . ah . . . looking for my dad. He works here. I got something really important to tell him. About my . . . um . . . mom. She's sick and I can't get him on his Link and so I thought I'd come looking for him. He's probably busy and that's why he's not answering. I mean, of course he's busy. He works in City Hall!" I trail off with a short laugh.

Beard narrows her eyes. "Who's your father?"

Oh jam.

I make something up. "Steve Monnnnkerrrrly?"

"Steve Monkerly," Beard repeats.

"Yeah. That's him."

My skin is as slick as butter and the mask peels away from my forehead. I have to get out of here fast.

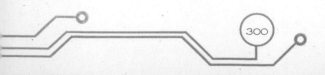

"His office is right down there." I point over Beard's shoulder. "I'll just go see if he's—"

"No." Beard grabs hold of my shirt and yanks me in the opposite direction. "You can wait in the lobby and we'll have him paged."

"But he's right down there. It's no big deal!"

"Unauthorized visitors are not allowed on the second floor. How you managed to make it up here is beyond me. Perhaps I need to have a conversation with the guards—"

It's now or never, Trout!

I duck down, hunching my shoulders, and twist as I stagger back. Beard tightens her grip, so I twist again and shimmy away, right out of my T-shirt.

Beard stands there, frozen, looking from me to my shirt clutched in her hand, then back at me. My mask pulls away from my cheeks, then my eyes, then droops off my forehead like a soggy pancake.

"What in the—" Beard says.

"Chop," I breathe.

"Guards!" she shouts.

I barrel down the hallway, cut left down another. "LT!" I scream. "LT!" I don't know where I'm going. I don't know which door they're hiding behind.

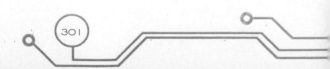

I take another corner. LT and Ratch race toward me. "Beard!" I shout. "She's coming!"

Her heels clop behind me. I skid past the robots as they remove their masks and clothes. LT doesn't question the reason why I'm shirtless, but he tosses me his anyway.

"Good God," Beard says when she sees what LT and Ratch are beneath their disguises.

LT doesn't take his eyes off Beard as he says, "Trout, run."

So I do.

THIRTY-SIX

OX AND VEE meet me in the hallway. My backpack is slung over Vee's shoulder.

"Where are the bots?" Vee asks as I race past. "What happened?"

"Beard happened."

We pile up at the next checkpoint. I insert the tag into the reader. The light slides to green and the lock clicks open. We take the stairs past the third floor, and up to the fourth. Without LT to guide us, we have no idea where we're going, but I figure Po's probably being guarded, so I keep my eyes open for anyone positioned outside a door like a sentinel.

It doesn't take long to find the room.

At the end of the hallway, two guards stand outside a door, their arms clasped behind their back, guns holstered at their sides.

I have no idea how to get through them. I have no

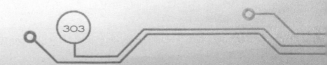

plan at all. I'm just running because I'm easily twenty feet away from my brother and I just want to see him.

It's Vee who saves us.

"Robots!" she screams. "There are robots on the second floor! Run! Run!"

The guards turn to each other, their hands poised over their weapons. "How did you kids get up here?" the woman on the left asks.

"The bots took out all the checkpoints, so we ran," Vee says.

"My dad works up here," I add. "We're looking for him."

The PA system crackles to life. "Code twelve-forty. I repeat, Code twelve-forty. All guards on alert. Seal all exits."

The woman's mouth drops open. Her partner, a short, thin man pulls out his gun. They take off at a jog, the gear on their belts clanking and clattering together.

We're finally alone.

I stand on the tips of my feet and peek in the square window set in the door the guards had flanked. Po is inside, pacing. When he comes back around and notices me, he freezes and gives me a weird look.

The disguise. I forgot about the disguise. I rip off the wig and mask. "It's me!" I say. "Trout. Your brother!"

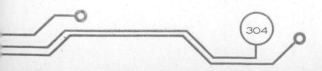

"Trout?" he mutters with a frown.

I fumble with Mrs. Dawson's Net-tag, jamming it in the slot. The door unlocks and I whip it back. My stomach goes squirrelly as I rush inside, wrap my arms around Po, and squeeze him tight. He smells like fried beans and sweat, but I don't care.

When I pull away and get a better look at him, I try not to dwell on the bruises that pepper his arms and the new cut that runs across his forehead.

"What the chop are you doing here?" he asks.

"I'm rescuing you, duh."

Lox and Vee group behind me.

"We gotta go," Vee says. "Like *now*."

LT shoots into the room. "They are holding off on the third floor."

"Holy jet smoke," Po says. You brought a robot into City Hall?"

"There is no time," LT starts, and turns toward the door as Ratch appears. "Are they moving in?"

Ratch says nothing. He reaches for the door handle and swings it shut with a clang.

"What's he doing?" Lox says.

"Why did he shut us in?" Vee asks, panicking.

LT goes rigid. I rush to the door and bang on it with my fists. "Let us out, Ratch! Beard is coming!"

His band of orange eyes stare at me through the window before turning to LT. "I'm sorry," he says. "But this is not what I envisioned for us when we saved Robert St. Kroix. I can't allow a human to run my territory."

"Ratch." LT's voice is low and throaty. I've never heard him sound like that. "Let us out. We can discuss this when all are safe."

Ratch shakes his head. "I can't do that. The bots need to take back what is rightfully theirs. And you've done nothing but become their slave. *Again*. Isn't this what we've been fighting for? Freedom? From man?"

"Ratch, please," I say. "Please let us out."

He doesn't even look at me. "Farewell, brother," he says. "You will be greatly missed." And then he jets away.

I bang on the door. I beat at it till my hands hurt, but it's no use. He's long gone, and there's no one there to let us out.

I slump against the wall and put my face in my hands. My skin is still sweaty and sticky from the mask. We're not getting out. That fact sinks in till I feel it burned into my bones.

"I should have seen this coming," LT says, his voice quiet now.

Maybe this is why Ratch helped Vee and me escape

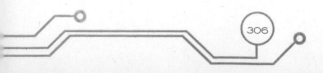

from Scissor's shop. He was setting us up the whole time, letting us sneak into City Hall, hoping we'd be caught. Well, he didn't have to hope too hard. All he had to do was shut the door on Po's cell.

"I take it that wasn't part of the plan?" Po says.

"No." Vee snorts. "We're cracked."

Lox drops onto the bed shoved up against the wall and sets his elbows on his knees. "It's been nice knowing all of you."

How long before Beard brings more guards? Does she know we're locked in here yet? Are there cameras? Sensors?

"We have to get out of this room," I say, and everyone looks at me.

"Well, duh," Vee says. "Except, how are we going to do that?"

Something Ratch said to LT about getting inside City Hall comes back to me. *Show the UD that their security and their brick buildings are no match for us.*

"LT, can you break through a brick wall?" I ask.

A light in his neck blinks. "Yes. Why?"

I nod at the exterior wall where a thick window looks down on the street four stories below. "Can you break through that?"

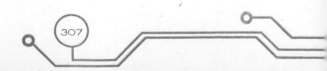

"What, and jump?" Po says.

"That was the plan anyway," I reply. "We were going to jump off the roof."

Po's face scrunches into disbelief. "To our deaths?"

I ignore him and take my backpack from Vee. "So, can you break through it?"

LT goes to the wall and plants the palms of his hands against it. "Twelve inches thick. Reinforced with re-bar. Weakening around the window casing. Water damage." He turns to us. "Yes," he finally says. "I can break through. It will take approximately six minutes, however, and I am uncertain of how long we will have before Beard arrives with her guards."

"Hopefully enough time. Start smashing through?"

"Cover yourself." He pushes us toward the door, then lifts the bed off the floor and props it on its side so we have a makeshift wall to hide behind. "There will be debris," he explains.

We crouch, and as I empty out my bag, LT takes the first hit. The floor vibrates. Something cracks. He hits again and pebbles of brick fly through the air.

I give Po the scrambler I got for him and he slips it over his head. Then I pull out the hoversuits and hand one to Vee, Po, and save one for myself . . .

I look up at Lox, and stop dead. "We don't have a

hoversuit for you." I suck in a breath and rise to my feet. "We don't have a hoversuit for you because you were supposed to wait in the car!"

Po wrenches me back down and I narrowly miss getting pelted with a chunk of brick.

Lox makes a face. "Ehhhh. Sorry?"

"Sorry!" I grab him by the arms and shake. "How are we going to get you down without a hoversuit?"

"I don't know! How was LT going to get down? He doesn't have a suit."

"Robots don't need hoversuits. They can jump that far. Darn it, Lox. You should have stayed in the stupid car!"

Po breaks us apart. "Calm down."

"Plan B," Vee says. "It's no big deal. He can ride down with me."

"What?" Lox and I say at the same time.

"Just don't let go," Vee adds with a smirk.

"Will that even work?" I ask.

"No. No." Lox shakes his head and scuttles away. "Even I think that sounds like a bad idea. And I'm not afraid of anything! Well, except for seagulls. They're always cawing and pecking and staring at you with those beady—"

"Lox!" I shout. "How else are you going to get down?"

Vee slides on a foot plate. "I promise I'll get us to the street safely. It's not even that far."

Something slams into the door behind us and we all jump. LT punches his arm through the wall and bricks explode in all directions. People shout from the hallway. I think I hear Beard, but I can't be sure.

"We don't have any other options," I say.

Lox sighs. "Okay, fine! But if I end up splattered like a bug on a windshield . . ."

Vee tightens a strap around her elbow. "You won't. I've been riding these things forever."

"Speaking of those *'things,'*" Po says, "what are they?"

I give him the short version and he watches me suit up. LT takes two final punches and the wall opens into a gaping hole. Morning sunlight pours in, blinding me.

"Someone open this door!" Beard yells from the hall.

LT tosses the bed aside. "Move," he orders, so I do. He puts his back against the door just as the reader on the other side beeps and the lock pops. LT digs in with his feet as the door is shoved open and the floor tile spiderwebs beneath him.

"Go!" he shouts.

"Mr. St. Kroix . . ." Beard calls through the door. "If you want your family to stay alive, I suggest you turn yourself in."

We hurry to the broken wall and look down. It seems so far away. The glowing rails give us a lit landing pad,

but this hasn't been tested, so who knows if it works.

"So we just jump?" Po asks, raising his eyebrows, and I give him a nod.

"Should probably get a running start," Vee says. "We can't jump straight down or we'll hit the sidewalk. We have to make it within the force field." To Lox she says, "Hold on tight. It's a good thing you're skinny."

"I'm lean. Lean!"

Lox looks ill as he climbs on Vee's back. I feel sick too. I got Lox into this. I got us all into this.

"Here goes." Vee takes off running. She doesn't get a lot of speed, what with carrying Lox, but I cringe and pray it's enough.

When she leaps through the hole, I rush to the ledge to watch. She spreads out her arms and legs like she's a flying squirrel leaping from tree to tree. Lox screams all the way down. The rails catch them, and Vee finishes like she's a ballerina.

I huff with relief. "Thank the universe."

Behind us, the door starts to give way. LT holds on tight. "Are you coming?" I say to him.

"I will come down soon."

"LT," I start, but he shakes his head.

"You must go. Now. I will be safe."

"Are you sure?"

The door cracks. LT's eyes narrow. "I am sure."

Po and I back up. Wind rushes into the room, ruffling my hair. "I can't believe I'm doing this," Po says.

"Are you gearing out? This isn't a time to gear out!"

"I'm not!" He wipes his hands on his pants. "All right. Go!"

We sprint toward the edge and jump.

"Ohhhh chooooop," Po howls.

I scream too as the wind blasts me in the face, making it hard to breathe. The building across the street whips past, floor after floor. I spread my arms out, put my head down, like a hunting falcon instead of a trout floundering in the water.

When the hover rails catch us, I crash against the force field, skitter down the street, twisting and flailing. Po lands in a crouch, like he's done this a million times. Vee skates over and helps me to my feet.

"Come on!"

I look up. "We have to wait for LT!"

Where is he? When is he coming down? He couldn't have held on much longer.

And then Beard and her guards appear at the opening in the wall, guns pointed at us. The coiled barrels turn fire orange as we're sighted in.

Vee yanks me away. The first gunshot blasts right over

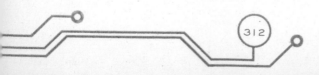

me, incinerating a mailbox to nothing but dust. It's the first time I realize Beard doesn't care whether we live or die. Seeing that pile of ash, feeling the leftover heat of the trail of the shot slams me into action.

We turn left toward where the car is parked and see a patrol car zooming our way, red and blue lights bouncing off the glass and metal surrounding us. We backtrack, head straight down another street, then another. Sirens wail in all directions.

"Get off the rails!" Po shouts over a shoulder. "We need cover."

At the next intersection, we hop over the rails and start running. Po arms his way through a door and we burst inside the darkened interior.

"Where are we?" Vee's voice wobbles in the darkness once Po slams the door shut.

"I think it's an old parking garage," Po says.

I can just make out the shape of a thick support column in front of me. Our voices echo around us.

"How did you guys plan to get out of the city?" Po asks. I tell him about Lox's car and where we left it. "Okay, so, we're two blocks away." Po's foot plates scuffle along the concrete as he paces. "If we can find another exit on the other side of this garage, maybe . . . maybe we have a shot of making it."

He jogs away and we stumble after him. He finds another door and cracks it open. "We're in an alley," he whispers. "When I say go, you go. Got it?"

We nod.

Sirens blare in the distance.

"Go," Po says. We file out. Run down the alley. Po holds out a hand when we reach the end. He peeks around the edge, then waves us on. We cross a service street behind a bunch of shops, slip into another alley. We're midway when a patrol car pulls up at the mouth of the alley behind us.

Vee grabs me by the wrist and yanks me down beside a Dumpster. Po and Lox use a tower of empty wooden crates as cover.

"You check down there," a patrolman says when he gets out of the car. "I'll take the alley."

"You got it," his partner calls.

Footsteps crunch closer. I squeeze my eyes shut. Vee trembles beside me. We're only one block away from the car. Can we make it if we start running now? Will they chase us out of the city and all the way to Texas?

I hold my breath.

I'm a sliver away from running when a radio expels a burst of static. "Reported sighting on east Fifty-fifth Street near Kritcher Law Offices," an operator says.

"Copy that. Unit seventy-eight headed there now," the man says, and jogs away.

I blow out the breath I'd been holding. Vee slumps against the Dumpster. "That was close," she whispers.

When we're sure it's clear, we scurry from our hiding spots to the opposite end of the alley. I can just make out the front end of Lox's car up the street. There are no patrolmen in sight.

"On three," Po says. "One. Two. Three."

We burst from the alley at a sprint. A man jumps out of our way, a shopping bag banging against his hip. "Watch it!" he calls.

Lox is the first one to the car. He presses his finger to the print reader on the driver's-side door. The lock clicks and Lox whips the door open. "Let me drive," Po says. Lox climbs through to the passenger side. Vee and I slide into the backseat.

Po hits the car's tinted glass button and the windows darken. The engine whirs to life and Po pulls out of the parking spot slow and easy. We stop at the next intersection for a red light. People zoom past on hoverboards. A couple walks through the crosswalk, two kids running ahead of them. We don't say a word as we wait.

When the light changes, Po steps on the gas and takes us toward the Geissa Section. We pass one patrol car, but the lights aren't on, and the two officers inside don't give us a second glance.

We make it outside Brack. Po taps on the radio and tunes in the news feed.

A journalist appears on the screen in the dash. "Breaking news. We have word two robots just attempted to break into City Hall and rescue the recently apprehended robot supporter Mason St. Kroix, son of suspected terrorist Robert St. Kroix. Officials have yet to comment on the situation, but from what we've been able to gather, Mason St. Kroix has, in fact, escaped. It's safe to assume he is armed and dangerous, possibly aided by additional robots . . ."

Po flicks the news off. No one says anything.

We make it to the freeway and Po points us toward Texas. I want to celebrate—we're safe and intact and I got my brother back—but a heaviness hits me square in the chest when I remember what Ratch did, when I remember that LT is gone, for good. He sacrificed himself for us. Now he's in Beard's hands and there's nothing I can do about it.

THIRTY-SEVEN

WE MAKE IT to Dekker's a few hours later and he looks like he's been through a hurricane. His rainbow hair is sticking straight up. There are empty energy drink cans in a row beneath his desk that weren't there when we left and there's a smear of something on his chin, like jelly or ink.

Lox collapses into a chair. "I thought we were notched."

"That was awfully close," Dekker says.

I lean over the back of the couch. "If the patrolman hadn't gotten that call at the last second—"

Dekker smirks. "You're welcome for that."

We all look at him. "You did that?" I ask. "How did you—"

"The worm device, remember? The one I put on Lox? I was watching the live feed. When I realized there was a cop on you, I hacked into the communication system at a local grocery store, so when I called in with a fake report it looked like I was calling locally. Makes it more believable, you see."

Vee folds herself into the corner of the couch and I sit down next to her. "That's so split," she says.

Po introduces himself to Dekker and they shake hands. "Thank you, dude. You have no idea."

Dekker tries to look cool. "It was no big deal." But secretly I think he's soaking it up.

"What's the news feed saying about the rescue now?" Po asks.

Dekker's expression immediately switches from proud and happy to sad.

He turns back to his computer. "See for yourself."

He cues up the news feed. A woman's voice plays over a vid of City Hall, where patrol cars surround the scene. "Known robot supporters broke into City Hall this morning to collect one of their own. Five parties escaped, but what they left behind tells a greater story."

The vid cuts to Beard. "We have reason to believe a robot extremist group known as the Meta-Rise plotted a terrorist bombing on City Hall. They left behind a robot with an internal detonate program coded into his operating system." The vid flicks to an image of LT strapped to a vertical table, his insides totally gutted.

My throat catches. I grit my teeth. "She's lying. There was no detonating program!"

"Thankfully," Beard says, "we were able to dismantle the robot before it carried out its objective, but there may be more attacks. We must be vigilant in reporting any bot sightings. If anything seems suspicious, please call the emergency hotline."

No one says anything for a long time.

Po is the first to speak. "You shouldn't have come for me."

I rise to my feet. "Dad was going to turn himself in! I bet all my creds you would have done the same thing."

"Did Dad know what you were doing?"

I shuffle my weight around. "Well, not exactly."

Vee levels her shoulders. "We did this on our own."

Dekker steps in the middle of everyone. "So what is your plan now? You know they're going to watch the borders back into Bot Territory."

I run my teeth over my bottom lip as I think. "We sicced the worm device on Beard. If we listen in, figure out their strategy, maybe it'll help us figure out ours."

Dekker sits in front of his computer. "I'm bringing up the worm feed right now." His fingers thump over the keyboard. "Okay. Here we go."

We gather around as Beard appears on screen. "We, the government, have an obligation to our people." She's in a big office with three tall windows behind her. She paces back and forth, hands clasped in front of her. "If they were willing to break into a government building to retrieve a boy, imagine what else they're capable of with the motive and the right resources."

She pauses and turns toward the windows. "We've always been a nation that stood up for what was right, and did whatever needed to be done to protect our freedom. If we allow robots to continue on as they are, turning humans into half machines, building more robots, better robots, I fear what our future will look like.

"We must keep our promise to our people and keep them safe at all costs. Sometimes that means sacrificing others to get from point A to point B."

She twists around, her hands clenched into fists. "And those little *weasels* broke into my building!"

"Congresswoman," someone says outside the range of the camera, "we got a lock on them near the Texan border."

There's a pause, then Beard says, "Let them go. They'll be dead soon, regardless. The attack on Edge Flats, Texas, will commence at three p.m. today as we've planned. Let's

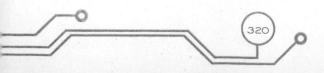

hope Robert St. Kroix and his team are there when it happens. Strike first at the police station and then spread the attack outward. When the news broadcast hits, make sure you place the blame on St. Kroix, his brats, and the Meta-Rise."

Footsteps shuffle out. A door shuts and Beard drops into her desk chair.

Dekker pauses the feed.

I glance around our group, hoping that someone heard something differently. But they all look as geared out as I feel.

The attack that I thought was planned for Old New York is meant for us.

"They planned this all along," I say, as everything comes together in my mind like the gears in a machine. "They told Dad to be in Edge Flats at three p.m. today. Instead, they're going to attack the city, starting with the police station where Dad was supposed to turn himself in." I take a deep breath. I feel like I might barf. "If they place the blame on the Meta-Rise, they'll finally get District approval to start up the war and get rid of robots and their ThinkChips once and for all."

"Waitwaitwait," Lox says, holding up a hand. "Three o'clock, but that's like . . ." He looks at the clock.

The color of Dekker's face almost matches the green stripe in his hair. "We've got less than thirty minutes before the first attack."

Po snaps his fingers. "Who has a Link? We have to call Dad. Make sure he isn't en route to the police station."

"I have one," I say, "but I don't know Dad's number. I've never had to call him."

Dekker throws me his Link. "Your dad is number twenty-four on speed dial."

I hit twenty-four and the Link beeps. A message blinks on the screen: *Unable to connect.*

I toss the Link to Vee. "Call your dad. He'll be with mine."

Vee punches in her dad's number and shakes her head when no one picks up. "If they're in the tunnels, it'll be hard to reach them. Reception is spotty down there."

I look at the clock. Twenty-five minutes before the attack.

"Come on, you guys." I scratch the back of my head as I think. "We've got evidence that Beard is planning an attack on innocent people. That's valuable! What if we—"

"Broadcast it." Po grabs a soft foam ball from Dekker's desk and squeezes it as he talks. "Like you did, Trout,

with your vid. We broadcast the stream. Get the people out of the city. And, we show the nation the UD has gone nuclear."

"I like that." Dekker points a finger at my brother before swiveling back to the computer. "All I have to do is isolate the feed, upload it to my site, and . . ." He trails off, stares at his screen, then taps the ENTER key over and over again. "Jam it!"

I lean over his shoulder. He smells like peanut butter and jelly and mint. "What is it?"

"They notched my signal!" He growls at the screen. "I'm the Net star with the big mouth and they're making sure I don't open it. If only they knew what kind of dirt I have on them." He types in a few commands.

"How long will it take to fix?" Po asks.

"I'm going to reroute to a local feed here in Texas. That'll give us something to start with. At least it'll help get the people of Edge Flats outta . . ." He throws his arms up, curls his hands into fists. "They've taken out all the local feeds. They're isolating us. I got nothing to jack into."

Vee cracks her knuckles. "That's why we can't get our dads on the Link. *All* the signals are out."

Lox shakes his head, unblinking. "We're notched. Totally, completely notched."

We're down eight minutes.

I try to ignore Lox's Doom and Gloom. "Do we have a plan B?"

Dekker taps away at the board. "Go big or go home, right? I'll hack into a UD feed, something low level, something they won't expect. From there, I'll set up a dummy sig point, bounce it off a shellbox, and run it through the UD's news feed. That sig can reach anywhere, even here."

I snort. "I have no idea what you just said."

"Basically what it means is that I have a lot of work ahead of me, but when I'm done, if I can do it before three o'clock, I'll broadcast Beard's confession to the entire continent and then some."

Vee ties her hair back with a rubber band from her wrist. "What can we do to help?"

"One-man job, unfortunately."

"We need to get to the police station," Po says. "See if we can intercept Dad. And maybe the police will have another way of getting a message out to the city."

"There might not be enough time," I say.

"How far are we from the police station?" Po asks Dekker.

"Ten-minute run."

"We need to start warning people in the area," Vee says. "If they can take cover, maybe they'll stand a chance."

I wish LT were here. I had no idea how much I liked having him by my side when things went south. And I left him behind for Beard and her guards, left him to be junked.

"All right," I say, "so how are we going to get people to believe us?"

It takes Dekker two minutes to manually upload Beard's confession on a few old Links.

"Play that for them," he says, "and they'll have to believe you."

We're down twelve minutes when we file toward the door. Vee has to shake Lox out of his stupor, but he finally gets moving.

At the top of the stairs, I pause. "Hey, Dekker. Keep trying my dad?"

He waves over his shoulder. "You got it, little dude."

THIRTY-EIGHT

A S SOON AS people see Beard and hear her say the UD is gonna start bombing Edge Flats in a matter of minutes, they take notice. It doesn't hurt that no one can call out on their Links. That makes them gear out for real.

Vee and Po go one way, to the right. Lox and I go left. We shout from the streets, knock on doors, run into shops blasting the warning. It takes people a second to register what we're saying, and then once it sinks in, they just stare at us, like their brains have gone on freeze mode.

"Come on, people!" Lox claps his hands in the produce aisle at a food market. "Get somewhere safe!"

People start bouncing off each other, they're in such a rush to evacuate. Lox and I pour from the store and Lox cuts left. I start after him, but something catches my eye. I look up. Hundreds of flutter-flies descend from the sky.

"Lox!" I call, and point to the cloud of metal wings glinting in the sunlight.

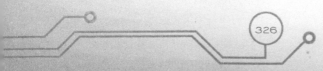

People stop running on the sidewalks to watch. Flutter-flies on their own aren't weird, but seeing hundreds of them is. The first one lands on the edge of a rooftop across the street. The wings rise and fall and rise again. We are transfixed by the sight.

And then suddenly it explodes.

I shield my face with an arm. Bits of stone pelt me in the back. I scramble for an alcove and hunker down. Lox crouches beside me. Another blast. People scream. The air thickens with debris. A huge chunk of brick slams into the hover rails and the blue glow crackles and dies.

Another explosion. And another. I put my hand over my mouth as the smokiness of the debris fills my lungs. Blasts start going off everywhere, which means the attack is happening. NOW. No way is it three o'clock yet. They're attacking early.

What if a flutter-fly bomb takes out Dekker's place?

Lox and I get the same idea without saying a word to each other. We backtrack toward Dekker's, steering clear of anything that flies. As the rails die out everywhere, cars hovering at the curb and in the street crash to the ground in a ruckus of smashing glass and twisting metal.

We dodge a falling billboard, the screen snapping and sizzling as it lands in a heap on the corner. I read the street sign—we're on the corner of Tannamont and Thirty-fifth

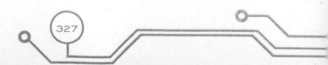

Street. I have no idea where that is. And no idea how to get back to Dekker's. I tap at my Link, but it's no use. Only its operating system is up. It's no longer connected to the Net, so I've got no way of loading its nav system.

"We lost?" Lox asks, his shoulders heaving up and down, he's breathing so heavy. Dust rains from the sky.

I put my hands on my knees and bend over. Another explosion makes me jump. Suddenly everything looks like fluttering butterfly wings.

"I think so."

Lox lunges in front of a woman running down the street. "Ma'am, please help me! I'm lost and I need to get home! Which way is the old Fort Worth fire station?"

The woman keeps running, but calls out, "Go straight, take a right, then a left. I hope you get there safely!"

"Thank you!"

I straighten. "Dude, you're a genius," I say right before an explosion rocks the city. Lox and I hunch our shoulders, even though it's a good three blocks away.

"That sounded close to Dekker's place," Lox says.

I start running. "We gotta hurry!"

The first thing I see when the fire station comes into view is the gaping hole in the side of the red brick building. A sinking feeling fills me head to toe, like I'm drowning in quicksand. The security system is out when I reach

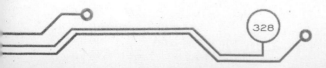

the side door. I barrel up the stairs and find Dekker in the living room, the lights flickering on and off. He's still tapping away at his computer, sweat pouring down his forehead. His rainbow-striped hair is covered in dust.

"I'm almost there!" he shouts.

"Have you heard from my dad?"

He shakes his head.

"We gotta go." I tug on his arm, but he pulls out of my grasp.

"I'm not leaving. The UD isn't getting away with this. I almost got a line into the news feed, but my signal keeps shutting down. I think my Kaster was taken out in that blast."

"Yeah, and they're blasting the rest of the city!" I shout as another one goes off.

Dekker pauses long enough to look at me. "The UD took your brother. They want to kill your father. They gutted LT. We can't let them get away with this, Trout. You think these small bombs are the worst of it? No way. This is just the preliminary attack. If they want your dad dead, they're going to send something bigger to take care of that job."

Please don't say that, I think, but Dekker is right. Maybe this is the warning attack, to get innocent people out of harm's way. The big bomb is probably lying in wait, its

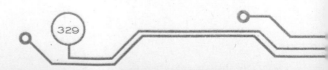

target the police station. If Dad was on time, he's probably already in the city.

Another blast rocks the ground. The lights wink out and flicker back on.

"What can we do to help?" I ask.

"Fix the Kaster," Dekker shouts.

I look at Lox like, *What's a Kaster?*

"Satellite," he answers. "Sends out the signal."

"Where's it at?"

"On the roof," Dekker says.

"Can we fix it?"

"I'm good with that kinda stuff," Lox says. "And Kasters are made outta meta-pol."

"We just need a UV light."

"And duct tape," Dekker adds, his back still to us. "Electrical gauze too. First cabinet down in the workshop."

Lox and I gather what we need and speed up the stairs. But when we reach the flight up to the third floor, we come to the gaping hole in the side of the building, the one I saw from the street. The bomb not only took out the wall, it took out the stairs too. The wood hangs twisted and smoldering. I can see clear down to the second floor, to one of the bedrooms.

The next landing is too far away to jump. And there's no other way to the roof.

"Now what?" Lox says.

I scan the hole in the wall, the hole in the floor, anything jutting out that I could use for a handhold. There isn't much. And I'd risk major slivers if I tried.

"I think I can climb up outside." I know exactly where I'll start.

"Okay, well, that's great, except what about me? I'm not a tree frog. I can't scale buildings."

Frog. The frog whipper!

I back down the stairs. "You gotta find Vee. She has this thing . . . it'll help you climb. I'll go up now and get started. It'll save us some time."

I stick the UV light in my pocket. The duct tape, I slip onto my wrist. The electrical gauze goes in another pocket.

Outside, Lox takes off down the street and I go around the side of the building to the nearest corner. The red bricks—the bricks that make up the walls of the building—are perfectly stacked, so there are no catch-holds like there was on the church way back in The Glitz. But, when they built this place, they used decorative white bricks on the corners, from bottom to top. The bigger bricks stick out from the others, and that's where I'm going to climb up.

I wipe my sweaty hands on my jeans before latching

on to the first brick. I'm shaking so bad, my kneecaps practically rattle against each other. It only takes another minute, though, and then I'm in the zone. Cool. Calm. Focused.

My fingers find plenty of grab points and my feet are steady as I slide up the building's corner seam. The higher I get, the thicker the dust is and I have to stop for a second to catch my breath. My eyes burn and my tongue feels gritty with dirt.

"Keep going," I mutter to myself, because it's got to be close to three o'clock, if it isn't already, and I don't know if the UD plans a bigger attack than the flutter-fly bombs. If they send missiles this way . . .

Don't think about that now. I gotta do this for Dad. For LT. For Vee's dad. For everybody in Edge Flats.

The muscles in my legs start to shake when I'm just four bricks away from the top. Usually climbing isn't hard for me, but I've been running all day. I'm tired and sore. I reach up for another brick on the right, but my hand slips and my shoe scraps away from its holding. And then I'm hanging by one hand. My fingers shudder and I dig in deeper.

Don't let go.

I pull in a breath, taste the smokiness of the air in my throat. I get my right hand back on track, fingers latched

on to the brick. I grunt, pull myself up. Find a good footing. Steady myself. Three bricks to go. Then two. Then one. Almost there.

I stretch, push with my legs. My calves burn. I get a good grip on the roof's edge and pull myself up. One more heave and I'm over, scrambling onto the roof. I raise my arms above my head. "Woooohoo!"

I look out onto the city and all the triumph leaks outta my bones. Plumes of smoke rise from the nearby buildings. One of the bubble-like buildings, with the glass ceiling, is shattered, leaving behind nothing but its black skeleton. There isn't a working hover rail in sight. Some of the billboards continue running their ads, so there's still a Net connection running somewhere. That must be what Dekker wants to tap into.

"All right, focus, Trout. Focus." I turn back to the roof and the scattered pieces of brick and plastic. I don't know where to start. I don't even know what a Kaster looks like. Thankfully, there isn't a lot of hardware up here. So I start piling up as many pieces as I can find. The biggest one is shiny black, with a long rectangular head and a skinny metal base. The base is cracked in two and when I try to stand it up, it topples over.

That's where the duct tape will come in handy. I wind a long piece around the crack, making it as tight as I can.

When I stand it up again, the base teeters for a second, but evens out. Okay, one thing down.

The rest of the pieces I'm not sure about. I leave the electrical stuff for Lox because I don't want to screw something up.

Another bomb thunders in the distance, but I stay focused. When I've duct-tapped everything I possibly can, I move on to the meta-pol. It has a rubbery, gritty feel to it. It makes up most of the back side of the Kaster.

I set a few pieces on the ground, lining them up as best I can. I flick on the UV light and wave it back and forth over the cracks. The poly heats up and glows like an ember. Within seconds, the gap closes, the poly melting around itself like beads of water forming a bigger puddle.

I'm halfway through when the frog whipper latches on to the rusted-out remains of an old ladder next to me. The whipper zings as it's wound up and Vee leaps over the side of the roof.

"Heard you could use some help." Her hair is dusty and rust-colored. There's a smear of something black on her chin. Ash, maybe. I'm so happy to see her, I want to hug her. She tosses the whipper over the edge of the building and shouts down to Lox. "Only press the button once!"

"Got it!"

"How can I help?" Vee says.

"I think I'm missing a piece or two. Can you search the roof?"

"You got it."

Lox climbs onto the roof a few minutes later, breathing heavily. "Butter my gears, that was wrenched. Everything about this girl is awesome. Can you be my girlfriend?"

"Lox!" Vee and I shout.

"Get over here and start rewiring this thing!" I add.

"Okay. Okay! Geez. I can ask a girl out and save the world at the same time, you know." He takes the Kaster outta my hands and looks over the wiring on top. "Gauze, please." I hand him the roll. To me, it looks like he's picking wires at random, but he seems to know exactly what he's doing. He twists the severed wires back together and then reinforces it with the gauze.

Vee hands me another shiny black piece for the Kaster's head. "That's all I could find."

"I think that'll be enough."

"Yo!" someone shouts from the ground.

Vee pokes her head over the side. "It's your brother," she tells me. Then: "We're almost done."

"It's two fifty-seven! If you don't get that thing cranking, we're all dead!"

My stomach bottoms out. Lox holds the last piece in place and I run over it with the UV light. The poly melts and bends and blends until the gap between the pieces is gone.

A bomb goes off next door and we all leap back as brick and wood and glass blast our way.

"Don't drop the Kaster," I shout over the trembling of the buildings.

"I got it," Lox says. "Something's not right, though."

"Is there power running to it?"

Another bomb goes off. I flinch. Vee gasps.

"The power light is on, but it's not sending out a signal. You can tell by this light in the head whether or not it's latched on to a ping point, but . . ."

"It's not tall enough," I say. "We're missing another piece from the base, I bet."

"Look," Vee says. She points to a brick column at the far corner of the building. "Something used to be there. I bet that's where the Kaster was installed. The bottom is still screwed into the brick."

Lox and I run over. I climb up. Lox hands me the Kaster. People shout down below and sirens echo through the streets. The city is filled with smoke and crumbling buildings, but it's not dead. And I'm not gonna let Beard or the UD destroy it.

I keep one foot on the column and stretch out, putting my other foot on the edge of the roof. I thrust the Kaster as high as it'll go, hoping it can find that invisible connection to the satellite in outer space. Vee wraps herself around one of my feet, anchoring me down. Lox does the same on my other foot.

"Hold still!" Lox says. "It has to find a signal."

I freeze. I'm a Popsicle. I won't move. Can't move.

The Kaster whirs to life. A bomb rocks the ground and the vibration goes from the column to my feet to my knees to my brain.

If this doesn't work, we're done for.

A billboard two blocks to the west flickers, goes dark, then comes on again. The vid plays and there's Beard, pacing her office. Her voice fills the streets. "They'll be dead soon, regardless. The attack on Edge Flats, Texas, will commence at three p.m. today as we've planned. Let's hope Robert St. Kroix and his team are there when it happens. Strike first at the police station and then spread the attack outward. When the news broadcast hits, make sure you place the blame on St. Kroix, his brats, and the Meta-Rise."

The feed loops back. The streets go silent. People look up toward the remaining billboards as Beard's confession plays again.

When the vid crackles out, Po is there, standing against a backdrop of Dekker's book stacks. His eyes are watery and bloodshot. His shoulders are covered in dust. He licks his lips before speaking. "As many of you know, I'm one of those brats Sandra Hopper was referring to. My name is Mason St. Kroix, but everyone calls me Po ever since I lost my leg in the war." He snickers to himself. "That's a long story, and trust me, you don't want to hear it."

"What's he doing?" Lox says.

"Shhhh," I say, trying to stay still.

Several more bombs go off in the city. Po continues. "This attack on Edge Flats was a cold, calculated move by Congress to get District votes to start another Bot War. Why?"

Po raises his fingers. "Because of two things: money and fear. The country is broke since the bots fled and left the manufacturing and service industries dead. Why did they flee? Because the UD knew they'd made bots into something more than just cheap labor. They made them into something closer to human.

"Which brings me to the fear. Once bots started acting human because of the ThinkChip, the UD worried bots would one day evolve into something better than us."

Po takes a breath and looks away for a fraction of a second as he gathers his thoughts. "I guess in some ways,

I'm afraid of that too, but only because we've made a lot of mistakes in the past. Dumb mistakes. We've fought a lot of wars. We've turned against each other. We've made fools of ourselves in a thousand different ways.

"But you know what? We can learn from them, just like they learn from us. Never, in my life, has a robot intentionally harmed me. And my dad, Robert St. Kroix, he was injured so badly in the war that half his body had to be replaced with bot parts.

"If I turn my back on machines, I turn my back on my dad."

Po shakes his head and exhales. "And I can't do that. I can't turn my back on my family. Because isn't that what it's all about? Family? Protecting those we love? For the families who owned bots before the wars, how did you feel when the bot was gone? Did you miss him or her? Do you still?

"We not only made bots more human, we made them family."

My eyes sting as Po stares out from the billboard. It's like he's looking straight at me.

"My little brother, Trout, did everything in his power to bring our family back together, and the UD, *Sandra Hopper*, she wanted to take that away just like they took the bots away."

Po grits his teeth and steps closer to the camera. "I'm not going to let that happen. So listen up, Beard." He grinds out her name like it's a rotten tomato. "We St. Kroix men, we stick together. Family sticks together. We are the Meta-Rise, and we will fight you with everything we got."

Flutter-flies fall from the sky, their wings unmoving. When they reach the streets, they disintegrate into ash.

I've been standing still for so long, my knees are numb, but I can't look away from the billboard and my brother. My stomach is all knotted up inside. I feel like I might burst with pride.

My brother is totally wrenched.

"The bombs," Vee says, letting go of my foot, "they've been disengaged!"

Lox lets out a whoop. My legs start to shake and I lose my stance. The Kaster disconnects and the billboards go dark.

I strain, listening to the city, worried that the vid didn't go out to the UD, worried that a bigger bomb is on its way. But nothing comes.

I leap off the brick column and lunge at Lox. I hug him big in a dude-hug, then turn to Vee, who shrieks and laughs in my face, but I don't care.

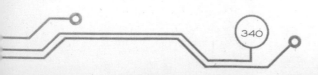

People cheer from the streets.

I raise an arm in the air. I feel light all over. Like I'm sailing down the rails. Like I just saved the world.

And I guess I kinda did.

THIRTY-NINE

WHEN WE CLIMB down, we find Dekker and Po in the living room of the fire station cracking open something that looks suspiciously like a beer. The house is a mess, and nothing is in its place. I wonder how long it'll take Dekker to start straightening things. For his sake, I hope he gets enough time to enjoy our victory.

Dekker takes a long drink out of his can and then turns to Po. "Dude, I thought we were dying. And no offense, but I don't know you well enough to die with you."

"That's all right," Po says. "I'd rather die with someone hot."

"Like Mar—" I start to say *Like Marsi Olsen,* but Po cuts me off with a big-brother scowl.

Vee collapses onto the couch, pushing her currently blackish silver hair behind her ears. "I think I could sleep for a week."

"I think I salt and peppered my underwear," Lox says.

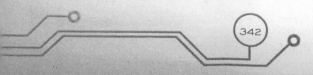

Everyone laughs, but when the door bursts open downstairs, we go quiet.

Po grabs a nearby lamp and wields it like a baseball bat. But when the first person appears at the top of the stairs, it isn't an enemy.

"Dad!" I call, and run to him. He wraps me in a hug and lifts me off the floor, and I don't care at all that my friends are watching. I'm just so glad he's here and he's alive and the UD didn't get him.

He squeezes, with one bot arm and one human arm, until I feel like I can't breathe. He doesn't put me down till he sees Po hovering in the background.

"Look at you, old man," Po says as a smile creeps onto his face. "I have to say, the bolt in the neck is a nice addition."

Dad half cries, half laughs as he wraps Po in a big hug.

"I missed you, Dad," Po says, his voice shaky.

"I missed you too, boy."

Dad pulls away just enough to motion me over. "Come on, group hug."

As the shortest St. Kroix, I get smushed between them. I look at Dad and see his heart, or what used to be his heart, glow a constant, steady blue.

I don't know what that means, but in my head I tell myself it means he's happy and proud. And if I had a

bot part for a heart, mine would be glowing blue too.

Someone else comes up the stairs behind us, and Vee shrieks. "Daddy!"

Lox says to Dekker, "Wanna hug it out too?"

Dekker chuckles. "Sorry, little hyper dude. Not the hugging type."

Dad maneuvers between Po and me, putting his arms around us. I get the bot arm. "I'm glad you two are okay, but if you ever pull a stunt like that, I swear, so help me—"

"I got it," I say.

"Loud and clear, old man," Po says.

"All right, boys," Dad says as he pulls us toward the stairs, "we've got a mess to clean up. And Lox, I think it's time we get you home."

"Ahh, come on! I'm having fun!"

"Lox!" Dad calls.

"Fine," he grumbles.

It's like nothing's changed at all.

Dad drives Lox's mom's car to the border between Texas and the UD. Po drives one of Dekker's cars so we have something to return in.

Lox's parents meet us on the side of the road. They're so mad, they're practically boiling red. But as soon as they

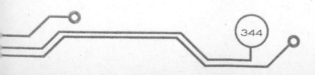

see Lox, and see that he's okay, they melt like ice cream. Lox soaks it up.

"If anyone asks," Dad says, after the reunion is over, "tell them Trout stole your car."

"What?" I shout. "I didn't steal—" Dad silences me with a look.

"I apologize for what my son did," Dad says. "And he is more than happy to take the blame to cover for Lox."

I cross my arms over my chest, but don't say anything else.

"I had someone check the vid feed in Brack," Dad goes on, "and it doesn't look like they got a good picture of Lox without his disguise. I think he'll be fine."

Lox's dad, Neil, eyes Dad's robotic arm before finally looking at his face. "Thank you for returning our son, but I think it's best if he doesn't see Aidan for a while—"

I'm not surprised to hear that, but it still hurts anyway.

"I understand," Dad says.

The trees rustle in the wind on the side of the road. A car slows as it passes us, then speeds up again. Probably someone trying to escape the chaos in Texas. Not like the UD is any better.

Kim, Lox's mom, pulls him close to her side. "It's not that we don't like you, Aidan," she says, "but after everything that's happened in the last twenty-four hours . . ."

"I know." I squint up at her. She's always been nice to me. Like the mom I never had. Mostly I'm sad that I got Lox in trouble.

"I'm sure it would be all right if you two chatted by vid," Neil adds. "I don't see anything wrong with that."

"And someday soon I'll sneak into Bot Territory," Lox says, "and we can have a slumber party."

"Loxley!" his mom says. "You will not be running away to Bot Territory!"

Lox grins. "Yeah. Okay Mom." He steps forward and we slap each other in a gear-lock. "Till next time, bolt sniffer."

I snicker. "Yeah. All right, drain clogger."

When Po turns the car around and heads back toward Dek's, I wave at Lox one more time before his car zooms outta sight.

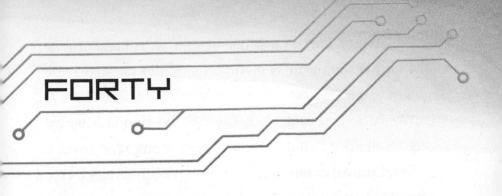

FORTY

THE DAY AFTER the attack on Edge Flats, President Callo holds an emergency news conference. He announces to the entire nation that Sandra Hopper was working with LT on the plot to attack several cities across the UD and Texas.

They play footage of her arrest for three days straight.

I'm glad she's no longer running any part of the UD government, but we all know the story Callo spun is a lie, and I hate that they used LT to do it. I also can't help but wonder if Callo was in on it too.

We found out just after the attack ended that Po's vid did go out to the entire country and some of the world too. Dekker said Po is turning into a Net star overnight, and Po tries to act like he's too cool for fame.

But we both know who was the first famous St. Kroix. That'd be me. FishKid.

No one heard from Ratch after he turned on us in City Hall. He didn't go back to the Fort, which is probably good for him. Dad ordered his people to dismantle Ratch the second they set eyes on him.

I hate that he's out there somewhere, still free.

We stick around Dekker's for the next few days, patching up the fire station as best we can with what we got. Dekker moves around the place readjusting things, lining things up, tapping light switches and cups as he goes.

Edge Flats fluctuates between celebrating their survival and mourning their injured and dead. Fortunately, there were only seven deaths, and only thirty-two injuries. It could have been a lot worse.

On Saturday, the city throws a memorial party in the park and that's when we sneak back into Bot Territory. When we pop into Scissor's workshop, I instantly miss LT. It hits me like a heavy weight in the chest. He's gone because of me and there's no way the UD will give him back.

He's probably in pieces by now. Gone for good.

Early Sunday morning, I lie awake in bed staring at the ceiling. I can hear Po snoring from his room down the hall. I think about stealing his prosthetic leg for old time's sake, but before I can, Vee pokes her head in my room.

"Clanker?" she whispers. "You up?"

"Yeah. Why?"

"Scissor says she's got something to show us."

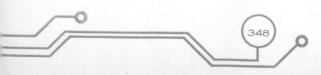

The sun isn't up yet, so the city is thick black like licorice. The streets are quiet and still. There isn't a cloud in the sky.

"Whatdoya think she's got?" I say when we hit one of the city's center squares.

"I don't know." Vee sticks her hands in her sweatshirt pocket. Her hair is twisted up tightly on the top of her head. "Maybe she invented something totally wrenched. Like a jet pack."

I snort. "Yeah right. There'd be people crashing into trees all the time."

"Well, lucky for you, you're already a pro at that."

"Ha. Ha. Ha."

"Oh, hey," she starts as I open the front door on Scissor's shop, "my cousin is crossing the border tomorrow. It's her first time in Bot Territory. Her dad's worried about her safety in the UD, so she's coming here for a few months. You wanna help me show her around?"

"Sure. Where's she from?"

"She's from Fifth District. Maybe you—"

"I'm in the back!" Scissor calls. "Hurry!"

We leave the main part of the shop and wind around the maze of tools and parts and worktables in back. We find Scissor leaning over a robot lying on the table. The operating lights are dark. The bot's front panel is open,

revealing the inner workings of his system—wires, gears, and metal bones.

Vee crosses her arms. "Please don't tell me this one has a soundtrack too."

"Awwww," Scissor's audience says. Her LED panel has a teal blue zigzag pattern on it today. "I will pretend you didn't say that. No, what I have here is something far better. Something magnificent!"

She whirls around to grab a little black box on the counter behind her and accidentally knocks over a pile of gears. The gears clink-clank to the floor. The high-pitched sound makes me wince.

"Sorry," Scissor says. "Anyway." She pops the black box into the robot, flicks on the operating system, and shuts the torso panel. The lights wink on. The eyes open and close. The fingers twitch. Vee and I share a look.

Why did Scissor get us out of bed in the middle of the night to show us a robot?

The bot sits up, looks around. The eyes blink again before resting on me. When the voice sounds through the voice box, I know instantly who it is.

"Trout. You are safe."

A lump works its way up my throat. "LT?"

"In the flesh!" Scissor says. "Er . . . well . . . in the metal, as it were."

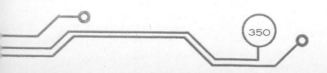

LT slides off the table silent as a cat. Even though he's a robot, and metal, and cold, I still hug him and he hugs me back, which shows that robots can feel something that's more than just programming.

"How did you . . . I don't understand . . ."

"It's a backup emergency program," Scissor says. "Something new I've been working on."

"When I knew I would not make it out of the building," LT explains, "I started downloading my system to a remote receiver."

"The little black box," Scissor says.

Vee's eyes grow big. "That's brilliant."

LT nods. "I had never done it before, so I was not sure it would work. It takes quite a while to download a robot's data, but I was able to hold off Sandra— "

"Beard," I correct him.

"Beard for as long as I needed to finalize the transfer. By the time they gained access to Po's cell, my shell was empty."

"So, you're back for good?" I ask.

LT nods and smiles a robot smile. "I am back for good."

I whoop and maul Vee. Then maul Scissor, then leap at LT. I never thought I'd say this, but I think I have a robot for a best friend.

FORTY-ONE

I CALL TELLIE THE next day and she answers on the second ring. "Hello?" she says, and when she sees it's me, she breathes out in one long rush. "Trout! Oh my God I'm so glad you're okay. I was worried. I heard you broke into . . ." She stops talking instantly and fixes her hair. "Never mind. You're okay."

There are a kajillion things I want to say to her. *Thank you. I think you're pretty. I'm glad we're friends. You saved my life. You helped bring my family together.* Instead I say, "Yeah. I'm okay."

She gets closer to the screen. "My dad told me you used my temp Net-tag to get into City Hall."

My face burns with embarrassment. "Yeah . . . about that . . ."

She waves off the apology before I can get it out. "Don't apologize. You were trying to save your brother. That's all that matters."

"Did you get in trouble?" I ask.

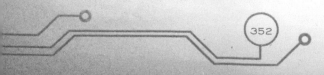

She shrugs. "I got my extended privileges taken away from my tag. And my vid account was suspended. But who cares. What was I using my vid account for anyway? Nothing worthwhile. Until I posted your vid, anyway. My dad said he admires your bravery, by the way."

"That's wrenched."

I have to admit, I'm still unsure about Mr. Rix. I saw him hitting Po in the last phone call he made to me before I left the UD. But every time I overheard Mr. Rix talking about the attacks, he was against them.

And I have to remind myself that a lot of people in the UD think my dad is a bad person because he's a bot supporter. Maybe Mr. Rix thought the same thing about Po.

"Has your dad said anything else? Does he still hate bots?"

"Of course he does. It's hard to think of them as anything other than machines." She frowns. "I know you like them, but just the other day, I overheard my dad talking about a group of bots on the East Coast claiming they were the ones responsible for that robot LT's detonate program. They're saying it won't be their last attack."

"There was no detonate program!"

"Who cares if there was or not? They're threatening the UD. That's what matters. Not all bots are good."

I think of Ratch. She's right about that. "Not all humans are good either," I point out.

"I guess that's true. I don't know." Tellie picks at the nail polish on her thumb. "Do you think you'll ever come back home?"

I hear Po and Dad talking out in the kitchen. Vee pipes in with something. I like it here. A lot. "I think I am home, but that doesn't mean I can't sneak in for a day. We can get ice cream or something. On me."

Tellie grins. "I'll hold you to that."

"Hey, Trout!" Vee calls.

"I gotta go," I say. "Thanks, Tellie. That's what I called for. To tell you thanks for everything you did. And that I'm really sorry you got into trouble because of me."

"It was for a good cause. And look, you got your dad back. Which is what we set out to do. Mission accomplished."

I laugh, because we set off a lot of other crazy stuff with that one vid. It seems like forever ago when I made it with Tellie at my side.

"Later," I say, and wave at the camera.

"Bye, Goldfish."

I flick off the Link and head down the hall. Dad and Po are at the table. Po is emptying out a bag of chips. Vee is pacing the room.

"What is it?" I ask.

"My cousin is supposed to be here any minute!" she shrieks. She clears her throat. "It's just been a long time since I've seen her and she's one of my favorite cousins. So I'm excited."

Merril pulls a cake out of the oven. Instantly the room smells like vanilla. "Y'all, this is one special cake."

LT pops open a can of frosting.

Vee's Link buzzes in her hand. "She's here!" She skips the elevator and takes the stairs instead.

I plop down next to Po. "How old is the cousin?"

"Don't know." Po shrugs and stuffs his face with a handful of chips. "I hope she's cute."

Dad shakes his head. "To be young again."

A few minutes later, the elevator dings and the doors open. Po wipes the chip crumbs from the corner of his mouth.

"You missed one right there," I say, even though I'm lying. He swipes at his mouth. "No, right there. You almost got it."

"Shut up." He punches me in the arm.

"Ahh, geez, clanker! That hurt."

Vee appears around the corner and tugs her cousin into the room. "Everyone, I'd like you to meet—"

"Holy jet smoke," I breathe.

Po swallows loudly. "Marsi?"

Marsi widens her eyes. "Po? I didn't know you were here. I mean, I knew you were here, but not *here* here—"

"Oh, this is so wrenched," I say.

"You guys know each other?" Dad asks.

"It's Marsi Olsen!" I exclaim. "Po's had the biggest—"

Po clamps a hand over my mouth and gives me a look. He's totally gearing out. It's like we're back in the middle of Brack on our way to the Heart Office. Everything has changed, but nothing has changed.

You should kiss her, I say with my eyes.

No way! he says with a frown.

You're a big clucking chicken, I reply.

He lets go of me and rises to his feet and walks over to Marsi. And then he stands there, looking at the ground. "Hey . . . I . . . um . . ."

Marsi giggles. "Po St. Kroix, how is it you can address an entire nation on the Net, but you can't say more than two words to me?"

He looks up. "I don't know."

"Three words." She smiles and dimples appear in each cheek. "We're making progress." And then she takes two quick steps, grabs Po's face, and kisses him right on the lips.

Vee gasps. Dad looks stunned. But me? I cheer Po on. That's what brothers are for.

ACKNOWLEDGMENTS

First and foremost, always much love and thanks to my husband, JV, for being my cheerleader, my supporter, and Trout's earliest fan.

To my agent, Joanna Volpe, who saw something in this story long before I did. Who continues to be the voice of reason in my frequent states of neurosis. She is the best agent anyone could ask for.

To my editor, Kate Harrison, for her wisdom, her insight, and her mega love for Trout! For giving him a home, and for helping me make the characters, and bot world, so much better. This book would not be where it is today if not for her.

To Deena Lipomi, for reading Trout in his earliest form, and for encouraging me to keep going.

To Patricia Riley and Danielle Ellison, thank you

for keeping me sane through multiple deadlines. You always know how to make me laugh.

And lastly, to my friends and family, for their support. And most importantly, to the grandparents, for endless hours of babysitting. You guys are awesome.